DIARY

OF A

CONFUSED

FEMINIST

For anyone who's ever felt a little bit confused

SIMON & SCHUSTER BFYR

An imprint of Simon & Schuster Children's Publishing Division
1230 Avenue of the Americas, New York, New York 10020

Simon & Schuster: Celebrating 100 Years of Publishing in 2024
For information about special discounts for bulk purchases, please contact
Simon & Schuster Special Sales at 1-866-506-1949
or business@simonandschuster.com.
The Simon & Schuster Speakers Bureau can bring authors to your live event. For more information or to book an event, contact the Simon & Schuster Speakers Bureau at 1-866-248-3049 or visit our website at www.simonspeakers.com.
The text for this book was set in ITC Franklin Gothic.
Manufactured in the United States of America
First SIMON & SCHUSTER BFYR edition January 2024
2 4 6 8 10 9 7 5 3 1
CIP data for this book is available from the Library of Congress.
ISBN 9781665937948 (hc)
ISBN 9781665937931 (pbk)
ISBN 9781665937955 (ebook)

DIARY

OF A

CONFUSED

FEMINIST

+ a novel by +

Kate Weston

SIMON & SCHUSTER BFYR

New York   London   Toronto   Sydney   New Delhi

Tuesday, September 4

Ways that I, Kat Evans, am going to be an excellent feminist this term:

1. I will organize a *small* bit of activism on the first day—*tiny*—just to ease us in. A bit of red spray paint never hurt anyone, right?
2. I will make the switch to a menstrual cup henceforthly becoming a model *eco-friendly* feminist.
3. I will definitely ask Miss Mills about writing a weekly feminist column on the school blog called Feminist Friday, and not just spend the whole term thinking about it and doing nothing.
4. I will also keep this diary EVERY DAY because all the top journalists and writers say this is a Good Thing and definitely not something I will look back on and cringe about in approximately five minutes' time.
5. I will thusly become a BETTER FEMINIST and a PATRIARCHY-SMASHING JOURNALIST. Think Emmeline Pankhurst with a smartphone.

Wednesday, September 5
8:45 a.m.

The main playground, where Krishna "Comedy Krish" Anand once made Dave Edwards snort a sherbet fountain and he had to go to the hospital because they couldn't stop the sherbet bubbles coming out of his nose

"Who the BLOODY HELL is TIM?"

Mr. Clarke, our principal, roars at us, striding across the gray tarmac like an angry bald buffalo. We all scuttle into a line and try to look like brave and intrepid feminists.

Me and my two best friends, Sam and Millie, are dressed head to toe in black. Each of us has a small black veil covering half our faces, film-noir-style, and a slick of red lipstick.

Although it's a bit of a departure from our usual maroon uniform, the outfits are clearly not what Mr. Clarke is referring to. The thing he's pointing to and appears to be most upset about is the giant, bright red #Tim painted on the playground.

It was obviously supposed to be #TimesUp but he's caught us before we've finished, so it's stuck at #Tim. Something creepy Tim Matthews in our year will definitely enjoy. I don't know anyone who's ever believed his *The more you feel them, the bigger they get* spiel, and yet he still rolls it out at every house party.

We decided to be feminists a few weeks ago after an incident with a staunch feminist, some hummus, and a very expressive carrot (more on this later). Feminism's basically equality for men and women, and an end to all the patriarchy bullshit (I think—the carrot was a little vague here). Anyway, it felt apt for our first point of business to be something supporting #MeToo and the TIME'S UP movement.

The plan was to look just like the glitzy celebs arriving on the red carpet dressed in black at the Golden Globes to announce time's up. Though in the picture we posted on Insta this morning, I looked more like a goth who'd been drinking red wine. Already an old lush at fifteen.

"We're protesting in solidarity with the #MeToo and TIME'S UP movements, sir," Millie says with authority. "We want men to know that time's up and we won't stay silent any longer."

"And yet I've never known you three to be particularly silent!" Mr. Clarke rages.

Millie doesn't look like a lush—she looks glamorous and poised like the Hollywood celebs, fitting for someone who wants to be an actress. And Sam, she looks like an actual catwalk model. The lipstick color suits her perfectly and seems not to have fallen off her beautiful full lips the way it has with mine. But now that I think of it, are feminists allowed to look nice? Isn't the thing that we no longer conform to the idea of looking pretty and girly? Surely I'm a better feminist because I look a bit weathered? Like I've been actually protesting (with wine)?

Or maybe that's unfeminist of me and women should be

allowed to be pretty if they want to be pretty? Being a feminist seems to be quite confusing, actually.

I tune back in to the conversation just in time to hear Mr. Clarke tell us to clean off our lipstick. In my case it won't be hard as it's mostly on my teeth and chin by now anyway.

"It's an artistic representation of menstrual blood, sir. A symbol of the struggle women go through every day, all over the world. We bleed and yet we carry on. We can't clean it off unless you're against women menstruating, sir. Are you?" Sam stares at him questioningly while his face goes bright red. He looks confused and like his head might implode. I guess he wasn't expecting to talk about the female reproductive system before 9 a.m. on the first day back at school.

"G-g-g-girls . . ." Mr. Clarke is spluttering, trying to regain control of himself. It's not pretty. "I think we've lost sight of the point here. You cannot go around defacing school property, no matter what the cause. You'll be cleaning it off in after-school detention."

"You can't silence us, sir. We're fighting years of this kind of oppression and control from men. You're the patriarchy and we're going to take you down!" I rage.

"Wonderful, I'll be sure to tell the department of education of your plans to bring down principals. I must have missed that part of the TIME'S UP movement when I read about it in the news. I'll see you back here at three-thirty for detention."

"This is a dictatorship," Sam huffs.

"Yes. Welcome back to my dictatorship, ladies. Have a great day."

4

I kind of knew this would happen as soon as I saw the red paint, but you can't go at feminist activism half-heartedly. When you think about it, a detention isn't *quite* as bad as what the suffragettes went through. Although it *is* really hot today and I haven't brought sunscreen.

10:30 *a.m.*

The science block toilets—our toilets
No one else really uses them as they're so old and out of the way. And smell of decades-old urine. Lovely.

Sam, Millie, and I have been best friends since our first day of nursery, when we all showed up to school with the same weary expression, completely unconvinced that whatever was waiting for us here would be better than what's on the CBeebies channel at home. We were right, and the shared experience of being betrayed by our parents has bonded us ever since.

Today's the first day of Year Eleven, which means we've been together now for twelve blissful years. And, as of today, eight detentions.

The three of us stand at the three sinks, staring into three mucky, old, cracked mirrors in a pink toilet block which was painted in the nineties—the last time it was acceptable to do the whole "pink for a girl, blue for a boy" thing.

"Sorry about that, guys . . ." I mutter as I try to sort out my smeared lipstick in the equally smeared mirror. I'm a bit sheepish because this was my idea, but I think we all knew it would end in detention. . . . I hope we all knew that, anyway.

"Oh, pssh!" Millie says, swatting a hand at me while brushing her hair with the other at the sink to the left of mine. "We all knew that was going to happen. Didn't we, Sam?"

Phew.

"We did! But it was worth it. . . . Well, almost . . . if we'd have gotten the whole thing on the playground . . . or if we'd have Snapchatted it . . . or done any kind of social media . . . to show what we were trying to do . . ." Sam says, looking at Millie from her spot to my right at the third sink, where she's putting on mascara without even doing that open-mouth concentration face.

"Oooh, that would have been a great idea!" Millie says, turning away from the mirror and blinking to look at us both excitedly.

I'm staring at Millie. Sam's staring at Millie. Millie has not remembered that social media was supposed to be her job.

"I did post this really cute selfie on the 'gram, though. Do you think you can tell what you two are doing in the background there behind me?" She thrusts her faux-fur-covered phone in our faces. On occasion I have mistaken this cover for a rodent and screamed.

You can literally only see my hand and one of Sam's feet behind her beaming filtered face.

"Millie, do you remember how I was the artistic director, Kat was the operations director, and you were the *social media director* for this little feminist adventure?" Sam says, half laughing.

"Oooohhhhhhhhhhhhhh." Millie looks at us, hand in front of her mouth. "I just . . . there's a new Snapchat filter that turns you into a llama and I . . . sort of got distracted."

"That's okay. Probably for the best that we didn't immortalize the bit where we wrote #Tim on the playground, really, isn't it?" I say, turning back to the mirror to make sure I haven't still got lipstick on my teeth.

"Yeah. Definitely," Sam agrees.

"And at least it's distracting me from having to wait to find out whether I've got Juliet," says Millie, scrolling through Instagram absentmindedly. "They're releasing the cast list at lunchtime. FINALLY."

When she found out that she would have to wait until the new school year to see if she got the part in our school's production of *Romeo and Juliet*, I thought we were going to have to get an exorcist in. She went full head-spinny, possessed by rage and stress.

Millie really wants to be an actor and she's good at it too. Of course, as a staunch feminist (as of nearly a whole month now) I'm a hundred percent sure that wanting to be Juliet is in no way affected by her lifelong crush on Nick Deans in the year above. The boy who will, without a shadow of a doubt, be cast to play Romeo. That definitely has nothing to do with it, even though she's on record as having said that the nurse was the best character and WHY would anyone want to play "simpering,

1

spineless" Juliet. But it's completely, absolutely, got nothing to do with Nick D. Sure.

"How do you feel?" Sam asks.

"Confident!" Millie sings, which is good because it's been swinging one way or the other all summer.

"Attagirl!" says Sam, walking over and patting her on the back.

"Who else would they give it to, anyway? No one else is half as good as you," I say, and I mean it—she's amazing.

"And if they do give it to someone else . . . an accident can be arranged . . ." Sam says, flexing her hands.

She's joking, by the way. We're not bad people. There are some in our school, but we're not them.

Sam's phone buzzes in her hand and her face lights up. "Dave says that he really enjoyed our disruption this morning. Says we looked great!"

"Looking great is SO NOT the point!" I groan, ignoring the fact that I've been staring in the mirror for the past ten minutes.

"But we do look pretty fantastic. HAVE YOU SEEN US? What's happening with Dave, now?" Millie asks. Dave is THE Dave Edwards I mentioned earlier, snorter of sherbet, but also fancier of Sam.

"I don't know. We talk a lot, I guess," Sam says.

"Yeah! He likes you! How come you don't just get together?" Millie asks.

"I dunno. I think he's just messing around. Don't think he likes me that much," Sam says shyly.

He does. We all know he does.

8

11 a.m.

History class

I can't believe I'm back in this hellhole so soon. School is the only place where you can sit next to a huge open window and still feel claustrophobic. I find myself leaning more and more toward the window because someone in here appears to have *really* discovered aftershave over the summer and it's combined with the general . . . agricultural smell to make the school atmosphere even more oppressive than usual.

The whole room is tinged with an air of disappointment. Even Mr. Crick doesn't look like he's really come to terms with us being back as he drones on about 1800s America.

I'm not even in the same classes as Millie and Sam this morning, which is just torture. I hate it when they're in classes without me. I worry that they're going to become better friends and start leaving me out of things and eventually forget about me altogether. I mean, they'll both definitely be working on the play together—Millie will obviously get Juliet and Sam's going to be working backstage to build the set.

Sam's amazing at art and anything creative. Her mum once took her to a life-drawing class and she came back with something so realistic it was borderline pornographic. Even though Sam said the guy was so old his danglies looked like pug faces.

It makes me uneasy that there'll be a whole huge part of

their lives I'm not going to be involved in. But I worry a lot about stuff like this.

I also worry that no one else worries quite as much as I do. I don't think my friends do, and I don't know why I worry so much more than everyone else.

Sometimes I worry that worrying is my greatest talent.

12:30 p.m.

The bench outside the drama block bulletin board, anxiously waiting to FINALLY find out if Millie has the part

Millie's notably less calm than she was earlier and keeps twitching every time someone walks past. I get it, though— she's been waiting to find out for so long, it feels cruel that they're dragging it out even longer. The suspense is ridiculous.

Our school is kind of a mishmash with one main playground and other little hidey-holes between blocks where different groups hang out/hide out. So, the music kids hang out by the music block, mathletes by the math block, athletes by the sports field (also frequented by anyone looking to get frisky, although I personally have NEVER been very athletic)—and the drama block is where the smokers hang so they can sneak out to the alleyway next to it and make an absolute holy mess of their lungs. You can tell as much. It's really smoky over here and we're all struggling to stay cool.

"Oh my god, there she is!" Millie squeaks, grabbing our

hands as the head of drama appears around the corner.

"Congratulations, Millie," Ms. Withers says, pinning the list to the board and then walking away.

"Oh my god, I can't look!" Millie says dramatically.

"She has LITERALLY just told you that you've got it," I say as Sam and I both roll our eyes.

"OH MY GOD, I GOT IT!" Millie says, reading the list with a theatrical gasp.

"Congrats!" Sam and I say together, grabbing her in a group hug and jumping up and down. Millie's taken it to the next level, though, and started dancing, except calling it "dancing" is really a bit of a stretch. It mostly looks like she's trying to be a chicken, only less coordinated. I guess she's excited.

I'm sure that as a feminist she's still absolutely not even a little bit bothered that Nick Deans is playing Romeo, but I can see him approaching, watching her "dance," and I feel like I need to find a way to warn her that she may look SLIGHTLY ridiculous right now.

"Ahem! Romeo," I mutter, hoping for subtlety and trying to make her stop being so dramatic before she hits mortification levels.

"Oh my god! Yes! Nick is playing Romeo! Finally, he'll have to notice me! Romeo, Romeo, wherefore art thou, HOT SEXY ROMEO!" she says, dropping down to one knee before pretending to faint with her hand across her forehead.

"You must be my Juliet, then!" Nick Deans says from behind her.

Millie falls the short distance left to the floor with shame.

12:45 p.m.

Emergency toilet debrief

"DID HE HEAR ME?" Millie is crying at us in such despair that a lost Year Seven girl has just scuttled out in fear. "What's he even doing here? The Sixth Form don't start until next week!"

"He definitely heard you, but it might not be that bad?" Sam says.

"I've made a complete twat of myself already, haven't I?" Millie asks.

"I've done worse!" I say cheerfully. I'm kind of a walking disaster for this stuff and I don't mind saying it if it makes her feel better.

"She has!" Sam says even more cheerfully.

Rude. But it's made Millie smile.

3:30 p.m.

The hottest detention known to man

It's so hot out here that I can feel my skin burning—it's more or less bubbling—as I'm cleaning. Thanks, climate change, for this hideous and unseasonal heat wave! What if I'm permanently disfigured from the sunburn I get during this detention?

I do feel intrepid and bold, though, like a proper suffragette.

Although, thinking about it, I bet the suffragettes never had to deal with creepy #Tim Matthews. As predicted, he's absolutely overjoyed with it all.

"Ladies, if you wanted my attention, all you had to do was talk to me. Such an extreme romantic gesture was not necessary. Not when you're as fiiiiiiiiiiiiiiiiiiiine as you three." His elongation of the word "fine" unleashes some excess spit all over the place.

Urgh. I am definitely going to throw my sponge at him if he doesn't leave soon.

3:35 p.m.

Oh god, as if this wasn't all awful enough, here comes Terrible Trudy sauntering past with her crew. I was hoping she just hadn't come back this year, that maybe her family got stuck on a superyacht somewhere forever or, better still, kidnapped by pirates. I'm not normally this mean about people, by the way, but Trudy's the exception. She's the most popular girl in school (she reigns only through terror) and she's my archnemesis.

The conflict between Trudy and me started on my second day of nursery. She tried to take away my favorite bunny because it was better than hers. I didn't let her have it (it was MINE!) and thusly I made an ENEMY FOR LIFE. It was one bunny, but boy, can she hold a grudge. Though to be fair, I've NEVER tried to be as accommodating of her as everyone else

13

is. And why should I be? She treats her friends like crap, let alone everyone else.

Over the years, Trudy's taken her grudge out on me in many different ways, such as sticking a tampon to my back with a note that said "I'm on my period!" (period shaming AND completely unfeminist, AND I REFUSE to be embarrassed by being on my period, actually!) and trying to tell people that I wasn't wearing any knickers one time even though I WAS and it meant that boys spent the whole day trying to look up my skirt. Perverts. And that's without even mentioning all the times she's tripped me up or pushed me over.

Part of the reason she gets away with so much stuff (apart from being terrifying) is that her mum's a big record producer, so allegedly there are always celebrities at her house and people want in on that. She comes back from holidays with the most completely unbelievable stories about who she's hung out with. She claims to have once gone on a date with Harry Styles. Common sense suggests this is a COMPLETE LIE but apparently I'm the only one who gets that.

Even if you didn't believe her, before you ever got to tell her that she was chatting utter nonsense you'd have to get through her crew. The Bitches—or, as I like to call them, TB, the name of a terrible, disgusting Victorian illness—are around her twenty-four seven. One of the rules for joining TB is apparently that Trudy Must Never Be Left Alone—diva. Another rule is that if Trudy doesn't have a boyfriend, then you can't have one either—ridiculous.

The Bitches consists of:
- Amelie—Second Bitch in Command, who follows Head Bitch around like she's leeching oxygen off her
- Tiffany—really wants to be Second Bitch in Command. Must suffer daily being Third Bitch in Command
- Nia—Fourth Bitch in Command. Resigned to carrying bags and standing in Amelie and Tiffany's shadows, not to mention Trudy's
- Tia—doesn't seem to understand hierarchies so lives in blissful ignorance

Although, now that I think about it, is calling them all The Bitches actually unfeminist? I don't think you're supposed to call another woman names at all, really. Maybe I should try a bit harder this year to get along with them all?

"Losers think they're feminists now," says Trudy. "As if they're anything like Hollywood stars. Silly little cows. You're only in the school play, Camilla—you're not Jennifer bloody Lawrence."

Maybe not, then, actually. Maybe feminism doesn't count when the woman in question is a complete MONSTER. Like with Margaret Thatcher . . . maybe Trudy is the Margaret Thatcher of our time?

3:40 p.m.

Still scrubbing at the playground like a Tudor kitchen wench.

Oh god. Hot Josh is walking toward us. Everything's gone a

bit blurry. . . . Arms and legs suddenly . . . weak . . . and I can actually hear my heartbeat in my head.

This always happens when I see HIM.

Hot Josh is amazing. I don't say that lightly. He's the absolute sexiest boy in school and possibly the entire county, if not the country.

Definitely in our town.

He's done modeling for ASOS and only started at the school at the end of last year after his family moved from London. He's really cosmopolitan. I can count the conversations we've had on one hand. They usually consist of one word from him and, only once, a bit of dribble from me. As he approaches, I swear I can hear an actual choir of angels heralding his arrival.

Suddenly, I remember that I am currently on all fours, scrubbing creepy Tim's name off the playground. Great.

I do a sort of sideways crab movement on all fours to move closer to Millie and Sam, seeking the safety of my pack like a baby lion.

"What are you doing, crabby? You look weird," Mills says. Helpful.

"Oh, I see!" Sam nudges her. "Hot Josh, dead ahead."

"Ooooohhhhhhh!" Millie and Sam look delighted. They love watching me get all fluttery and red in the face.

"Your face matches your lipstick now." Sam can be such a cow sometimes. I never do this when she's flirting with Dave.

Hot Josh appears to be heading straight for me. Or us? Oh god, it's me.

"Hey," he says.

I seem to have continued being crouched down on all fours, staring up at him. Paralyzed. I worry I may look like a cat caught going to the toilet. The other two have obviously, sensibly, jumped up to normal standing positions. My legs are apparently unable to support that movement, unfortunately.

Hot Josh appears to be holding out a hand, and all I seem able to do is stare at it, like I've never seen a hand before, and stay in my weird crab/cat position on the tarmac.

What is he going to do with that hand? Is he about to delicately brush my cheek and tell me he loves me?

"Er . . . want me to help you up?" he finally says after what feels like ten THOUSAND YEARS.

"Oh yes. Fabby. Thank you."

I appear to have just said FABBY? WHO SAYS FABBY? SOUNDS LIKE FLABBY!

FFS.

I take his hand and stand up, trying to hide my pink cheeks.

"I really love what you guys did today." He seems to be talking directly to my actual face. "It's such a buzz in the industry right now. So woke of you guys to support it."

Oh my god.

Oh my god.

Oh.

My.

God.

I'm suddenly very aware of my vagina. Why? What? What's

happening? Why aren't I talking? Oh my god, he's going to think I'm so weird.

"Thanks," says Sam. Thank the baby Jesus Christ for Sam and her ability to talk real words in the face of extreme sexiness.

"Power to the pussy!"

Oh god, who said that?

That just came out of my mouth, didn't it?

What am I doing with my hand? Am I making a vagina sign with my fingers? I MEAN, REALLY?

"Errr yeah, great . . . sooo . . . laters!" Hot Josh walks away and takes with him any chance of me EVER having dignity or poise.

"POWER TO THE PUSSY!" Millie and Sam sing after he's out of earshot (I hope). I sink back down to the ground. No amount of scrubbing is going to erase the shame of that little incident.

I shall never speak again. I cannot be trusted.

6 p.m.

Back Chez Moi

I can hear Dad, my fourteen-year-old brother Freddie, and our next-door neighbor Matt in the living room. They're whispering, and it sounds like they're up to no good.

As I cautiously put my head around the door, I see them all sitting in a line on the sofa, staring blankly at the TV.

Each of them has #Tim written on their foreheads.

Eugh. How do they know? Did Freddie find out and pass it on? Traitor.

I bet the forehead thing was Dad's idea. He used to be a stand-up comedian and still likes to think he's "funny." I hope they've accidentally used permanent marker.

"Power to the pussy!" the three of them sing in unison after a few seconds.

"URGH! Children!"

"Could you not have waited until next week when I was in before you menstruated all over the school?" Matt teases. He's going into Lower Sixth this year so he starts with Nick next week.

"Great feministing, Kat!" says Dad. "Who is this Tim lad, though? I'll need to know for Nat's next storyline."

Nat is the daughter in Dad's sitcom about a single father raising a teenage girl. Every week, millions of people tune in to watch thinly veiled stories from my actual life, while Dad rakes in the glory.

"Oh great. Yet again, changing the first letter of my name makes for a masterful disguise. Last month that woman from the weird house at the end of the road congratulated me on starting my period!"

"Aww, that was kind of her, love. Fabby!" Dad says.

"It is not fabby! And, I started my period YEARS AGO, Dad."

Of course. It's HIS bloody fault I said fabby earlier. I've picked it up from him!

"Well, better late than never!"

"Why can't you just get a normal job like Mum?" I huff. "I'm going upstairs! Matt? Are you coming?" He is, after all, MY friend, not theirs. "You wait till Mum gets home and I tell her you were making fun of feminism! And you KNOW it was supposed to say #TimesUp!"

Mum is a staunch feminist and a serious scientist. She'll sort them out. She's how I got started on all this. Last month, after three bottles of wine in our kitchen, she and Matt's mum Sandra started explaining the patriarchy to me. Which ended with Sandra waving a carrot stick around and dipping it in hummus, quite aggressively, actually, before shouting: "And that's ALL they want to do, Kitty Kat! They just want to dip their carrot in your hummus and then waltz off." Then she fell off her stool, taking her carrot with her.

Bea, our beautiful black Labrador and my only current female ally, follows me upstairs. Seems she's had enough of the boys too.

Worth noting that Dad didn't find menstruation quite so funny when she was "in season" on his record collection a few years ago. We had to get her some doggy period underpants. I think she quite liked them. They were soft and bouncy—excellent for sitting.

6:15 p.m.

Debrief on the floor of my room with Matt, watching Drag Race

"So, did anything else happen today? Aside from you sticking it to the Man?" Matt asks, tickling Bea's tummy.

Matt moved in next door about ten years ago after his dad left him and his mum for his PA. Sandra painted all the walls in their house bright red—as a woman now, I'm starting to understand her—and Matt's been seeking shelter with us ever since.

"God, loads!" I say. "How much did Freddie tell you?"

"What? Oh, no, Freddie didn't tell me. It was all over Snapchat," Matt says.

Makes sense. Matt's the most popular boy in school so he has everyone on Snapchat, although that also makes it super weird that he spends so much time with me.

"UURRRGH!" I groan. Goddamn you, social media.

"This will cheer you up: Mum shouted at those boys again when we were out in town. They weren't even doing anything this time."

"What—the ones who were little dickheads after you came out?" I ask.

"The very same. It's so embarrassing, though they look so much less hard when my mum's calling them 'little knobless pricks.'" He chuckles to himself.

Matt came out last year. I was so proud of him and so pleased that he felt like he could finally be himself and be open with everyone. Unfortunately, some dickheads from school started shouting things at him, calling him names. He was trying to ignore it and wouldn't even let me kick them in the shins, but then his mum heard and went full lioness-protecting-her-cub on

21

them. "Little knobless pricks" is actually quite tame compared to the things she told them she'd do if they carried on. As well as the fact that she threatened to report them to the police for homophobia. Matt was both mortified and relieved.

"Go, Sandra! In other news, unfortunately Trudy didn't die at sea on her parents' yacht." (Massive **unfeminist thought** to wish death at sea on another woman . . . MASSIVE.)

"Shame. Any members of One Direction on the yacht this year?"

"She was too busy taking the piss out of us to tell us. But I'm sure Zayn was there rubbing sunscreen into her back while Harry Styles waited on her naked or something."

"Obviously."

"Millie got the part of Juliet."

"Amazing! Bet she's pleased!"

"Do you think Nick knows that Millie's in love with him?"

"EVERYONE knows that Millie's in love with him," Matt says.

"Well, we shall wait and watch with interest!" I say.

"We shall!" Matt agrees.

Our love lives may be nonexistent (especially as one of us just made a vagina sign at their crush) but at least we get to watch other people be happy. There's always that. And that's lovely, isn't it?

6:20 p.m.

SOME kind of interest would be nice, though. Please.

6:25 p.m.

WHEN WILL IT BE MY TURN?

6:26 p.m.

But obviously I'm a strong, independent, feminist woman, happy to be on my own. I don't need a man.

6:30 p.m.

I can hear Mum getting home from work downstairs. She works in a research lab at the hospital analyzing test results and being a cool science-y lady. She was a child genius. I'm pretty sure she'd already won about ten thousand science prizes by the time she was my age.

"Hey, Matt! Hey, Kat!" she shouts up the stairs. She sounds excited. "Heard about your activism, Kitty Kat. Can't believe they oppressed you before you got the whole word on the playground. It's just a shame about that sleazy boy in your year being called Tim too. . . ." She appears at my bedroom door.

She looks like she's about to laugh. She'd better not laugh. She's weeping slightly at the corner of her eyes. I can see a collection of water and her shoulders are shaking. Matt's just started laughing, so now she's laughing.

THANKS, MOTHER. THANKS, MATT.

"MUM! I can't believe you of all people are laughing about this! And Matt! Whose friend are you, exactly?"

"Sorry, Kitty Kat, I do think it's a wonderful thing that you've done but, you know, you have to see the funny side, really." She's the worst. Just when you think you can depend on someone. AND she knows I hate being called Kitty Kat. Everyone STILL does it, but it makes me sound like a toddler.

"Sorry, Kat." Matt's staring at the floor, but I can see his shoulders are still shaking.

For god's sake.

"If *you* won't even take me seriously, I shall stay in my room," I tell Mum earnestly.

"What about dinner?"

"I shall come down to dinner and then come straight back to my room. I shall not utter a word to ANY of you."

And I really mean it.

8 p.m.

My bedroom

After Matt left, I sat through dinner in silence. I did the washing up in silence. I came back up to my room in silence, and now I am continuing to read *Pride and Prejudice*. Apparently, Jane Austen was a feminist.

10 p.m.

In bed

The dog's just come into my room with a note attached to her collar.

It says #Tim.

11:30 p.m.

The mortification of today is swimming round and round and round my head. First off, I spray-painted the name of the school pervert onto the playground. Then I made a vagina sign with my fingers at the boy I fancy AND said both FABBY and PUSSY. Such an idiot. I spend a lot of time in bed worrying on a normal day, even without all that. People say bed's supposed to be a relaxing place, but it doesn't seem to be for me.

Have you ever found yourself worrying about really bad things happening when you're on your own? Whenever I'm alone for too long, I find my mind wandering to scary things.

Like, every year before we go on our summer holiday, I'm always convinced that the plane is going to crash and we're all going to die, or that my whole family will die and I'll be the last one left alive and I'll have to survive on a desert island alone, presumed dead.

I hate flying.

Or, what if someone breaks into our house tonight with a

25

gun and then they kill everyone, but I survive the horrible massacre of my family and then have to go into witness protection? And what if they can't find the person who did it and then I am framed for killing them all and I have to spend my whole life in prison?

Because things like that do happen. There are shows about it on Netflix.

Sometimes when I start thinking about these things, I get a funny feeling in my throat, like something's obstructing it, and I feel a bit sick and like I can't breathe.

I've been having thoughts like this since I was about six years old. I used to make deals with myself like, "If I touch the light switch three times before I fall asleep, we'll all make it through the night." And, "If I wash my hands three times, then none of us will ever get sick."

The light switch deal is the only one that I still do. It's not something I've ever told anyone about. I don't think my friends have these thoughts, but I'm far too embarrassed to ask and find out.

11:45 p.m.

Beep

> **Message:** WhatsApp group name changed by Sam:
> **POWER TO THE PUSSY**

Me: SAM!!!!!

Sam: ⟳

Millie: ⟳

Unfeminist thoughts: 1

Wishing Terrible Trudy had died during the summer holidays. It wasn't my fault, your honor—she made me do it.

Thursday, September 6
7:12 a.m.

The bathroom, sitting on the toilet, willing the misery to end

My womb is a man. I'm sure of it. It's the only way I can get my head around the idea that something inside me is causing me this much pain.

Fun Feminist Fact: *In the 1800s some people considered men-struation a dangerous disease and it was suggested that women stay horizontal. Previously women's menstrual blood was also considered to have evil powers so women were given a wide berth. Today I wish I was either Victorian or considered to possess evil powers via my vulva. I think vulva is the right word. Does anyone really know what's vulva and what's vagina?*

7:15 a.m.

Do you know who profits from our periods, by the way?
    MEN.
    I read about it on Insta on the @PeriodFactsCompletelyTrue account. The tampon industry is FULL OF MEN, earning money from our pain and misery. Well, #TimesUp, guys, because I've finally bought myself a menstrual cup. Yep. That's right. I've beat your hideous masculine system. SISTERS ARE DOING IT

FOR THEMSELVES (cleaning out their period blood from a small reusable silicone cup, that is).

In the Insta post they talked about how women are taking charge of their periods and as I am clearly now a woman—albeit with smaller boobs than I thought I would have—I am going to do it too. It's all about being woke and vocal about the experience.

The only thing is, I'm not sure if I've put it in right. I followed the instructions to the letter, but I'm starting to wonder if there's some secret of vagina ownership I don't know about yet because mine seems tricky. For a start, although the view from up here is obviously a little different, I don't think it looks like the one in the diagram. I also took one look at the size of the err . . . receptacle and frankly it didn't seem quite right to me that that would fit in THAT.

It's so unfair that we have to spend so much time worrying about our vaginas when boys whang their willies all over the place, just waiting for a chance to use them.

I feel like, in an EQUAL world, there would be more penis admin.

10:30 a.m.

The toilets with the girls

"Kat! I think we've synchronized!" Sam says coming out of the toilet, the most joyous I've ever seen her about getting her period.

29

"YESS! Moon sisters!" I high-five her.

"WHAT? Why haven't I bloody synchronized? I'm going to the toilet to check!" Millie says.

She stomps into the toilet while Sam and I stare at each other, a little bit nervous about the outcome.

"I KNEW IT! I'm ALWAYS the odd one out!" Millie shouts through the door. "NOTHING! Not even a speck!"

"Well, you did have yours last week," I reason. "It would probably be a bit annoying to get one again this week, and at least you don't have to spend the day worrying about leakage."

"Kat! Ew! No!" Sam says.

"That's true, and when I get my period my boobs get so massive and heavy, my back can't cope with that kind of struggle two weeks in a row. You're so lucky you don't have to worry about that, Kat."

"Oh, cheers, Mills! Now's definitely the time to bring up my flat chest," I say sulkily.

This morning I felt intrepid with my menstrual cup, but now I just feel uncomfortable. Never mind, I'll have to reshuffle it a bit. A tiny bit of discomfort is nothing if I'm helping to save the planet, right?

"And it's not like I get away with it! I've got horrible period pains, I'm properly bloated, and either my vagina or this bloody menstrual cup is abnormally sized, and I'm willing to bet it's my clearly abnormal vagina."

"Your vagina is NOT abnormal. I think it's a bit like breaking in new shoes or something. You just have to get used to it. Maybe wear it while you're doing the vacuuming," Sam suggests.

"Please no! Feminists DO NOT VACUUM!" I practically shout. Am I the only one who understands feminism? Or is that wrong now? Do feminists actually vacuum because we can do everything? Confused, AGAIN.

"I guess I've got PLENTY of other stuff to stress out about anyway," Millie carries on, ignoring me. "I spent all of last night looking at this script for *Romeo and Juliet* and I don't understand ANY of it, and even if I did understand it, there's no way I can remember it all!"

"Fair play," says Sam. "It's basically like reading another language, one that Google Translate doesn't even recognize."

But somehow this gives me an idea.

"What if I help you with your lines? English is the one thing I'm not too bad at. It can be my contribution to the play!" I say, pleased that I've finally found a way that I can be involved. I was starting to get FOMO.

"Oh god, yes please! I'm properly drowning in it all," Millie says, clinging to my arm joyfully.

"Wanna help me with the set too?" Sam asks hopefully, clinging to my other arm. Suddenly I feel very far from FOMOville.

"You know I'm TERRIBLE at art," I say. "Remember the time I tried to draw a fruit bowl and Mr. Forth asked if it was a rabbit?"

"Ack, yeah. I'd forgotten about that. . . . Yeah . . . maybe . . . not?" Sam says, clearly trying and failing to spare my feelings.

11 a.m.

Bored in biology (how apt)

I think the menstrual cup is getting better. I just did a small wriggle in my seat, and it shifted slightly. I'd timed it to the same moment that Dr. Woodcock was cutting open an eyeball, so the whole room was squirming. I'm sure I just looked squirmy, like everyone else, not like I was trying to shift a giant rubber shot glass in my vagina.

Is where it's sitting technically even still my vagina, though? Isn't that bit called something else? I really need to pay more attention in these classes. This is the second time today I've wondered about this. I'm sure it's the vulva that's the outside bit and the vagina that's inside. But then why do people always just call all of it a "vagina"? Might stick my hand up and ask. It's got to be more useful to us all than this eyeball business.

I think the cup will be okay. Unless it falls out. What if it falls out? And my knickers can't hold the weight of the immense amount of period goop I lose? And then the cup and biblical levels of blood come gushing out of my knickers?

My thoughts are suddenly all focused on my crotch. Is it feeling a bit weak? Is this science lab about to become the end scene from the horror film *Carrie*? I'll never take a sturdy gusset for granted again.

"Urgh!"

I hadn't actually meant that groan to be out loud. I'm hoping it was timed with some kind of eyeball goop falling out. I look over at Millie, who has one eyebrow raised at me and is mouthing, *You okay?*

I do a little nod and try to focus on the grossness of Dr. Woodcock picking at eyeballs. Some of the class seem to be really enjoying this eyeball dissection—psychopaths. I'm making a mental note of who they are for when there's a Channel 5 documentary about them being a serial killer in the not-too-distant future.

1 p.m.

I've had enough now. It's too stressful. I wait until I have the toilet to myself and exchange the cup for a tampon. I'll get the hang of it, but maybe Sam's right and it is the sort of thing you have to break in. Maybe I should do some squats and lunges with it in—really put it to the test so that I can feel confident in its abilities.

Thank god, no one comes into the toilet until I've finished washing and drying the cup. I quickly throw it in my bag just as a few Year Sevens walk in and I briskly walk out. Nothing to see here!

1:05 p.m.

Back at the lunch table

Sam's appalled.

"So your menstrual cup is just chilling in your bag now, babe?"

"Yeah," I say, shoving half a sandwich into my mouth almost whole. That's another thing, does EVERYONE get this hungry on their period? I'm starving.

I'm starting to realize, though, that the cup situation is a bit odd—that it was in my vagina and now it's in my school bag. But there's not a lot I can do about it at the moment. I need to reassess this whole cup thing entirely.

"Oh, man, that's grim!" she wails, throwing down her ham sandwich.

I note this is a poor choice of sandwich for someone to be eating while having a chat about vaginas, and, with that, lunch is over for all of us.

4 p.m.

The playground, heading out of school. I've nearly made it through the day without any embarrassing events at all!

HOT JOSH APPROACHING! HOT JOSH APPROACHING! After yesterday, as well! He's talking to me and for some reason, I find myself twirling my hair around my finger and having to restrain myself from falling at his feet. WHAT IS THAT? I spend the rest of my life behaving like an almost-normal human, then he says one word to me, and I crumble into some girly, stuttering, fabby-shouting mess.

"Back in uniform today, then? That's a shame. . . . I liked the goth look on you."

Is Hot Josh flirting with ME? OH MY GOD, HE'S FLIRTING WITH ME EVEN AFTER I VAGINA-SIGNED AT HIM? I can feel Sam and Millie on either side of me, their eyes growing wider by the second. Must not make an ass of myself. Must be normal and not do anything vagina-y with my fingers. I'm just going to reply in a calm and considered way and not sound like a hee-hawing donkey.

What the hell? Is that a football hurtling toward me? How did it get there? Where has it come from? I seem to be completely powerless as it smacks me in the face and I feel myself falling backward in slow motion like a sack of potatoes.

I'm lying on the floor like some kind of upturned turtle, scrabbling to get myself together, skirt up around my eyeballs, and I wish so badly that I'd gotten a better grip on bikini-line hair removal.

This is SO embarrassing. I'll never get over this. Why is it taking so long for me to recover my modesty? Am I so mortified that I'm having some kind of out-of-body experience?

On a bad day my nether region looks a bit bear-like. On a good day, I can get it looking more like a squirrel's tail, and that's a GOOD day. Lord knows what type of animal Hot Josh (and the Entire World) are seeing hibernating between my legs. I don't think feminists are supposed to worry about waxing. But I wonder if that still applies when you're showing your pantaloons to the whole universe?

35

For the second time today I'm thinking about my crotch as Hot Josh once again offers me a hand up (gentlemanly in the face of my awful furry exposure). I think I might be able to ride this out after all. Although, what's Sam doing?

Is that my menstrual cup on the floor? Oh my god, she's picking my menstrual cup off the floor. She's quick, but not quick enough. Everyone's seen it.

It must have fallen out as I went down. And yet nothing else seems to have fallen out of my bag, of course it was just that. As if it joyfully jumped out to GREET EVERYONE and RUIN MY LIFE. I'm mortified. I can only hope that Josh doesn't know what it is. But he looks pretty embarrassed.

I leap up and grab my bag from the floor and my menstrual cup from Sam. I'm getting out of here as fast as possible. I can hear Hot Josh calling after me. Is he asking if I'm okay?

"Completely fine! Thanks!" I shout back, hopefully in a casual, cool tone while RUNNING AWAY.

As I turn the corner, I can see Terrible Trudy approach him from the shadows, practically rubbing her hands with glee. Like an actual cartoon villain. I think I know exactly where that football came from. It's the bunny all over again.

4:15 p.m.

The walk of shame

So, in two days my interactions with Hot Josh have involved me:
· Saying "Power to the pussy!" to him

· Throwing my menstrual cup at his feet with my skirt up around my eyeballs
· Scrabbling on the ground like a crab/cat/turtle TWICE

My life is over.

We're going back to Sam's house to debrief now. I need to hide.

"I shall have to leave the country. What are schools like in Switzerland? That's where people go to disappear, right?" I say, slightly dazed.

"Sure," says Sam. "If you've committed a political crime. I don't think dropping a menstrual cup at a guy's feet and showing a playground your underpants is quite that, though, babe."

"I honestly barely saw anything." I know Millie's lying but it's sweet that she's trying.

I'm inclined to think that the flashing of my hairy bikini line is in fact a political crime. It certainly doesn't look right down there to me. Switzerland is probably the best idea.

"She's right. You're spiraling, no one saw anything, it all happened so quick," Sam says.

"Also, so what if they did? FEMINISM! Remember? You're the one that was telling us we shouldn't be period-shamed anymore!" Millie says.

"YEAH! Or furry-vagina-shamed," Sam joins in.

"Okay, yeah, good point," I admit reluctantly.

"Now, how about we distract you by running some lines? I'll let you be the nurse again if you like. She's got the best bits anyway," Millie says.

I bloody KNEW she only wanted to be Juliet because of Nick. I KNEW IT.

5 p.m.

Sam's bedroom

I'm trying to concentrate on playing the nurse to Millie's Juliet, but it's actually quite hard to forget you've just embarrassed yourself in front of the whole school AND the love of your life, Mr. Dream Sex God. Sam's house is nice, though. Maybe I'll just hide out here forever.

Sam's dad's an architect who built their house when she was a baby. With her mum being an interior designer it's altogether pretty great. There's also art all over the walls that her parents bring back from their yearly visits to Trinidad to visit Sam's grandparents.

Her parents fell in love at fifteen and moved to London at eighteen to go to design school together. It's such a cute story. High school sweethearts. Her whole family's artistic—Sam's sister Jas left last weekend to start a degree at Central Saint Martins.

"Do you girls want anything?" Sam's mum comes in for the second time since we've been here.

"No, Mum, we're still good. Thanks, though!" Sam says.

"Okay, well, let me know!"

Sam ushers her out of the room.

"Mum's starting to do my head in. It's been four days

since Jas went to uni and she's spent all those days fretting about her 'nest' emptying and SUFFOCATING ME with her attention."

I'm trying to be supportive and listen but I keep thinking about my extreme menstrual cup mortification.

"Last night while I was building a prototype set with bits of cardstock at the kitchen table, she started trying to help me. It was so weird."

"She just cares, and that's nice. My mum and dad are at work so much at the moment that Issy and I don't even see them till bedtime," Millie says. Both her parents are lawyers. Her nan moved over from Greece to help take care of her and her little sister when they were young, but she died last year. It hit poor Millie really hard.

"I know—I shouldn't complain. I've just got so much to do. I've got the sets and then I found out that if I'm going to apply for the art-camp scholarship that Jas used to get then I need to get my portfolio to them in SIX weeks. So far, my portfolio is three things."

"I thought Jas didn't go to camp until Sixth Form?" I ask.

"She didn't but the earlier I can get in, the better," Sam says.

"You've always been an overachiever," Millie says.

"Yes, and I intend to stay that way," Sam replies.

5:30 p.m.

Using Sam's bed as a stage with Millie

39

I've been doing some of my absolute greatest acting as the nurse, but I still can't stop thinking about what happened at school and worrying. I'm just going to text Freddie and see if he heard anything.

Me: Freddie, have you heard anything that people at school might have said about me maybe?

Freddie: What's it worth?

Me: If you don't tell me then I will wedgie you until your balls retract up into your stomach when I get home.

Freddie: Urgh. Rude.

Freddie: Just that you fell over, flashed your knickers at Josh, and then threw a condom at his feet.

Freddie: Oh and Terrible Trudy says you're desperate.

Freddie: Kind of sounds like you are to be honest.

Freddie: I'm going to disown you by the way. I can't be seen related to someone so embarrassing.

"Noooooo!" I start shouting at my phone screen and bury my head into the cushions on Sam's little bedroom sofa.

"What?" I realize then that Millie is still in character as Juliet and thinks that I'm referring to her acting skills and line interpretation, so I show them both my phone.

They read with eyes growing wider by the second.

"Babe, what are you going to do? That's so much worse than the cup!" So good of Sam to manage to stifle her giggles for long enough to take note of the gravity of the situation.

"I KNOW!" I cry. "I'm going to have to move schools! Actually, other schools will probably hear about that level of hideousness. I'll become one of those urban legends! I'll have to move countries. Maybe Switzerland isn't far enough away for them not to hear about it. Maybe I should join the Mars One mission?"

I sit with my head in my hands while the girls start to formulate a plan to integrate me back into polite society, into which I clearly cannot be trusted.

When I lift my head, Millie has a webpage up called "Debrett's Etiquette and Modern Manners."

6 p.m.

Shamed in Shamesville

My phone buzzes on the floor. I've been lying on Sam's sofa for an hour now with the cushions over my head, trying to work out how I can stay here forever.

Matt: Is it true that you threw a condom at Hot Josh then writhed around on the floor trying to give him a demented lap dance?! Xxx

Me: You KNOW it's not!

Matt: Yep, but it's a great story. Trudy told Krish who just told me. I haven't told anyone but you though 😊 XX

Me: You better be telling the truth.

Matt: Does your shame want some company after dinner? Xx

Me: Please xxx

8 p.m.

My room—crisis talks with Matt

I'll never leave the house again. Matt says it's not that bad and that he's been defending my honor to everyone.

   MY HONOR DOESN'T NEED DEFENDING.

   IT WAS ALL TERRIBLE TRUDY'S FAULT FOR BEING TERRIBLE.

9 p.m.

I'll have to be homeschooled.

9:30 p.m.

No. I will not be ashamed.

   I will not be period-shamed, slut-shamed, or clumsy-shamed.
Or squirrel-shamed.

   None of the shaming.

   No siree.

   Nope.

9:37 p.m.

Except everyone thinks I was trying to seduce Josh with my bear fanny and an unwrapped condom.

And yes, I did mean to write "bear" rather than "bare" then. It's certainly more bear than bare these days.

9:38 p.m.

How on earth could they think that was a condom, though? It's got a big long thing hanging off it. What on EARTH do they think that bit is? Some kind of fanny lollipop?

9:40 p.m.

I'm a feminist. I can overcome this. Think of all the women who have been oppressed, imprisoned, silenced.

The suffragettes, Taylor Swift('s music), the women who entered the Big Brother house year after year . . .

10 p.m.

Oh, sod it. I'm starting to wish that the suffragettes never got us anything. At least then maybe I could just be left at home to wither in bed on my period. None of this would have happened.

10:10 p.m.

What did the suffragettes do about their periods, though? Were they all protesting in diapers?

Might google it. It could be great for my Feminist Friday blog. Reminds me, I need to ask Miss Mills about that ASAP. I should stop distracting myself with boys and get back to the matter at hand!

> **What did the suffragettes do about their periods?**   🔍

10:30 p.m.

Okay, so I found this article by someone named James Griggs (A MAN) called "What did women through history do about periods?"

Well, it's interesting you bloody ask, James "A MAN" Griggs.

10:35 p.m.

Actually, this is quite good. My favorite bit is about the linen rags that Roman women used to put into their knickers: "'menstruous rags,' as they are referred to in the Bible . . ."

MENSTRUOUS RAGS. So aggressive. I'm definitely going to start using that expression.

11 p.m.

It'd be a great insult: "Stop being such a MENSTRUOUS RAG."

IIII

11:30 p.m.

Finally rolled up in the safety of my bed

I touch the light switch three times before I go to sleep. Today's been a bad enough day as it is. I won't even question it.

At least I distracted myself from all the shame with the menstruous rags.

At least I didn't throw a menstruous rag at Hot Josh.

12 a.m.

But which bit is the vulva and which bit is the vagina, though? Does ANYONE know?!

Would google it but I'm afraid of porn.

12:15 a.m.

Sod it, just going to google. It's embarrassing to be the daughter of a top scientist and not know this sort of stuff. Mum would be so ashamed. If she isn't already. As long as I don't look at any images or videos, it'll be okay.

Which bit is the vulva and which bit is the vagina?	Q

12:17 a.m.

I know I said I wasn't going to look at images or videos but there was something on there that looked fucking loopy. I'm just going to take a quick look. . . .

12:45 a.m.

Oh, dear god, no. My vagina cannot do that, nor should it.

The internet is a bad place.

BAD.

Unfeminist thoughts: 3
1. Not knowing the difference between a vulva and a vagina.
2. Wanting to use my period as an excuse not to make the most of my education and privileges hard won for me by feminist activists of the past.
3. Feeling ashamed of my menstrual cup—even if it was just for a short while.

Friday, September 1

I AM FATIGUED BY SUFFRAGE!

I mean maybe that's a little dramatic, but I stayed up for most of the night reading about the suffragettes and they really had a poor deal. I'm very pleased they got us the vote. I feel awful for yesterday.

7:30 a.m.

My bedroom

I AM NOT ASHAMED! I am disappointed at my attempts at feminism so far, though, considering I've:
· Graffitied the name of the school pervert on the playground
· Turned my attempt at supporting TIME'S UP into an advert for said pervert, via the addition of a hashtag to his name
· Failed so badly at using a menstrual cup that the whole school thinks it was a condom that I was using to seduce a boy. At least it was clean, though (small mercies, people)
· Although thinking about it, I did demonstrate the feminist bush in my knickers by falling over yesterday

Bea has just walked in looking guilty and come to sit at my feet. I cuddle up into her soft fur. Thank god for Bea.

"Are you a feminist, do you think, Bea? You're not interested in boys, are you? I mean, I know that's because we had you done, but frankly I wouldn't blame you for not being interested in boy dogs. Their bits are so . . . dangly . . . all out on show. There's no mystery there, is there? Imagine if we walked around with all our bits hanging out? Fallopian tubes just dancing in the wind."

She's just dropped something at my feet and put her head on my leg, staring sheepishly up at me.

It's my menstrual cup—chewed to bits, barely resembling its former self. A metaphor for my attempts at feminism, dignity, and poise from this week. FFS.

I'm unsure how I feel about the fact that the dog has eaten something that has been in my vagina. I don't even want to contemplate the reasons why she may have thought it a suitable chew toy, and it certainly won't be going back up there now.

She's quite clearly neither a feminist nor an eco-warrior.

As I contemplate whether Bea was trolling me or doing me a favor, I hear the doorbell ring and Freddie screaming that Millie and Sam are here.

The girls glide into my room in black berets and sunglasses looking like they're hungover in Paris.

"Err . . . bonjour?"

"We thought we'd all go incognito today, following your little *faux pas*." Millie looks proud of herself for using a French phrase while wearing her beret.

"Also we were going for the Beyoncé-in-Topshop-trying-not-to-be-noticed look—how did we do?" Sam huffs.

"Oh yes, I see it now."

I put my beret and sunglasses on too and unfortunately

look more like a drunk in Topshop, but one for all and all for one and all that. Intrepidly we head off to face another day fighting the patriarchy. Or, in today's case, fighting the false rumors of sluttery.

I had hoped we were past the stage where women would be judged for this sort of thing. If a boy dropped a condom, he'd be a hero.

Just saying.

8:30 a.m.

Hiding behind a bush outside the school gates, waiting for the bell to ring

I'm trying to avoid being seen in case:

A. Whatever I do or say now gets mistaken for me trying to proposition someone.

B. Terrible Trudy or one of her Tuberculosis buddies launches another attack on me.

C. I see anyone or anyone makes a comment about my knickers, a condom, my cup, or #Tim. Although, I definitely don't feel shame. (If you say something enough, does it make it true?)

We're all huddled peering around the side of said bush, our eyes peeled, afraid that someone may see us.

"Here's the plan!" Sam says. She appears to have drawn a bloody map and is enjoying this WAY too much, if you ask me.

"We go into the school here." She points to the gate we're standing right by. "Once inside, we need to get to here—our homeroom—without being seen by people as we pass through here—the main playground—or here—down the corridor."

"How do we do it?" Millie asks intensely.

"We pull our berets down to hide our eyes. No one utters a word until we're home and dry at the dropping-off point. We both hold Kat's hands so that she cannot fall over or throw anything fanny-based at anyone."

"For god's sake. Let's just go!" I say. "Surely nothing can be worse than yesterday."

"Don't tempt fate. We're trying to help you. You're stuck in some kind of mortification spiral right now and we're going to get you out of it," Millie says, saluting like she's in the bloody Special Air Service.

8:40 a.m.

We enter homeroom as stealthily as possible. However, the three of us clattering in all at once in berets and sunglasses is, on reflection, not as stealthy as I'd have liked, and Miss Mills looks heartily amused by the sight of us. I'm starting to wonder if she might actually be a bad feminist.

When I arrive at my desk, there's a folded-up bit of paper with my name on it. I approach with massive caution. This cannot be good. I pick it up between thumb and forefinger, remembering that I have a small bottle of hand sanitizer in my bag and I'm not afraid to use it.

Kat,
If you wanted someone to deflower you, you should have just asked. My body is yours for the taking. I'll be the Greek god to your goddess. The Adam to your Eve. The Paul Daniels to your Debbie McGee. Let me know when you're free.
All my lust,
#Tim x

I throw it to the floor in disgust and immediately set about the task of sanitizing my hands. I wonder if I should just ask someone to hack them off for me. I will never feel clean again.

9 a.m.

I remember Debbie McGee from last year's *Strictly* and I'm pretty sure that Paul Daniels is (A) much older than her and (B) dead. Not sure why #Tim (as he will now be forever known, thanks to my inability to spray-paint fast enough) would want to be an old, dead magician.

11 p.m.

Safe bed

For once, the rest of school was pretty standard. Matt came over this evening and we had film night and talked about his first day of Sixth Form on Monday.

I touch the light switch three times, pleased that today was a little less (period) drama. Maybe I'll survive this term after all?

Unfeminist thoughts: 1
Feeling resentment toward the menstrual cup after yesterday and relief when Bea destroyed it so I don't have to look at it anymore. Bad Kat—it's not the cup's fault.

Saturday, September 8
10 a.m.

Still in bed

I've got all morning to do absolutely sweet nothing, so I'm in bed with Bea and I've just finished *Pride and Prejudice*. Bliss. Next on my reading list is one I plucked from Mum's shelf called *Divine Secrets of the Ya-Ya Sisterhood*.

10:30 a.m.

Bea is happy, I am happy. I've even made myself a cup of tea, I'm never moving again. . . . Oh my phone's going off like crazy. Ack.

> **Revenge of the squirrel fanny**
> Sam, Millie, Me

> Millie: SOS SOS!!!

> Millie: MAJOR PLAY DEVELOPMENT!

> Millie: Sophie Steiner's mum is coming!

> Millie: THE AGENT.

> Millie: She's coming!

Millie: WHAT IF THIS IS MY BIG BREAK?!
I DON'T UNDERSTAND THE LINES!
I DON'T UNDERSTAND ANY OF IT!
KAT!!! HELLLLPPPP!!!!

Me: This IS SO EXCITING!! THIS COULD BE IT!!!
YOU'RE GOING TO BE AMAZING! Come over!
We'll get you agent ready in no time! xxxx

Sam: On my way too. This is so exciting!
Don't worry, lady. We got you Xxx

Oops. There goes the peace and quiet. No more bliss over here. I get up and Bea does a small whine.

Sorry, girl.

2 p.m.

The kitchen

I'm currently being Romeo to Millie's Juliet, but it's not going massively well, if I'm being honest. She really does have a very poor grasp of what any of the words mean.

"Why don't you just watch the film?" Dad says, looking over his laptop at us.

"Dad . . ." I start.

"It was a modern retelling, Kitty Kat. Leonardo DiCaprio was in it. It was a swoon fest!"

Gross.

"What's this?" Mum says, coming in.

"Dad thinks we should watch the film of *Romeo and Juliet*." I huff.

"With Leonardo DiCaprio?! It's been years since I watched that! John, that's a great idea. Kat, you'd love it. He's SWOON-worthy."

For god's sake, will my parents stop saying SWOON?

2:30 p.m.

The sofa

"Oh, Leo! Hubba-hubba!" Dad's saying to the TV screen.

It's annoying because (A) this is actually pretty good, and (B) Dad is right. I would so be all over Leo if I were Juliet. So what if you've got family drama, love, have you SEEN him?

More unfeminist thoughts. Bad Kat.

3 p.m.

Millie, Sam, and I are sitting in complete silence all wide eyed, transfixed by Leo. No one's so much as taking a breath as we watch them in the swimming pool. The only noise is the occasional sound of popcorn being chewed. Even Bea is silently appreciating Leo.

"FUCK THE FUCK OFF AND GET OUT FOREVERRRR!" suddenly comes from Matt's front garden. All of us jump, spin around on the sofa, and pop our heads up to the windows to see what's happening.

"OH EM GEEE!" we all say at once before putting our hands over our eyes.

"What is it?" Dad says as he and Mum come over.

"Terry," I manage from behind my hands.

"And his todger!" Mum gasps.

"Jesus, Terry, mate, this is a family street!" my dad's shouting out the window as Terry tries to cup the, errr, offending article.

I cannot believe the first penis I've ever seen in real life belongs to Matt's mum's old, gross boyfriend.

3:15 p.m.

The sofa with Matt while Mum and Dad decant wine into Sandra in the kitchen

"So Terry was in the shower and his phone kept going off and Mum got annoyed with it and went to put it on silent, and she saw all these messages from TINDER. From three different women on there," Matt's recounting.

"NO!" we all say.

"It turns out Terry has been on Tinder thrusting his todger about and pretending to be TEN years younger than he actually is."

"Fucking hell," I say.

"Your poor mum!" says Sam.

"MEN!" says Millie.

"It's okay, he's only been around six months, if that. And he always calls me 'champ.' She can do better," he says.

The. Drama.

11 p.m.

In bed

So much for my day of rest. On the bright side, though, there's still tomorrow. And I'm quite loving the *Ya-Ya Sisterhood*.

I still cannot believe that I saw my first real-life penis under such circumstances. I mean, I've touched one before, just not looked one in the . . . um . . . eye. It was on French exchange. I was making out with one of the French boys and he put my hand in his trousers, but I didn't really know what I was supposed to do so I just sort of held it for a bit, then pulled my hand out and RAN AWAY.

I touch the light switch three times. It's necessary after today.

Unfeminist thoughts: 1
Not rooting for Juliet when I should have because I was BEDAZZLED by Leo's hotness.

Sunday, September 9
3 p.m.

The sofa

Sundays in our house are so beyond the valley of boredoms-ville. Especially today when Freddie has mysteriously disap-peared, and Mum and Dad are sitting in the kitchen in dark glasses, crying into their coffee cups due to wine-o-rama with Sandra yesterday. I'm mayor of Boring Town right now. The absolute queen of NOTHING.

Might see what Angry Angus the cat is up to on Insta. He's a cat who's always angry—duh!—but also always funny. Ooh, today he's sitting in a sink. Looks angry. Fun. Now what?

BEEP

OH, THANK GOD. A TEXT! Who will it be from?! Someone exciting?

Oh, it's just Matt.

Matt: SOS, KITTY KAT! I need help picking out an outfit for the first day of Sixth Form tomorrow. Mum's too hungover to function. PLEASE HELP MEEEEE Xxxx

Me: I'm coming over. But I cannot leave Bea here in this house of hangover and doom xxx

Matt's bedroom

Matt's mum doesn't actually seem that bad compared to my parents. She's capable of words and even the odd sentence. Mum and Dad have only managed noises today.

Bea and I, however, are exhausted. We've reviewed twenty outfits in all. Fortunately, the last one turned out to be the winner.

"You won't forget about me when you're in your Sixth Form common room, will you?" I ask.

"Um, no. You're still right next door to me. . . ." Matt rolls his eyes.

"I know, but people say that Sixth Form's different and you're more grown up in Sixth Form and everyone else is a loser when you're in Sixth Form," I say, really laboring the point that he's in SIXTH FORM there for him.

"Nahhh. You're already a loser and I'll never be too grown up to hang out with you, Kitty Kat." Matt slings his arm around my shoulder, singing "You've Got a Friend in Me" from *Toy Story*.

We've sung this song to each other since we were about six. Mostly when one of us fell off our bike and hurt ourself. Matt once had to sing it to me three times after a particularly bad spat with some stinging nettles.

8 p.m.

Sitting at the living room window with Mum, Dad, and Freddie

"Imagine having the balls to do that after showing the whole street your bits," Mum says, stuffing popcorn into her mouth and then passing the bowl along the line.

We've been watching a thankfully clothed, but sadly not sober Terry serenading Sandra outside their house for the last half hour. In that time we've had "The Lady in Red," "Sorry Seems to Be the Hardest Word," "Candle in the Wind," "If I Could Turn Back Time," and, most disturbingly, Justin Bieber's "Sorry."

"Do you think she'll come out?" Dad asks.

"NO!" Mum and I shout together.

"Should we throw water on him or something?" Dad says.

"Probably not a bad idea," Mum replies.

"CAN WE USE THE PRESSURE WASHER?!" Freddie shouts, delighted there's some part of this he can get on board with.

"Okay, it's time to put Terry out of his misery," Dad says. "I'm going to have a word."

Mum, Freddie, and I stay on the sofa. My phone lights up again with a message from Matt. We've been texting throughout the ordeal. He and his mum are like hostages right now and I'm their line to the outside world.

Matt: Dear lord, make it stop.

Me: We've sent Dad in to negotiate.

Matt: Thank GOD.

10 p.m.

In bed

It took Dad ages to convince Terry to go home. AGES. He finally left about half an hour ago when Sandra slung the window open and said she'd call the police. So much drama for a Sunday night!

10:30 p.m.

Please don't let Matt forget about me when he becomes a Sixth Former tomorrow. I touch the light switch three times just to be sure.

Unfeminist thoughts: 0
I don't think I've had any thoughts all day, let alone unfeminist ones.

Wednesday, September 12

So, I know I said I'd write every day, but some days are just too uneventful to bother.

10:30 a.m.

The toilets

"Did you hear Polly Perkins's parents are away so she's having a party on Saturday? The whole of Year Eleven and most of Sixth Form are going. Fancy it?" Sam asks.

"I bet that means Nick'll be there!" Millie's eyes light up and she looks like she might explode with joy. As if she's not already spending enough time with him in rehearsals!

"I should think so . . . and Hot Josh. . . . We won't let you near him alone after last week, though, Kat." Sam chuckles to herself. Smart.

My stomach does a gymnastics move worthy of the bloody Olympics. Parties make me anxious; any social situations with lots of people make me anxious. Hot Josh being there is like the massive, anxious cherry on top of the big anxiety-filled cake. But I'd also be more anxious about missing out. So, weighing those two options of anxiety or anxiety, I guess I'll go. What could really go wrong?

"And Dave will be there," Sam says. "He's the one who messaged me about it, so that must mean he wants me there, right?" she asks hopefully.

"I would say that's basically him asking you out on a date!" I say.

The sofa with Mum, Dad, and Freddie

We're watching *EastEnders* after dinner. It's something we do every now and then so that Dad can give his impressions a run-out. He does a great Mick and an uncanny Dot Cotton. My talents are Kat and Bianca. Mum does a good Sharon (demure, quietly furious about everything) and Freddie likes to do Phil Mitchell, which he's actually terrible at. Matt would normally be here doing characters like Stacey and Mr. Trueman (he's got a very diverse acting range) but he seems to be MIA tonight.

Dad's trying to be menacing right now but actually he just looks like he needs to poo, and when he switches to Dot Cotton abruptly he looks relieved, like the poo has been passed.

Most families play board games together; we pretend to be characters in an East End soap. God. Why can't we be more normal?

I've got half an eye on my phone, connecting with the world outside this house for stability.

> **Me:** Where are you, Matt? You're missing a cracking EastEnders episode. Mr. Trueman has been drinking rum! Xxx

Matt: Didn't leave school till about 5 because I was messing around with the guys, and now I have to do so much work before tomorrow 😭

Me: Uh-oh. I guess that's what being a big Sixth Former is all about Xxx

Revenge of the squirrel fanny
Sam, Millie, Me

Millie: Oh god, what am I going to wear to the party?! It'll be the first time that Nick has seen me outside of my dingy school uniform. I need to look nice! Xxx

Me: EER HELLO! MILLIE?! NO! We're feminists?! We do NOT make ourselves look nice for men! We make ourselves look nice for OURSELVES Xxx

Sam: So you won't be making yourself look nice for Hot Josh then? Xxx

Me: I will be making myself look nice for me Xxx

Millie: So for Hot Josh then Xxx

Bollocks. Busted! I'm TRYING, though.

10 p.m.

Please just let me have one social event with Hot Josh present

64

where I don't embarrass myself, expose myself, or throw myself at him. What if I do something so bad that my family and friends all disown me?

I touch the light switch three times.

Unfeminist thoughts: 1

But it's a blurry line. I mean, I know it's not feminist to want to look nice for a boy (right?), but is it okay if I want to look nice for me so that I feel confident in front of the boy? Can I be a sexy feminist?

Thursday, September 13
9 p.m.

My bedroom

THIS IS NOT FOR A MAN. THIS IS FOR ME.

I know that you're supposed to show off your best assets when attracting a man . . . I mean . . . dressing for yourself. The thing is that I don't know if I've really got any "assets" so I've purchased some of those chicken fillet bra things or, as I like to call them, "fillets à boobié"—said in a French accent.

I know they're quite old-school, but I'm hoping they'll stick to my boobs and create the illusion, at least, that I've got some kind of womanhood factor going on. Also hoping Dad won't see them in the laundry basket and give me a lecture about how I'm lovely just the way I am. Like he did when he found out I was planning to dye my hair pink last year. I'm still furious I didn't get to do that.

I know this is very unfeminist of me not to be happy with my body as it is, and I'm really trying my best to be better. But it's hard to change the thoughts in your head to match up with what you THINK you should be feeling rather than what you're actually feeling.

At least once a day I worry that I don't feel very womanly and that I don't have "womanly curves." And maybe that's why I'm connecting with feminism so much. I feel like it's a step toward feeling more like a woman even if I don't have the curves or the sophistication. It seems unfair not to feel very womanly when you still have to deal with menstrual cramps, though.

So maybe I am just making myself feel more womanly and feminist with these fillets à boobié, and I am actually still DOING GOOD FEMINISM?

Who am I kidding?

Unfeminist thoughts: 2
Thoughts made of silicone—a fillet à boobié for each breast.

Friday, September 14

7 a.m.

My bedroom

It's the end of the second week of term and I STILL haven't asked about doing the Feminist Friday blog. STILL. I'm letting myself down and all the women who need to be talked about. I keep finding new and inspiring women to talk about too. For instance—**Feminist Friday Research Fact**—a woman invented the sanitary belt!

She was called Mary Beatrice Davidson Kenner, but no one wanted to buy the patent from her because when they went to meet her, they saw she was Black and said that they were no longer interested. People need to know about Mary Beatrice Davidson Kenner, and I am going to tell them!

I'll post a picture of her on Instagram. I've got 150 followers, that's as good a place as any to start.

I wonder if Mary Beatrice ever wore fillets à boobié? She was DEFINITELY a feminist.

9 a.m.

Cannot believe my post has only been liked by my mum. I have so much educating to do. Millie and Sam need to pull their fingers out—quite literally—and like it.

11 a.m.

Biology again. Yawn

Dr. Woodcock has just put a gigantic penis up on the electronic whiteboard. It's not supposed to be that big, but something's broken, so we're all snickering while he tries to get rid of the twenty-foot penis that's currently looking down on us all.

The whole thing is not helped by the fact that he is called Dr. Woodcock.

11:05 a.m.

#Tim just announced to the class that a vagina would be more to his taste and Comedy Krish (our school funny guy. I mean. He's quite funny. He's not THAT funny—let's be honest) announced that would be a bit like staring into a cavernous cave.

I'm going to bet that neither of them have ever actually seen a vagina before.

11.07 a.m.

Giant penis is starting to a feel a bit threatening now. Like the King Kong of penises. Slightly afraid it will jump out of the whiteboard and attack us all.

11.08 a.m.

When you think about it, the giant penis is a bit like a meta-phor for the patriarchy—bearing down on us, suffocating and squashing us, casting a shadow over our days.

11.09 a.m.

The patriarchal penis still reigns supreme.

11:10 a.m.

Hooray! He couldn't fix the image, so he just went to the next page on the electronic whiteboard and it WAS a giant vagina next to a very spacious womb. Now #Tim is getting his wish, though, and that's a bit grim.

Never seen ovaries so big. Millie's laughing so much that she nearly fell off her chair and I had to grab her to stabilize her.

I can hear Comedy Krish from the back of the room saying things like, "My eyes!" And, "Please, god, no."

Apart from his own birth, I believe this will definitely be the closest he ever comes to a vagina.

11:15 a.m.

Dr. Woodcóck has had to leave the room. He said it was to get technical support but we think he might be having a giant-genitals-related nervous breakdown.

11:20 *a.m.*

Krish is drawing teeth on the vagina like it's a mouth. He's also given it two eyes and a speech bubble saying, "Hi, I'm Virginia Vagina."

11:23 *a.m.*

Dr. Woodcock is back. Krish's got detention.

2:30 *p.m.*

Unsure if it's one of those urban legends or something, but someone's just told me Dr. Woodcock's first name is Richard.

Dick Woodcock.

I can't even.

4:30 *p.m.*

Millie's living room sofa

Millie's house is the next street after Sam's. As usual, her parents are still at work, so we've let her little sister Issy hang with us too. She's in Freddie's year but she's MUCH more grown up than him. Like MUCH.

"Do you think that I could ever look like Cara Delevingne?" Millie's asking, scrolling through Cara Delevingne's profile on Insta.

"No, because you look like Millie . . . and Cara Delevingne looks like Cara Delevingne. . . ." I say.

Millie sighs deeply. "I guess."

4:45 p.m.

"OH MY GOD. HELP! HELP! HELP!" I'm flapping my hands around like a bird unable to take flight.

"What?" Millie and Sam are staring at me like I'm a lunatic, and Millie's little sister has taken her headphones off and come to peer over my shoulder at my screen.

"I've double tapped! I've double tapped! Help me!"

"What did you double tap? WHICH ONE?!" Millie is as frantic as I am because she knows exactly what I've been looking at.

We've been stalking boys on Insta again. I was looking through Hot Josh's hot pictures. I guess I lost control of my thumb at the excitement of it all.

What is wrong with me?

"I'm sure it's not as bad as you think. Which picture?" Sam always manages to stay calm in a crisis.

"It was this one. Of him half-naked on holiday with his parents TWO MONTHS AGO." I turn the phone around slowly to face them.

72

"Ohhhh, have you unliked it? I think if you unlike it quickly enough, it makes it okay again! QUICK, UNLIKE IT!" Sam's jumping up and down, flapping her arms as well now, so I know it must be bad.

"I HAVE, but what if he still gets the notification?"

"Oh yeah, he will," says Issy casually. How DARE she? No respect for her elders.

I feel like it's time to get serious and start googling:

How can I freeze the internet?   Q

Is there a way of breaking all of Instagram so that someone can't see the one hundredth hideously embarrassing thing I've done this week?

And more sensibly:

Can you stop someone from seeing that you've liked their picture on instagram?   Q

None of these googles are coming up with anything useful. It's just chat rooms of people who sound as anxious as I am.

I'm fucked.

6 p.m.

My bedroom back at home

"Hahahahaahaha! Kat! Did you click like on a half-naked

73

picture of Josh from two months ago?" Freddie screeches as he runs into my room.

Urgh, so he knows, then.

"Trudy told her friend Sharon, and Sharon's little sister told Stacey in my year, and now you're all anyone's talking about for the ten thousandth time this term. You're such a loser!"

And so does everyone else.

Great. Thanks, Freddie. Which weasel told Trudy?

My phone's buzzing:

Matt: Are you going to Polly's party tomorrow? Xxx

Matt: Did you like the half-naked picture of Hot Josh on purpose? Xxxx

Me: NO!!! Please help me xxx

Me: And yes, I am going to Polly's party tomorrow Xxx

Matt: I'll see you there, from afar probably. I don't know if it's safe to be associated with you now

Me: *GIF of lonely girl*

Matt: Just joking, I'll come round yours tomorrow and we can head over together. Don't touch anything until then. Don't talk to anyone, don't do anything. Just sit still and be quiet. You are a walking disaster this term.

Unfeminist thoughts: 1

Probably should not be ogling naked pictures of men as technically this is objectifying them and thou shalt not do things to others if thou does not want to be ogled oneself.

Saturday, September 15
6 p.m.

My dressing room (it's the same as my bedroom, just wanted to make myself seem fancier. Did it work?)

Moon Sisters
Sam, Millie, Me

Sam: I'm on my way over. Hot Josh is definitely going to be there. He's posted loads of pictures of him half-naked getting ready for the party. Kat, you're not allowed near it in case your thumb twitches with excitement again Xxx

Me: Oh my god I want to see.

Millie: You know the rules, you can't be trusted to look at his page unattended. We'll show you when we get there but you must not touch the phone, it must be at least one meter away from you and your tappy fingers at all times. We love you but you're a disaster.

Me: I promise not to double tap it with my eyes Xxx

Sam: Does anyone else think it's a bit twatty to post so many half-naked selfies, though? Xxx

6:15 p.m.

Still languishing in my dressing room

"Mind if I come in?" Matt says, knocking and walking in at the same time.

I turn around wearing my kimono dressing gown (fillets à boobié suctioned in place) to see his eyes practically pop out of his head.

"Jesus Christ, Tits McGee! Someone's inflated you!"

"Do you think it's too much?" I ask, approaching him.

"GET YOUR DIRTY PILLOWS AWAY FROM ME!" he cries, shielding his face and batting me away.

Oh god. I thought they'd make me look nice. Older. More sophisticated.

6:20 p.m.

I can hear Sam and Mills racing each other up the stairs. Such children. I wonder when our poise and sophistication will kick in? This coming from me, the smuggler of fillets à boobié. At least they'll be more supportive of my newfound breasts than Matt.

Both of them come crashing excitedly through my door. Sam looks amazing, wearing a brightly colored casual-looking dress with a black suede biker jacket over the top, and some mega heels that she's definitely stolen from her sister's wardrobe of things she left behind when she went to uni.

Millie's wearing a lovely floaty top, some jeans, and the coolest pair of leopard-print sneakers I've ever seen. They've got a pink, ballet-style bow tying them neatly up and I feel an extreme amount of jealousy that she owns them and I do not.

"WHERE DID THOSE PUPPIES COME FROM?" Sam gestures at my boobs while Millie stares at them agog. She gives them a bit of a poke, but I cannot feel it. Such is the shock-absorbing power of the fillets à boobié.

"Might have put in a bit of fillets à boobié action."

"They're massive! Should you not have tried something a bit more natural?" Sam's appalled. Easy for her to say when she's got a full chest.

"THAT'S WHAT I SAID!" Matt agrees.

"Will you give yourself a bad back with those, though?" Millie appears to have confused them with actual breasts, not just ones made of lightweight silicone.

"I need someone to make a snap decision for me. Jeans or skirt?" I say, ignoring their childish assessment of my tits. I'm clearly trying something new and I think they should be more supportive.

"That skirt is very nineties. Go with that, a black top, black biker jacket, and your little suede boots." Sam finds dressing so easy that it hurts. Why can't I be more like Sam? Or Millie? Or maybe just anyone but me?

Le sigh.

7:30 p.m.

Polly's house

AKA the biggest house in the world. Who actually lives in a house like this?

To be honest, I didn't know that there were this many teenagers in the entire county. I think some of them are from the other two schools in the town, though. They're all sprawled out down the driveway and I'm relieved that we made my dad drop us around the corner.

Polly's parents are away, but I feel like when they get home they might have a small inkling that this party has taken place. As we walk through the door I hear something smashing, but Polly already seems to be too far gone to care. She's currently trying to lean sexily over the island in the kitchen while a Sixth Form boy observes in a concerned manner. She looks like she's winded. She's giving less of an impression of allure and more of an impression of an old-age pensioner who's fallen and can't get up.

I'm scanning the room looking for Hot Josh, Millie's scanning the room for Nick, Sam's scanning the room for Dave, and Matt's trying to find the booze. All I can see right now is #Tim, wearing a bow tie (?) and waistcoat (?! maybe he really IS going for the Paul Daniels thing?), and moving from girl to girl, trying to talk to them. I can imagine the sorts of things he's saying: *I've got a magic trick for you. . . . I can make my hand disappear . . . into your bra!* And I'm sure he'll have already rolled out his classic *The more you feel them, the bigger they get!* at least twice.

As if by actual magic, Hot Josh, Dave, and booze appear to be together, with Nick not far away. The four of us make a bee-line for what appears to us to be a very desirable kitchen counter. Matt peels off toward Nick and the other guys from his year when we get there.

Hot Josh looks . . . hot (wow, my writing skills are journalist-ready—yes?). He's wearing a white T-shirt and jeans, and you can see his muscles through the thin material. If this were a sexy romance novel, I'd say that they were rippling. But it isn't. This is feminism.

I try to walk toward him in the sexiest way I can. I've got my boobs pushed out, my head up high, and I'm trying to put one leg in front of the other in sort of a slow-motion slinky way.

"Kat, why are you walking like that?" Mills whispers.

"I'm being sexy."

"You look like you've shat yourself." Don't mince your words, Sam.

Looking like I've shat myself isn't the most appealing way to walk, though, so probably a good thing she told me. The thing is that with these fillets à boobié in place, I feel like I need to keep a watch on where my boobs actually are. They're bigger, so small spaces are harder to negotiate. I've already smacked a couple of people with them trying to get through the living room and Matt's shaking his head at me ever so slightly but enough to know I need to sort it out.

After everything this term, I think I might have reached peak weird.

"For Christ's sake . . . just be normal. Can't you just be normal?" Sam has a point, but right now apparently no, I cannot be normal. And she should have known me long enough to know this now.

"Here." Millie puts her arm around me so that we can walk together. She's so considerate.

"Is there any rosé?" Millie asks Nick.

I mean, bloody hell, Millie. I'm pretty sure it's just the unwanted spirits from people's parents' liquor cabinets and the occasional warm, stolen beer. Rosé? Optimistic.

"Errmmm, I have some peach schnapps?"

"Oh, perfect. I love SCHNARRRRPPPPS." Millie tries to make it sound sophisticated, but it just sounds like she's done a sneeze or a hiccup halfway through. Good work, Millie.

"Hey, Kat," Hot, HOT Josh says.

Don't do anything weird.

Don't do anything weird.

Don't do anything weird.

"Hey, ho— . . . Josh. HEY, JOSH."

I don't know why I (A) nearly called him Hot Josh to his actual face and (B) then congratulated myself for not calling him Hot Josh by SHOUTING the greeting again once I'd gotten it right. He's definitely going to think I am socially challenged now.

"Fancy a beer?"

"I'd love one! Thanks."

Hot Josh takes a bottle of store-brand warm beer and opens it on the side of the counter like a pro. This isn't his first time at a shit house party, clearly. He's handing it to me, and my plan is to take a sip casually and then say, "Thanks."

What is actually happening right now, in slow motion, is that I take a sip and it appears to be fizzing up and entering my nose. I've got no control over it. It is now dribbling out of my nose and I am powerless to stop it. I've started choking and the beer bottle is bubbling over. The fizz just keeps coming.

I am a human beer fountain.

I want to suppress the coughing but trying has made it much, much worse and so now I'm doubled over, with Josh patting my back like he's burping a baby.

He's patting quite hard, so hard that unfortunately while he's patting I can feel the fillets à boobié come loose inside my bra. Please god, please no. Haven't I been through enough?

Before I can do anything to stop the impending doom, I see my fillets à boobié shooting out across the kitchen. Millie swiftly catches one and Sam the other. Like a pair of tit-fielders.

"What was that?" I was so hoping Hot Josh hadn't seen but I guess two silicone fillets flying across a kitchen out of my bra are hard to miss.

"Nothing! We were just playing catch with some of those party-feet things from our shoes! I've got HUGE blisters," Sam sings sweetly. I think she might be about to demonstrate by putting my fillets à boobié in her shoe. . . . Yep, she's doing it. She's taking off her boot, and, yep, it's in there.

"Mmm, so comfy now. Thanks, guys!"

Sam half limps, unable to get her foot back into the boot properly because of the sheer size of the offending boob fillet.

I've stopped choking (probably due to the amazement at the lengths that Sam will go to for me) but I can't bear to make myself upright again and look at him directly. My eyes have been watering, so I'm 100 percent sure that my eye makeup is now anywhere else on my face but my eyes, and I know I'm bright red because I can feel how much the blush is warming my face.

Okay, I'm just going to have to do it. After a count of three I'm going to stand up straight and we're just going to have to laugh about this. I need to make some kind of joke. Something sophisticated.

"Hahahaha. I promise I'm not a choker normally."

Both girls are staring at me. I can't bear to look at Josh but I'm certain he's looking at me like an alien just landed from Planet WTF. Oh. GOOD. GOD.

"HAHAHAHA. Babe, that was so funny." Millie puts her arm around me. "She's such a joker. Always messing around, aren't you, babe?"

"Right . . . well, I hope you're okay!"

I finally look up. Josh seems to just be a bit puzzled by the whole thing. I don't blame him. He's had to just basically burp a fully grown person who is seemingly incapable of drinking warm, probably flatter-than-average, store-brand beer, and watch her breasts shoot out across the room.

He's walking away and I'm really just going to let him. I can't be trusted to do anything else.

"I think I'll just pop into the bathroom," I whisper to Millie and Sam. I need to sort out the probable absolute shit-show that is now my face.

"We'll come too," they say.

At least there's safety in numbers. I'm sure nothing else will happen, right?

9 p.m.

Back in the kitchen, AKA the scene of the crime

Miraculously, the rest of the party's been okay so far. I've gone back to being au naturel in the chest area and I have to say I much prefer it. The reason I have small boobs is probably that I'm a bit better balanced that way.

I'm still trying to keep a low profile after the drama, though. Millie's gone over to chat with Nick about the play and I'm sort of third-wheeling with Dave and Sam, trying to work out an appropriate time to cut loose before I look like more of a loser. It's making me feel even worse that Sam can just talk to Dave normally. Whenever I talk to Josh I turn into some kind of slap-stick comedy sketch.

It seems like everyone else finds this whole boy thing so much easier than me. I just want to be more normal. I want to be more like everyone else.

9:15 p.m.

The garden

I've wandered out into the garden as everyone seems to be either coupled up or busy, and I've completely lost track of where Matt went. This place is huge. I feel so out of place and awkward that I keep just looking at my phone so that I feel like I have a purpose. Like a safety blanket. I'm just going to take a seat somewhere and pretend to be doing something important on it.

At least outside there's some air. The house has become so stiflingly hot inside, I was starting to feel dizzy and a bit sick. Though that's often just how I feel around lots of people. Maybe the girls are wondering where I am. Maybe?

No, there are no messages from them. I'll just give them a nudge.

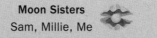

Moon Sisters
Sam, Millie, Me

> **Me:** I'm in the garden in case anyone was worried about where I'd gotten to . . . or you know . . . noticed I was gone in the first place . . .

Maybe they'll see that and realize that they've both basically ABANDONED me.

I look at the @FeministFacts page. Which always gives me a bit of a boost of womanly courage and strength. They've put a link to something called @I_weigh on one of their stories.

It looks pretty cool, actually. It's this actress called Jameela who has looked at a picture of the Kardashians that lists their weight next to their faces and decided "fuck this," and she's gotten women to put on their pictures what their actual weight is. Not their physical weight but their mental and emotional weight. So, people have put things like "Survivor" and "English degree." It's really inspiring to read all these. Some of them are ones I can relate to, as well. To start every day now I think I'm going to write an @I_weigh statement to myself—not for anyone to see—just to keep myself pepped up and remind myself that we're all strong and it's not about how we look.

I'm definitely going to tell Millie and Sam about this when they've finished making boys the center of their universe for this evening. Tut-tut.

9:30 p.m.

I've been so engrossed in this new Instagram revolution that I didn't notice someone coming over. I look up and see Hot Josh standing in front of me, and my stomach flips.

"Hey, fancy a walk?" he says.

I nod because I'm not to be trusted with actual words anymore. We set off walking toward a pair of swings at the bottom of the garden.

"So, what else does the school feminist have planned?" he asks with his little dimples, and his gorgeous eyes, and his lovely tanned arms, all very, very close to me.

Right, I need to answer his question. In a normal way. Without doing anything weird, awful, or certifiable.

"Not sure yet. We've got a few different ideas. I'll keep you posted!" Okay, not too weird. The keeping posted thing is maybe a little businesslike, but not too bad.

"That's so cool. You're so much more woke and interesting than the other girls at school, you know."

I feel like when he says "interesting," he probably means weird. I'm definitely weirder than the other girls at school.

But as we sit down next to each other on the swings, I realize that I'm quite literally beaming from ear to ear. My face (and the rest of me) really needs to calm down. I probably look deranged.

He's staring at me really intensely. Even though it's dark, I can still see how beautiful his green eyes are, and there's moonlight bouncing off his sandy hair. I've read that in saucy books from my mum's secret stash, but I didn't realize it actually happened. Did I mention his tight T-shirt before? I can see every curve of his toned chest and arms. I'll be surprised if I don't leave a puddle on this bench, if I'm being honest.

Mostly, though, I can't believe that he's even talking to me. Especially after the choking, the menstrual-cup-throwing, and the finger fanny.

"Are you okay after earlier? You seemed to totally wipe out," he asks. Still intense with the eyes.

"Oh, me? Yeah! Course. Just a little cough. It was nothing!" I'm trying to sound blasé. It was literally the most dramatic thing ever.

"I know it wasn't a condom the other day," he says.

I can feel my face go redder and redder. Why does he have to talk about this? Why can't we pretend it never happened?

"I mean, people like you and me know what condoms look like, don't we? It's just immature idiots who would think that was a condom, isn't it?"

My face is scarlet. I'm so pleased it's dark. He thinks I'm experienced enough to have spent a lot of time with condoms, when in reality, as we know, I am not.

"Oh yeah, TOTALLY." I'm hoping I sound sophisticated, unfazed, and sexy.

"Hey, so why don't we go out sometime, just by ourselves? You can tell me more about feminism and stuff. Would be great to spend some alone time together without everyone around, you know?"

This is the greatest moment of my life. I can't even process the words he's saying, and now his fingers are moving slowly toward my face. What's he doing? Where's he going with those fingers? Oh god, is he about to put one in my mouth? Am I supposed to suck his finger? IS THIS A SEX THING? HE ALREADY THINKS I AM *AU FAIT* WITH CONDOMS!

Oh no, it's fine. He's pushing a bit of hair back behind my ear so he can stare at me more intensely. This is the greatest moment of my whole life and all I want to do is run away and giggle in the corner.

I'm full-on jelly. I can't believe this is happening.

"Oh, yes, please." Did that just come out of my mouth?

What? What did I just say? I said, *Oh, yes, please*? Like when your mum asks if you'd like a biscuit. Christ, next thing I'll be clapping like a seal at him. What am I doing? I'm so pleased that Sam and Millie aren't here to see this absolute display.

"Great. I'd love to get to know you a bit better, you know?"

He's staring into my eyes and I could swear that he's not blinked in at least three minutes, which, to be honest, is slightly freaky. I'm just staring at him, hoping I don't do anything else embarrassing right now, like fart, because all my concentration is going on staring at him as much as he's staring at me. I'm suddenly far more aware of my bum than I was before, and I've started clenching. I'm clenching my bum and staring really intensely at a hot boy who's staring at me, and all I keep thinking is how awkward it would be if a squeaky little fart came out now. I'm not sure this is quite how it happens in the romance novels Mum has. I feel a bit like this is all happening to someone else, not to me, and I'm watching it, like it's a film or something.

In a film a girl like me would definitely laugh. But in reality I would laugh and then fart. I'd LART.

Suddenly I notice something out of the corner of my eye. Terrible Trudy is standing in the shadows a few feet away, glaring at us murderously.

I'm not sure how long Trudy's been there but I'm willing to bet long enough. She looks furious. Hot Josh seems to have seen her too and he puts his arm around me, which is harder than it looks when you're both on a moving play apparatus. A small petty part of me is so pleased that she's got a front-row seat to this after years of her being so awful to me.

If I had to stand up now I'm 100 percent sure that my legs would not support my weight. He's pulled me closer to him. He's warm and solid. I feel baking hot and I'm pretty sure if my vagina was in charge she'd be gyrating up against him right now. Not now, vagina!

With that, he kisses the top of my head (I shall never wash my hair again) and says, "I'll text you."

9:45 p.m.

> **Moon Sisters**
> Sam, Millie, Me

> Me: SOS in the garden. I NEED YOU!

It takes them a full five minutes but I can finally see them rushing out the back door. Nice to know that I'm a priority. I mean, what if I were actually being murdered out here or something?

"Are you okay?" they both shout at once.

"I'm fine! The most amazing thing has just happened!"

Sam slumps to the ground and Millie falls on top of her.

"What the fuck, dude? We thought you were being abducted or something out here," Millie says.

"Have to say that you moved really, really slowly if that was the case. I would already have been halfway to a ferry port by now at the speed you two were going. ANYWAY, Josh has just been talking to me. He asked me if we can hang out, just the two of us. He TOUCHED me. He kissed me here!" I point to my head.

"WHHHATTTTTT?" Both Millie and Sam are staring at me open-mouthed. I think the "what" noise came from Sam while Millie just mouthed the word—too shocked to get sounds out. Good to know that they both had faith that I would eventually get the guy.

"I know! He said he'd text me!"

"Oh MY GOD. Guess what else? I just saw Sam making out with DAVE," Millie shrieks.

We both turn to look at Sam questioningly.

"Oh REEEEEAALLLLLLLYYYY?" I ask, slightly furious that she's stolen my thunder, to be honest.

"Oh yeah. He asked me to be his girlfriend. I said okay."

"YAYYYYY!" Millie and I sing, putting our arms around her, sort of head-locking her in excitement, actually. Oops.

"Oh my god, chill out," Sam says, trying to be cool.

"What about you and Nick, Millie?" I ask.

"Oh, we have a professional acting relationship now. You can't mix business and pleasure."

¶

"Er, Kit Harrington and Rose Leslie . . . ?" I interject because frankly there are loads of actors that I can think of that have mixed business and pleasure and I'm perfectly happy to list them all right now.

I don't care if the year's gotten off to a dubious start with all my little "accidents"—now I just know this will be our year. WE'RE ABOUT TO ABSOLUTELY SMASH IT AND BE FEMINISTS TOO.

One of us has an actual boyfriend now, another one of us is going on a date, and the third one of us is definitely going to kiss the boy that she fancies, even if it is all in the line of duty as a professional actor. A professional actor praying for a bit of tongue slipped in there. Like a total professional.

Although, now that I think about it, I'm not sure I should be defining having boyfriends as smashing it. So, for feminist purposes, you should know that I think we're smashing it because one of us has the lead in the play, another one is doing the sets AND will probably get a scholarship to a fancy art camp, and I am SMASHING THE PATRIARCHY WITH MY WORDS.

12 a.m.

In blissful bed

Matt walked me home after the BEST night of my life. He's livid he missed the Josh excitement. I was worried that Hot Josh doesn't have my number but Matt says he'll get in touch via the socials anyway. Everyone does these days. I still can't quite believe what just happened!

I touch the light switch three times. For the first time in ages, I'm excited about what tomorrow might bring.

Unfeminist thoughts: 10,000
Spent the whole day preparing for a party to impress a boy (except for ten minutes where I was reading an excellent feminist book called Girl Up). *Then I finished the party being all overjoyed that my girlfriends had boyfriends. Not a good day for feminism. Great day for sexy time.*

Sunday, September 16

I_weigh:

- One message-less phone
- A constant worry about whether or not it's unfeminist to wax my punani
- The possibility of being thrown out of the sisterhood if anyone ever reads my mind
- This is absolutely not how I_weigh was supposed to be used

9:30 a.m.

In bed, thinking about actual Hot Josh kissing my actual forehead

I forgot to tell Sam and Millie about I_weigh last night because I was distracted by all the kissing and boys. I am the absolute worst feminist in the history of all the feminists. Emmeline Pankhurst is probably turning in her grave right now and my ovaries are probably packing their belongings and prepping to move out and live in a better woman.

9:35 a.m.

But a sexy boy asked ME out, even after I embarrassed myself in front of him, and Trudy was SOOOOOOO jealous. Her face went so many different shades of red. It was wonderful. I loved it. All of it.

Again, not feminist. Must do better feministing. Must text the girls about the I_weigh thing.

9:38 *a.m.*

Hmmm I wonder when Hot Josh will message? Am I just to check ALL my social media accounts all the time until he picks one?

10:05 *a.m.*

Okay, no, nothing on any of them so far. But Angus the Angry Cat has been standing up on his back legs appalled in his kitchen this morning, and that was definitely a rewarding watch.

Bea is very unhappy that I'm:

A) looking at a cat; and

B) can't sit still for more than five minutes.

10:10 *a.m.*

For god's sake, need to text the girls about the feminism @I_weigh thingy. I bet Mary Wollstonecraft never forgot about feminism because of a boy.

10:15 *a.m.*

Just checked all social media again, and nothing from him yet. Can't remember why I picked my phone up in the first place.

11 a.m.

FEMINISM! I MUST TEXT THEM NOW!

11:15 a.m.

Sophie Steiner just posted a picture from the party last night and in the background you can see Josh and me talking.

Our first picture together.

I shall just sit here and look at this.

Forever.

11:30 a.m.

The girls are coming over. We are going to have a massive debrief after last night, especially now that one of us has a boyfriend and another one has a date. . . . I just don't know when. . . .

11:45 a.m.

FEMINISM. I WAS SUPPOSED TO MESSAGE THEM ABOUT THE FEMINISM AND THE @I_WEIGH.

I'll tell them in person. I promise.

12 p.m.

My bedroom, away from Freddie's dirty prying ears—he's far too young for this talk

The girls have just gotten to my place and already Sam has sent Dave three messages and he's replied to all of them. I guess when you're actually in a relationship there are no rules about how often you should message them anymore?

"What if Josh messages and he wants to meet in the alley-way and do some top-level fondling and finds out that I don't have as much to fondle as it looked like I did yesterday? Also, am I supposed to fondle back?"

"What would you fondle?" Millie looks mystified.

"Um no, babe. No. You don't need to do that." Sam is firm. She sounds experienced? Millie and I immediately shoot her a look.

"Dave and I only got together last night, ladies—no judgment! But I know about stuff from listening to my sister talk. Which is why we should have a code for things like this. In case your brother hears!"

"Okay, let's call it . . ." Millie raises her hands in breast cupping motion and makes a noise like a donkey: "Hee-haw hee-haw."

I'm lost for words.

"Are you five years old?" Sam asks.

"Fine, you come up with something better!" Millie pouts.

We cannot.

1 p.m.

Matt: HAS HE MESSAGED YET?

Me: NO.

Matt: OH, sorry. He will though. He definitely knows your Instagram handle 😆

Me: Oh my god, now is not the time!

I think things are heating up really fast between Sam and Dave. He's sending her loads of messages.

"He wants to hang out next week, though, and I just don't have time. I've told him how much I've got going on right now and he seems to be understanding, but what if he gets bored waiting?" Sam says.

"He won't get bored! He's liked you for ages. And anyone who gets bored of you that easily wasn't worth it in the first place," I say, as if I'm wise about this sort of thing.

"Do you think he wants to get down and dirty by the art block?" Millie asks.

"I hope not yet, he'd never find anything through my bush at the moment." Sam mimes trying to find her way through dense foliage.

"I think it's okay to have a bush now, Sam. We shouldn't have to wax. Will he wax his man mound for you? I DON'T THINK SO! So why should you wax for him? And anyway, some of us have already shown the whole school their squirrel." I've stood up because I'm making an important feminist point right now about pubic hair equality.

"YEAH!" they both say.

7 p.m.

Mum made the girls go home about half an hour ago because apparently we should be preparing ourselves mentally and physically for the week ahead and making sure that we're well rested. Honestly, she's older than some of the antiques on *Antiques Roadshow*, and I bet she'd not even be worth much if one of the oldies valued her.

I'm fairly sure that there was something else I was supposed to talk to the girls about today that I forgot.

11 p.m.

@I_WEIGH! I meant to tell them about that!

I'll send them a text now. Better late than never.

11:05 p.m.

I wonder if you can have a boyfriend and still be a feminist. I might just google it.

Can you be feminist and have a boyfriend?	Q

How to be a feminist boyfriend	V
5 ways to find a boyfriend	V
What to do when you realize your boyfriend is sexist	V
Feminists who have had boyfriends	V

Aha!

11:10 *p.m.*

Germaine Greer had a husband, but technically only for a couple of weeks.

Mary Wollstonecraft only had a husband for a very short time before she died but had two affairs in a time when apparently sex outside of marriage for a woman was frowned upon. Good for you, Mary!

Emmeline Pankhurst had a husband, but he was really an ally for the feminists. He supported her. So, I think maybe it's okay to have a boyfriend as long as you're still doing feminism and they are also feministing?

Not that it matters. Still no message from him.

Unfeminist thoughts: INFINITY
MUST. DO. BETTER. FEMINISM. TOMORROW.

Monday, September 17

I_weigh:

The weight of all my filth because Freddie is always hogging the bloody bathroom.

8 a.m.

Rushing around trying to get ready.

The doorbell's just gone off and as usual I'm not ready because as usual Freddie spent a whole half an hour in the bathroom longer than he was supposed to. I don't know what he was doing in there, and god knows I would really never ever ask but I do know that it's impeded my preparation for what could be a very special day at school. (Maybe Hot Josh is waiting to see me to pin down a date!)

I pull my hair up into a messy bun and shove some glasses on—I'm going for intellectual, poised, and sophisticated feminist today—get my stuff together, and race down the stairs. Weirdly, I'm not greeted by the usual sight of just Sam and Millie, but Dave appears to be there too. Which I don't really understand because he lives on the other side of school. He would have had to leave his house an hour early to come over this way, only to go back the other way. All so that he can see Sam? Gosh, I guess love does funny things to a person.

"Morning, guys! Morning, Dave!" I shout in a way that I hope suggests I'm breezy and not at all surprised or perturbed by Dave's presence. Millie shrugs at me as Sam and Dave hold hands in my hallway.

I'm impressed with the effort that he's gone to, but I really hope he's not going to be hanging out with us ALL the time. That would be most annoying.

9 a.m.

Assembly

"TIMOTHY MATTHEWS, STOP MASTICATING!" Mr. Shaw, our head of year, bellows at #Tim across the assembly hall.

He thinks it's hilarious to shout this at anyone he catches chewing gum in front of as many people as he can, so that they never do it again.

The fact that he's shouting it at #Tim makes all our skins crawl, and I see Millie and Sam do little shudders at exactly the same time as me.

"Do you think #Tim does it on purpose to draw attention to himself and make people think of him masturbating?" I whisper to the girls.

They both stare at me, alarmed.

I've only got myself to blame for putting that image into their heads and I will admit I am now disgusted. I think about going to confession to see if I can repent for that sin, except I'm not Catholic and I don't think they let you do it if you're not. I think it's also actually worse than any sort of sin you might have committed if you lie and pretend to be Catholic too just so you can go to confession.

I'm scanning assembly to see if Hot Josh is around. I was hoping for a bit of steamy eye contact across the hall, but I can't see him anywhere.

Maybe he's sick? Maybe that's why he hasn't messaged?

1:30 p.m.

My locker

"Oops!" Trudy says, knocking the book out of my hands as I try to take it out of my locker. "Clumsy klutz! Just like Saturday when you dropped your tits," she says, her gaggle of TB laughing dutifully.

I bend down to pick up the book, desperately hoping that I can escape from this situation quickly and easily.

"Saw you talking to Josh on Saturday," she says as I'm bent over.

"What do you want, Trudy? Can you just get on with it? I'm late," I say impatiently.

"Back off him. He's not interested in you. He doesn't want a clumsy little girl like you anyway. He wants a real woman, not one who has to pad her bra and chokes all over the kitchen." Just then she produces one of my fillets from her pocket and starts pinging me in the nose with it.

How did she get them? Maybe they're not mine? Thinking

103

about it, what happened to them after Sam put them in her shoe?

"Urgh, Trudy, get over yourself," I say, closing my locker and walking off. How? HOW? Did she get my fillets? She's right, I was stupid to think that they'd help me feel like a real woman when I'm not.

How can one person make me feel so shit about myself?

3 p.m.

If Josh didn't want to go out with me, he wouldn't have asked me. Just because he hasn't gotten in touch yet doesn't mean anything.

10 p.m.

In bed staring at the ceiling with my headphones in

Still no message from Josh and I didn't even see him in school today at all.

Sam said he was in art, though, so maybe he was just running late. It must be hectic being a model AND doing school. Like having two jobs.

I shouldn't be so needy.

11 p.m.

I touch the light switch three times. Maybe he will message tomorrow now?

Unfeminist thoughts: literally a kazillion
All based on hanging around, pausing my life, waiting for a boy to text . . .

Wednesday, September 19

I_weigh:

A now completely message-less phone. There are no messages from anyone. I am in a black hole of communication.

7:30 a.m.

My bedroom

Maybe my phone is broken and that's why he hasn't messaged?

It beeped!

A message! Maybe it is fixed now and he has finally gotten through. I shall sue the phone company! SUE THEM for damage to my emotions!

> **Emmeline Pankhurst's BAD BITCHEZ**
> Sam, Millie, Me

> **Millie:** Running a bit late this morning as Issy took an inexplicably long time in the shower. Sorry! Xxx

Eugh . . . NOT HOT JOSH. More disappointment. WHEN WILL HE END MY MISERY?

9 p.m.

My desk, trying my best to work

Still no message from Josh. I start looking at my *Inspector Calls* essay to try to distract myself but I can't seem to get my head into it. This is absolutely rubbish feminism! I shouldn't be letting a boy distract me from my work! Especially not when you definitely need a good English GCSE score to be a journalist.

10 p.m.

In bed

What if Trudy was right and he's not interested in me? Why would he ask me out, though?

I touch the light switch three times. Maybe he'll text me tomorrow.

Unfeminist thoughts: 5

1. Wondering when Hot Josh will message me.
2. Why hasn't he messaged me?
3. Where is he?
4. Maybe he's sick?
5. Maybe I was supposed to message him? No, definitely not.

Friday, September 21

I_weigh:

Freedom. I've given up on Josh. I've moved on. I'm over it. (Well, I'm trying my best to be, anyway.) If he can't message me then he's missed his chance! Finally, I've used I_weigh the right way. FOR MYSELF.

10:30 a.m.

The toilets

"They announced the date of the play, finally. Did they tell you guys yet?" Millie asks.

"Err, no? And it'd be great to know so that I, you know . . . have the set finished!" Sam says.

"It's Friday, December 14."

My ears prick up.

"Sweet. That's loads of time!" Sam says.

I'm sure they've realized that's my birthday. The date of my actual sixteenth birthday. They won't have forgotten. And yet I'm looking at them and there is NOT A HINT of recognition on their faces. We've been having birthdays together for twelve years and NOTHING.

"That's a great date . . . ," I say hopefully.

"Yeah, not too soon and right at the end of term so we can all properly relax after," Millie says.

Right.

I don't want to make a big deal out of it, though. No one wants to be THAT diva, do they? Three whole months before their birthday, kicking it off like people have forgotten! They won't forget. I have to learn to relax. Like a koala bear. Be more koala.

But there are traditions to be UPHELD! Ones I really like, too. We always surprise each other on our birthdays. We've done it since we were about eight or nine. Two of us will surprise the birthday person with something completely unexpected. We've done things like: decorating their room like a castle (we were eight), having our faces painted as our favorite animals and pretending to be them for the rest of the night (you don't need to know how recent this was), and pottery class (for Sam, obvs). And it's my sixteenth so I bet they're already planning something great. They won't let the play get in the way of TRADITION.

"There's going to be a massive cast party too!" Millie says.

Um, WHAT? Right, that's IT. This koala is getting a little worried now. I'm just going to mention it, casually. Calm, casual koala.

"Um, not to be a diva, but you know it's my birthday that day, right?" I say.

"DUH!" Millie says. "But what better way to celebrate that day than at a massive party with everyone there that you don't have to organize yourself!"

"Yeah, you get a banging sixteenth birthday party with

EVERYONE from school and you don't even have to organize it. It's PERFECT!" Sam adds.

Of course, I should be pleased. A ready-made, super cool party. That's what every sixteen-year-old wants, right? What's wrong with me? We're grown up now. We do grown-up things. We can't go and get our faces painted and spend the evening pretending to be a zebra at sixteen. Grown-ups have parties, not activities.

Grow up Kat, stop being a child.

1 p.m.

Drying while Dad washes—as dull as dishwater

"Where's Matt gotten to? Sixth Form giving him a hard time?" Dad says.

It's a good question. Matt's usually at our place most evenings and I've barely seen or heard from him this week. And we always chill on a Friday night.

> Me: Hey, whatcha up to? xxx

I stare at my phone. I usually get an instant response from Matt. He's just one of those friends who you can always depend on to get back to you quickly.

Nothing.

8:30 p.m.

The sofa with Dad, trying to find something to watch post another cracking EastEnders

Still nothing from Matt. I don't get it. Usually he responds right away. This is so unlike him.

8:35 *p.m.*

Oh FFS. Be more koala, Kat. Maybe he's just out.

8:40 *p.m.*

WITH WHO, THOUGH?

8:45 *p.m.*

Maybe he's out with Josh who is out with Trudy and everyone is out without me and laughing at me?

8:50 *p.m.*

> **Matt:** At the pub with Simon and Steve from sociology. They know this pub that you can get served in without ID. P A R T Y—the only other people in here are over 75 xxx

Oh, FINALLY. Thank god. Of course he isn't out with Trudy or

Josh, and why would Trudy and Josh be together anyway? SILLY BRAIN.

I guess it's okay for him to have other friends. I mean. Maybe.

10:30 p.m.

In bed, contemplating life as a spinster

When I was younger, I thought that once I started my period I'd instantly feel like a woman, sexy and powerful and together. But it didn't happen. I'm still waiting for it. I'm still waiting to feel like all the other girls at school. We haven't talked about it but I know Sam and Millie feel like women. I'm stuck as a little girl. Like maybe I'm some kind of real-life Benjamin Button hybrid child-monster. On the outside I'm ageing but in my head I'm going backward until I'm just eating, pooping, and crying at everyone.

Okay. I need to grow up. I need to start doing the things that everyone else is doing. I can't seem to move on from being Kitty Kat. The girl whose hair people ruffle, who has a cute nickname and can't talk to boys. Not that boys are the most important thing, because I'm a feminist. Or trying to be. Why can't someone just teach me how to do it all? A bullet-point list of rules? So I don't have to feel like I'm just muddling about trying to piece it all together and absolutely ALWAYS GETTING IT WRONG.

First step: Forget about Josh. Feminist grown-ups don't need this much BS.

I've just touched the light switch three times without meaning to. I don't even have control of my own arms anymore.

Unfeminist thoughts: 0

Just feminist ones over here. NO BOYS ALLOWED. Feminist service has resumed!

Saturday, September 22

I_weigh:

Zen. I'm breathing in peace and love and I'm breathing out all the negative vibes and bad juju. A change is coming, and I am calm, centered, and poised.

9:30 a.m.

My bedroom on a yoga mat

"Out with anger and in with peace . . . out with hatred and in with love . . . out with fear and in with confidence."

This morning's yoga video has a handy bit of meditation at the end. Frankly, though, I'm finding the yoga lady's "soothing" voice is:

1. making me angry,
2. filling me with hatred, and
3. making me fear for my sanity.

So she's not exactly doing the best job of making me feel zen about the fact that Josh is clearly NEVER going to message me. Which was really the only reason I bothered to get all downward-doggy-style in the first place.

Item number three is probably because whenever I sit and try to be quiet or peaceful, my mind spirals. It's as if, when given a chance to slow down, my brain decides it's time to speed up. Today my brain has come up with the following:

1. Everyone has (or will soon have) boyfriends apart from me.

2. Josh does not want to go out with me, and maybe I imagined the whole conversation with him because I am crazy.

3. I am too ugly to ever have a boyfriend and will be single and alone forever.

4. But even if I am ugly, I'm not supposed to worry about my looks. Because feminist.

5. Oh god. It's all so confusing because I can't change the way I feel and surely I should be in tune with my feelings?

6. My friends will replace me with someone who they can triple-date with, who is easier to hang out with and better at feministing.

7. I will fail my GCSEs because, as well as not being very pretty, I am also not very smart.

8. I will then fail to get into any A levels and thusly be left behind while everyone goes to university.

9. I will then have to get a badly paid job in this very same town and live with my parents forever.

10. I will eventually probably get so depressed at having no friends and being so ugly that I will stop even washing. My hair will become tangled and I will probably acquire a small forest of woodland creatures living in it. This will also be true of my pubic hair, which will simply become a matted mess, obscuring the entrance to my vagina forever, though thereby giving a much-needed home to some friendly voles.

11. I will lose my badly paid job and be unable to get another

one because I look so awful and it is safer for the general public and their eyes and noses if I never leave the house.

12. I will always be financially dependent upon my parents and they will come to hate me.

13. What if my parents lose their jobs and we become homeless?

14. Actually, they could lose their jobs and we could become homeless at any point. What if that happens tomorrow?

15. What if someone breaks in and kills us all?

16. What if someone breaks in and kills everyone except me?

17. What if I go to prison because they get confused and decide it was me?

18. I'll probably die in prison. I'm not very tough.

19. Even if points thirteen to eighteen are avoided, eventually my parents will die and I will not know how to look after myself.

20. Then I will die—alone in the house I grew up in, having achieved nothing, and no one will notice because I won't have any friends and even Freddie will have blocked me out of his memory because, as he'll tell his wife and kids, It's For The Best.

21. The end is nigh.

9:35 a.m.

Opening my eyes from meditation hell

By the time I'm supposed to be opening my eyes in a calm and refreshed way, I'm actually opening them in a frantic and petrified way, rushing to the mirror to check that I am still young and have washed recently, still have all my teeth, and can hear my mum on the phone in the kitchen talking to Auntie Jane about some award that Auntie Jane has won for a breakthrough in treating arthritis.

Their house must have been a nightmare of overachievement when they were kids. It just reminds me even more that I'm probably not the child Mum was expecting to have. She probably presumed she'd have someone a bit more science-y. I'm also sure that she'd already won about ten awards by the time she was my age, and I haven't won any at all.

10:30 a.m.

My desk

Right, then. If the end is nigh, I am going to absolutely crack this *Inspector Calls* essay.

10:35 a.m.

Everyone in the world is out doing something exciting today. I looked on Instagram and it's just FILLED with loads of people having a great time. All of them. All the people. Just having endless, joyful, achingly cool FUN.

Urgh.

And I am here alone.

10:40 a.m.

I need to stop looking at my phone and do some work.

10:50 a.m.

Wonder what the girls are doing, though? Maybe I'll just see what they're up to?

11 a.m.

Play stuff. Right. Best get on with my essay.

11:10 a.m.

Is it unfeminist to lust after another woman's nose on Instagram? Although is that her real nose? I don't even know who she is. But she's got 150K followers and a tiny nose. What ARE Instagram influencers, anyway? I don't think they influence me at all.

11:15 a.m.

Those are GREAT sneakers, though. And there is a handy clicky link to buy.

Oh, bugger. Right. Yep. Influenced.

9 p.m.

In bed. I'm bored of today

I'm absolutely not thinking about the fact that it's been exactly a week since he asked me out. That's exactly a week of no message to set a date. I've taken myself to bed, because what's the point anymore?

11:30 p.m.

Beep
Urgh who on earth is messaging me at this time? URGH!

> **Josh:** Hey, Kat!

> **Josh:** How's it going?

OH MY GOD, OH MY GOD. I KNEW IT WOULD HAPPEN EVEN-TUALLY! FINALLY!

> **Me:** Hey, good thanks.

> **Josh:** What are you up to?

> **Me:** Just chilling.

I'm hoping that makes me sound cool rather than like a loser . . . oh god, what if he thinks I'm a loser and doesn't message anymore?

Oh no, it's fine. He's typing again.

Josh: So I just wondered if we could go out on Thursday after school?

YESS! YESS! YES YES YES YES YES YES YES YES YES YES YES YES YES YES YES YES!

Me: Sure.

Josh: Perfect. 3:30 by the alleyway?

Me: Sounds good.

Josh: Can't wait x

OH MY VAGINA! I KNEW IT! I KNEW I DIDN'T IMAGINE IT! I'm going to message the girls.

Emmeline Pankhurst's BAD BITCHEZ
Sam, Millie, Me

Me: HE MESSAGED!! He wants to go out on Thursday after school. He said meet by the alleyway! Does that mean he wants to get frisky?! Already? Guys? GUYS?!

Urgh they must be asleep already. Losers.

And that's another thing: It's Saturday night, WHY AREN'T WE OUT ON THE TOWN?

The very small town.

The admittedly very small and very quiet town.

Okay, I've just answered that for myself there.

12 a.m.

Literally no idea how I'm going to sleep now.

The only person I can talk to about what's just happened is Bea.

And she couldn't care less.

Unfeminist thoughts: 2

1. Does getting annoyed with the yoga lady's voice count? It's just so . . . yoga.

2. My mood dramatically lifted after hearing from Hot Josh. As a feminist, I should not be letting a man impact my happiness . . . I think?

Sunday, September 23
11 p.m.

Bed

Too excited about Josh all day to write properly.

    The girls think it's fishy that Hot Josh didn't get in touch for so long. I asked Matt what he thought and he said the same thing. Urgh. Why can't people just be happy for me? I know that they're looking out for me, but Sam's got Dave, Millie's clearly well in with Nick, why can't they just let me have my nice moment?

Unfeminist thoughts: 1
"Too excited about Josh to write properly" . . .

Wednesday, September 26

I_weigh:

I'm going on a date with the hottest boy in school LA LA LA LA LA LA LA LA! I_weigh pure EXCITEMENT.

1 p.m.

The dining hall

Haven't seen Hot Josh all week. It's like he's a ghost around school these days. I used to bump into him all the time, now he's barely around. I guess he's v busy with all the modeling and stuff.

Sam and I are just heading to meet Millie after her rehearsal. Dave doesn't appear to be with us just yet, but I'm sure it's really only a matter of time before he finds us. Not that I mind, obviously. I really like that she's got Dave. I'm really happy for her. Really. He's just around a lot, I guess.

I can see Millie talking to Nick as we approach the drama block. I wonder if they rehearsed one of THE KISS SCENES today. I'm dying to ask her but we can't seem to get her attention. In fact, she seems to be pretending we're not here.

"Is she pretending we're not here, Sam?"

"Yes, I think so. That means that we should be making ourselves a bit more visible, making a bit of a fuss. Don't you think?"

"Oh, absolutely! What shall we do?"

"Let's go over there!"

"MILLIEEEEEEE! HOW'S IT HANGING, BABES!" Sam launches herself wildly at Millie and does a weird sex-type dance move, like she's been fired from some kind of weapon of mass embarrassment.

Millie looks mortified. I've only ever seen her face go that red twice before, and one of those times was when she peed herself in preschool. Bad times. Feel a bit bad now. Fingers crossed she hasn't wet herself this time around. I'd like to think she has a better handle on her bladder these days, but you never really know what's going on in someone's pants. And there is a lesson for us all.

"Oh, hi, Sam. Hi, Kat." I think she's going for Cat Purring Voice, but really she just sounds like she's got a lot of phlegm. I must remember to tell her that Phlegmy Voice is not as sexy as she thinks. For her own good.

"Well, I've got to head off. But see you later, yeah, Millie?" Nick says.

"Sure." Millie tries to look cool and calm but instead looks slightly constipated.

We all stand watching him walk away in an extremely obvious way.

"YOU GUYS!" Millie says as soon as he's out of earshot. "Could you be any more embarrassing?! I'll remember that for the next time YOU'RE with Dave or Josh!"

"Sorry, Millie," I say, feeling genuinely bad.

"Surrree, sorr-eeeyyyy, Millie," Sam says sarcastically before

124

we all start laughing and Millie grabs us both in a hug.

3:30 p.m.

Heading out of school

This evening I must begin my date preparation. This involves a face mask, toe and fingernail painting, and a full-body exfoliation. Millie has another rehearsal and Sam has to crack on with the sets so I'll have to go it alone, but I've been given thorough instructions. They're still being supportive even if they are a bit concerned about his intentions.

I haven't seen Matt all week. I told him about my date with Josh and he just replied with "Be careful." Whatever that means. The house is quiet without him.

Maybe I should text Hot Josh? Something casual. Breezy. Chill.

> **Me:** Looking forward to seeing you tomorrow x

One kiss? Or two? Or no kisses? Is no kisses more casual? Should I be being more aloof? Maybe I shouldn't send it? I won't.

3:35 p.m.

Definitely won't send it.

3:37 p.m.

Have sent it.

5 p.m.

The bathroom

How is a girl supposed to relax in the bath when her brother keeps banging on the door yelling things like:

"I need a wee!"

and:

"I'm going to piss myself!"

and:

"It's starting to come out!"

I mean, really. I've put some of Mum's expensive oils into the bath and got myself her copy of *The Female Eunuch*. I skipped the introduction and went straight for the first chapter. "Body: Gender." I've managed to get about ten lines in before reaching the word "fungi." It's grossed me out already and I'm wondering if this is the book for me. But I feel like I need to offset all the time I'm spending obsessing over a boy by doing more feminist things. I take a flick through the rest of the book in case I can absorb any important feminist wisdom by simply staring at it. It all seems a bit overwhelming, but one line makes me stop:

"No woman wants to find out that she has a twat like a horse-collar."

What is a horse-collar? Is my vagina like a horse-collar? (Or do I mean vulva?) I grab my phone and google

What is a horse-collar?	🔍

There are two things I can say immediately when I look at the images:

1. My vagina/vulva does not look that much like a horse-collar—I don't think. . . . To be honest it's hard to tell from up here and also there's so much foliage to get through before you see any actual vagina/vulva that it's exhausting. Like hunting for very buried treasure.
2. Horse-collars do look a bit like giant vaginas/vulvas, though. Imagine being a horse and being forced to put your head through a giant vagina/vulva every day. No wonder the Royal Society for the Prevention of Cruelty to Animals needs so much funding.

Oh god, must resolve the vagina/vulva problem. Maybe that's why Germaine just called it a twat? Just a nonscientific, nonspecific twat. General twat.

New career idea: horse therapist.

Anyway, I'd better get on with the business of exfoliating every inch of myself to reveal a silky-smooth underskin. Apparently, you just need to rub off all the dead skin cells. I've never done it, so for all we know I am a princess under this reptilian outer sheath.

5:10 p.m.

Le sigh. I am not a princess. I am instead quite red and angry looking.

"Kat! That's it! I'm going to piss in your wardrobe!"

"NO, YOU ARE NOT, FREDDIE, YOU LITTLE FUCKFACE!" I'm racing to get out of the bathroom now to rescue the shoes and clothes that reside safely in my armoire. They don't deserve that.

So much for a relaxing bath. My clothes might be covered in urine, I'm bright red, and I'll never look at a horse in the same way again.

7 p.m.

Still nothing from Matt. Thought he might at least have popped over after school the night before my hot date. I know things are different in Sixth Form and everything, but he said he wouldn't forget about me. . . .

10 p.m.

In bed praying for tomorrow to hurry up and arrive

I told the girls about the horse-collar thing. They don't THINK theirs look like horse-collars either, but we've agreed we're going to have to keep an eye on that as we get older. Just in case.

128

I'm fizzing with nerves and excitement about tomorrow, but mostly nerves, let's be honest. I know I should be all confident and comfortable in my own now-extremely-red-but-very-feminist skin—but really I just want Josh to think I'm sophisticated and funny, and to be my boyfriend. I worry that the date will go badly and he'll realize I'm just a massive dork and won't want anything more to do with me. Come to think of it, he hasn't replied to my message. I'm sure he's just busy, though.

I touch the light switch three times after I've turned it off. I hope that might guard me against having a bad date tomorrow. My FIRST proper date.

Unfeminist thoughts:
Oh, sod off and just let me enjoy my moment with the hottest boy in school.

Thursday, September 21

I_weigh:

The pressure of trying to look good for a date while still in school uniform. American students really don't know how good they have it. In the films they're always allowed to wear whatever they want. I'm so jealous.

I also know that this is another misuse of I_weigh and I am going to start using it properly and doing proper feminism. Tomorrow.

I promise.

1 a.m.

My sexy boudoir

I think it's time to whip out something a bit special. Today, in preparation for my date, I am going to wear my Secret Thong.

Mum still buys all my knickers so they're the kind of massive ones that you get in a multipack from Marks & Spencer. Pure cotton. Pure shame. And not exactly sexy.

So, a few months ago, in preparation for events such as today, I purchased for myself a Secret Thong.

Today is the Secret Thong's first outing.

8 a.m.

On the way into school, buzzing with excitement

"Oh my god, I know it's in the script but he touched my cheek last night in rehearsal and I definitely felt something," Millie says.

"What did you feel?" Sam's asking, eyes wide.

"A bit sick," Millie says. "And like my knickers were about to come shooting off of their own accord."

Fair play.

"I think this is going to be the longest day of my life, guys. How am I going to concentrate on ANYTHING before the date?"

Seriously, I've lost all perspective; I'm wearing an uncomfortable thong and I can't focus because of a boy. Hurrah for feminism! I'm doing really well at it this week . . . not. I need to spend more time thinking about things like Malala, the girl who got shot just because she wanted to go to school, and less time thinking about my crush.

"Has he texted you since Saturday, babe?" asks Sam. "I've barely seen him around school—have you?"

I've wondered about this too, especially as he didn't get back to me after I messaged yesterday. But I'm sure he's busy, and I'm not that needy. ~~I am that needy~~. Surely it's normal not to hear from someone for a bit? Right?

"No, but I think he's probably quite busy. Modeling plus school must be like having two full-time jobs, I guess.

Especially with GCSEs coming up." I'm saying this with far more confidence than I feel.

I won't lie, it's made me doubt myself slightly, but we arranged it on Saturday so that's that, and I'm completely ready for it. I've spent every minute I'm by myself, most of the minutes I'm in class, and all the minutes I've been asleep, thinking about what we'll do on our date. We'll probably go for coffee or something really sophisticated like that. I should think he earns a fair bit with being a model so he can probably afford to pay for fancy caffeinated beverages.

I blame reading Mum's Jilly Cooper books too young for giving me high and probably very unfeminist expectations of romance. All the characters are super rich, ride horses, and ride men. I read this stuff at age twelve. Since then I've just presumed that's how everyone does it.

If we're being honest, I'm really lowering my standards not being met by a helicopter and whisked away to Rome.

"Yeah, I'm sure he's just busy, Kat, he wouldn't have asked you if he didn't want to go out. What would the point be in that?" Millie's so supportive. "Like you say, all that modeling and schoolwork must take up a lot of his time."

SEE, I'm not the only one who thinks that then.

"How did the lines we practiced on Tuesday go? Were they a bit better?"

"Oh god, so much! I actually understand them now so I know that I'm definitely making the right facial expressions. I think before I probably would have smiled when Tybalt died. I had no idea!"

It's true she really did NOT understand the play at all. There were several points where she asked if that was when they were supposed to kiss and one of them wasn't even with Romeo. I hope she thinks I'm being supportive too. Feminists have to look out for each other, after all.

12 p.m.

Math

This is the longest day in the history of all days ever. No one single day has ever been this long. I am ageing faster than time is ticking. What's the youngest that someone has ever gotten a wrinkle? Because I think I'm getting one at fifteen.

12:30 p.m.

The dining hall

Terrible Trudy looks smugger than usual today. She pushed past us in the corridor just now. Not sure what she's got to be so smug about, especially when I'm going out with Hot Josh later. I hope she sees us meeting and it wipes the smug smile off her face.

UNFEMINIST THOUGHT ALERT!

2 p.m.

French class

Hot Josh just walked into class and didn't even look at me. Maybe he wants to keep us on the DL. I'm sure it'll be okay when we meet later. He had his arm around me at the party AND he kissed my forehead, so he definitely likes me. Also, maybe he's actually quite shy. I could see he was trying not to look at me and I think it's probably because he's shy or doesn't want to rouse suspicion. I'm sure it's just that. A lot of models can still be shy, you know. I think?

I'm going to try to make sure I'm as alluring as possible with my French accent today when I answer questions. I will push my lips out into a sexy pout.

OH GOD, MY FEMINISTING IS GOING OUT THE WINDOW!

2:30 p.m.

I've been trying to get his attention but he's concentrating very hard. I guess models need to know foreign languages for all the shoots that they do abroad. So, he's probably really absorbed in doing something that helps his career and I should stop trying to distract him.

Only one hour until our date, anyway, and I'm a strong, independent woman with focus, poise, and important French to be learning.

2:35 p.m.

"Où sont les tampons? J'ai un flux lourd!"

About time I learned something useful. Shame I had to teach it to myself. I'm literally never going to want to tell a French person it's raining, guys. They can see that for themselves.

So. Basic.

2:45 p.m.

Madame Rauché just told me off for taking the piss out of French people with my lips out like that and said to stop being the class clown. So—sexy, yes?

She didn't even hear what I was saying. Had she heard, she'd know I was taking the whole thing VERY seriously.

A heavy flow is no laughing matter.

Oh god, I think I've become delirious with excitement.

3:30 p.m.

The playground

I'm just strolling over to the alleyway in a VERY CASUAL way because I don't want to look too keen, but I am keen, I'm super keen. I can see from here that he's not there yet, though. I can't see him around anywhere. He left French before me so maybe he's playing it cool too? Maybe he went to his locker because he'd left flowers and gifts there for me and he's going to shower me with them? That's probably it.

I don't really want to be the first one there. I was hoping that he'd be waiting when I arrived.

Sam and Millie offered to wait with me but I know they've both got places they need to be and I'm not that lame. I don't need to bring my friends on a date with me.

3:35 p.m.

The alleyway

I do need to bring my friends on a date with me. I'm all lonely and feel weird waiting around.

At least I can look at my phone. Maybe I'll look at some more @I_weigh posts. It's amazing what we women go through, and all anyone wants to talk about is our weight or our looks.

Although now I do feel guilty that I've been so shallow this week but I've really, really had to focus on getting ready for this date. It's the best thing that's ever happened to me. I know that also sounds silly and overdramatic, but I promise I'll go back to being a bit more feminist after this date.

I promise. Again.

3:40 p.m.

STILL waiting.

He's probably held up somewhere or something.

> **Me:** He's not here yet. You haven't seen him anywhere, have you?

Oh god, and Terrible Trudy and TB are on the approach. Why, why, why?

"What you doing here, loser? Looks like you're waiting for someone." TT is smirking like a smirk champion.

I am not responding to her. If I don't engage, maybe she'll just go away.

"It can't be your two loser friends, cuz I've seen them leave already without you, so you must be waiting for someone else. Who could it be? Let me think. . . . Is it a BOY?"

Trudy's standing right in my face, while Amelie, Tiffany, Tia, and Nia circle around me. This is their signature maneuver and not the first time I've experienced it. I still can't help but feel intimidated, though.

"I know! You're supposed to be meeting Josh, aren't you?"

How does she know this?

How? HOW?

"I already warned you to back off, and you didn't listen. Well, now he's taking ME to the cinema tonight. Not you. Me."

What?

Did I just hear that right?

I'm starting to feel a bit weird and I can't tell if it's because Trudy's so close to my face or what, but everything keeps going a bit blurry.

"I told him I don't go out with schoolboys so he used you to make me jealous. And now we're together. He's not coming to meet you. Loser."

I feel like I'm going to cry. I NEVER want her to see that she's made me cry, but especially not now.

"Oh, that seems to have made you sad. Look, bitches, look how sad she is."

"So sad," Nia and Tia say at the same time, still circling me while Amelie and Tiffany stand with Trudy. Like a pair of bodyguards. Like I would do anything. It's five against one, I don't have a death wish.

Trudy's phone beeps in Amelie's hand (she couldn't possibly carry her own) and she shows Trudy the message.

"Oh, look! That's him now!" Trudy says while Amelie thrusts the phone in front of my face.

Josh: Can't wait. See you there at 7 xxx

Three kisses. I only got one. How come Trudy's worth three and I was only worth one?

Everything's very blurry now. I want to curl up into a ball and cry but I need to extract myself from this awful situation first, and that seems impossible. I can hear a whooshing noise in my head, my ears are ringing, and I've got a wave of

nausea and dizziness sweeping over me. I feel like I'm suffocating.

"Leave her alone, Trudy!" Matt's voice comes from
behind me.

"Oh, look, it's your gay bodyguard. Come to rescue you.
What happens when he gets a boyfriend too? You'll be every-
body's spare wheel then!" Tiffany shouts. I know she's desperate to be Second in Command, but she'll have to try harder
than that. When Matt gets a boyfriend, I'll be really happy for
him. You idiot.

The four of them are now building a wall between Trudy and
Matt. Protecting their great and heinous leader. I'm so relieved
that he's here, though. I need to get away so I can work out
what the hell has just happened.

Matt takes my hand and leads me away from them all. I
can't believe that at fifteen I still can't defend myself against
Trudy and her satanic crew.

3:55 p.m.

**Sitting on a bench by "The Green"—the absolutely tiny bit of
grass near our houses**

Matt and I used to play on this patch when we were kids and it
felt much bigger. Everything seemed better back then, I guess.
Although back then we were small enough to be fooled into
thinking a raisin was a delicious, filling snack.

"Come on, Kitty Kat, what was all that about? You've barely said a word, which is—not to be rude—quite unlike you, and that looked pretty brutal even by Trudy standards." Matt pulls at the grass next to me.

"It was supposed to be my date with Josh tonight," I say. My voice is coming out much quieter than I expected it to, and it's actually an effort to talk because I'm trying not to cry at the same time.

"Oh, yeah! I'm sorry, I should have asked. I've been pretty distracted trying to get my head around Sixth Form workloads and everything. What happened? Did he reschedule or something?" Matt says, sweet but clueless.

"He's going out with Trudy instead," I mutter.

"What? But that doesn't make any sense. Why did he ask you out, then?" Matt's as surprised as I was about fifteen minutes ago.

"Apparently he was just using me to make her jealous," I manage.

"Eugh. What a creep," Matt says, putting his arm around me and pulling me into a hug.

This is the first time I've seen Matt in about a week and I'm crying all over him. I can't believe I didn't see this coming. I feel like such an idiot. OF COURSE Josh wouldn't want to go out with me.

"That's shady, and so stupid," Matt carries on. "You know that, don't you? You didn't do anything wrong. You're better off without someone who plays games like that. It sounds like he and Trudy are a match made in heaven, and anyone that's a match for Trudy is not a match for you, my love," he says, kissing my hair.

Matt gives me a tighter cuddle and starts singing "You've Got a Friend in Me." But today it just reminds me that I'm still a child and Trudy's a woman, and I didn't get the guy because I wasn't grown up enough for him.

That's not Matt's fault, though. It's mine.

4:30 p.m.

My bedroom

Matt had to head home to do work. Sixth Form sounds like it's quite full on. I've put the TV on in my room for background noise and I'm just staring blankly at it with Bea lying next to me. She followed me up to my room when Matt left.

I'm fifteen and I've just been stood up on the only date I've ever been asked on. I've only kissed a boy once and barely touched a penis. Sam has a boyfriend, Nick's definitely into Millie, I don't have anyone. Everyone's moving on and I'm not keeping up.

What if my friends replace me with someone who's more like them? Like Trudy. I try to shake the thought off as stupid, but I wondered before about Josh and Trudy and thought that was stupid. What if the things I worry about and think are stupid actually aren't? Maybe it's time for me to start taking my worries far more seriously.

141

5:10 p.m.

I need to get it over with and tell the girls. It just feels like it will make it real. And what if they're disappointed in me, or decide not to be friends with such a loser? This is a stupid thought but what if it's one of those stupid-not-stupid thoughts? My phone is buzzing like a malfunctioning sex toy with about a million messages from them asking how it's going. I think about muting the conversation. But it'll only get worse later.

> **Me:** Hey, so, he didn't show. Trudy and TBs did instead. It turns out he didn't want to go out with me. He's going out with Trudy tonight. He was just using me to make her jealous and he didn't even have the guts to tell me himself that he wasn't coming Xxx

5:15 p.m.

I can feel my phone vibrating again, but I can't face it yet. It'll just be pity messages from the girls and I'm too ashamed to look. The only message I really want right now is from Hot Josh telling me that Trudy was lying and that he likes me and not her, but I saw the evidence myself. That's not going to happen because I wasn't good enough for him.

5:20 p.m.

God, at least I can take this vile thong off now. Or rather

remove it from where it has lodged itself. Can you lose your virginity to an item of clothing? Because it's really gone up there. It's like it's launched an exploration mission of my nether regions.

Google: Can you lose your virginity to a thong?	Q

Can a thong break your hymen?	V
Lads, do girls wear thongs if they're virgins? Or is it a sign that they're real sluts?	V
How my thong made me infertile	V

Jesus, that was a fucking minefield.

5:30 p.m.

I'm sitting in front of the light-up mirror at the dresser I demanded for my fifth birthday, saying that all princesses needed somewhere to get pretty, something Mum gave me a big talking-to about. Now all it's lighting up is every massive pore, every spot and every acne scar, my greasy hair and shiny skin, and the way that my forehead is too small.

I look at women on Instagram who are so effortlessly beautiful and it makes me hate myself even more. I KNOW that there are filters on those pictures, but even filters don't make me look normal, let alone actually pretty. I need to be more like them.

I know that none of this is feminist. We're supposed to love our bodies, our faces, we're supposed to be confident in them. That's what feminists do. That's what real women do. That's what I can't do, and that makes me even more flawed.

I feel like I'm a half woman. Not quite fully good enough for the world.

6:05 p.m.

I'll probably end up being one of those hoarder spinsters you hear about who dies under an avalanche of her own belongings in her parents' house and isn't found for eight months. And no one will be able to identify me anyway because I'll look nothing like the filtered, faux-faced pictures of me on Instagram.

6:30 p.m.

I'm woken up by Dad banging on the door and shoving his head around it. Must have fallen asleep after I pulled the duvet over my head midcry.

"You okay, Kitty Kat? Not feeling well?" I wish everyone would quit calling me Kitty Kat too. It's just another way that people treat me like a child. How am I supposed to grow up if my own parents won't even let me?

"I think I'm coming down with something but I feel a bit better after a sleep." I'm not entirely lying. I do feel a bit better from the sleep, but only because it took me a couple of moments to remember why I was in bed with a damp, tear-stained pillow.

"Ah, well! Lucky for you dinner's ready. That'll make you feel better!"

"Okay." URGH.

I can see that my phone has about a kazillion messages from the girls now. I still can't face them.

6:40 p.m.

The kitchen table

Dinner appears to be some kind of bean thingy. Mum's gone vegan this week and maybe that's the kind of calming, poised, grown-up thing I need to do too, to make myself more sophisticated.

"You're very quiet tonight, Kitty Kat," Mum says.

"I think she's coming down with something, Claire—she's just had a sleep." Someone once said my dad was one of the greatest observational comedy writers of his generation. Spot on, Dad. But he's not yet realized that women can answer for themselves. "I'm sure she'll feel better after some of this hippie food." He winks at me and I can tell he thinks he's being hilarious. It's not, though, is it, Dad? We've all moved on a bit.

Mum's kicking him under the table and just made a small tittering noise. Honestly, their old age pensioner flirting is disgusting and it's completely unsanitary of them to be doing it at the dinner table.

Freddie's giving me a bit of a curious look and I wonder if he saw what happened with Trudy earlier. The younger kids at school are even more afraid of her than the rest of us. If he did see it, he's probably terrified that Trudy will connect him to me in some way.

7 p.m.

Back in my room

When I finally looked at my messages, I was weirdly sad not to see one from Josh telling me it was all a mistake, even though I knew I wouldn't. And it's seven o'clock now, the time his message to Trudy said he would meet her.

> **Emmeline Pankhurst's BAD BITCHEZ**
> Millie, Sam, Me

> **Me:** I'm ok, thanks, guys. I feel a bit better now. Who needs a man anyway, right?!

> **Sam:** Exactly! You go, girl! And don't worry about school tomorrow. We got your back. Neither of those two is coming anywhere near you. Love xxx

Millie: Did you not hear ANYTHING from Josh at all? LOVE x1000000 xxx

Me: Not a thing. If nothing else, it's very poor manners

Sam: I hope she gives him crabs that eat away at his danglies Xxx

Millie: Me too. I hope it turns out Trudy has vagina dentata and she gobbles his penis off with her fanny. I wonder if there's any witchy spells we can cast on them to make bad things happen to them? Xxx

Me: Sounds good, babe. Let me know what you find. Love you both xxx

I had to google vagina dentata. I mean, I wish I hadn't. Turns out it's a lot like what Comedy Krish drew on the board the other day with the massive vulva/vagina, just like that film *Teeth*. So what he was doing was, in fact, science, actually. Maybe if our biology teacher was a little better he'd have known that.

I don't know why I worried about telling them, or why I ever thought that they would stop being my friends just because I don't have a boyfriend. I should have known better than that. I'm so lucky to have such great friends. I should appreciate them more and worry less.

I think I was just doing my usual thing of imagining the worst-case scenario and presuming it had definitely happened. I think I'll go downstairs and see what the family is up to. Better than moping up here thinking about how Josh is with Trudy RIGHT NOW.

10 p.m.

In bed

The girls have made me properly laugh this evening with ideas for what we can do to Josh as payback. Matt even came over for a bit and sat with us all. He says his mum's on a date. I'm glad she's back out there. I'm going to be more like Sandra. I'm going to get up tomorrow, get myself and my feminism together, and I am going to show that it takes more than that to knock me down.

I touch the light switch three times. I need all the good vibes possible.

Unfeminist thoughts: millions
A misuse of I_weigh and many thoughts about bad murders I could do to Trudy—I'm a massive patriarchy enabler.

Friday, September 28

I_weigh:

The weight of a woman scorned. But I have returned to fight another day and I have gotten myself together. So, HA! Up yours, Josh and Trudy!

7:30 a.m.

My bedroom—moving on with poise and maturity

The first thing I will do is NOT call him Hot Josh any more. If he needs a name before Josh, it shall be Shit. He can be Shit Josh.

I got up early to do half an hour of yoga using a YouTube video so that I can feel stretched out and de-stressed. Though if I'm being honest, I mostly marvelled at how anyone can actually get themselves into those positions. I feel rejuvenated and ready to face the day, though, so something must have sunk in.

Millie has found instructions for voodoo dolls and has suggested that we make some of Josh and Trudy stat, which I think is a great idea. I'm going to accidentally focus the pins around Josh's manhood in the hope that it falls off.

Fingers crossed Millie was right yesterday, though, and he'll find out that Trudy has vagina dentata the hard way, when her vagina eats his penis, and Trudy will go to prison for being a toxic-vaginaed cowbag. And Josh will die.

Think I might have gone a bit far. Probably not feminist to wish vagina teeth on a woman. Or that a man's penis falls off/ is eaten. Probably not a marker of human decency in general, that. And I've not just gone too far with the bad thoughts about Josh and Trudy. I've gone over the top on the bronzer, too. Instead of looking like I've been in the sun, I AM THE SUN.

7:35 a.m.

The kitchen

"You look better this morning, love!" Mum's at the counter, juicing something involving kale. Ordinarily I'd stay well away from that sort of thing but today is a new day and I'm the new me.

"Yeah, I feel much better. Thanks, Mum. What are you making?"

"Spinach, kale, mint, and lime smoothie. It's my own recipe. Want one?"

"Yes, please!" Even though whenever she says "my own recipe," we all know it's fit only for the rubbish bin. Sorry, Mum, but Dad's really much better at this stuff.

Dad and Freddie look up from their iPads, and Mum looks up from her juicer. The kitchen is eerily quiet.

"John, did she just say 'yes, please'?" Mum says slowly, gripping the counter.

"Claire, I believe she did." Dad take his glasses off and stares at me in wonder.

Dickheads.

"Shit." Mum's miming being shocked like she's hilarious. Is this what happens when I try to improve myself? For goodness' sake, people. Can't a lady ask for a disgusting vegetable smoothie in the morning without the army being alerted?

I'm maintaining full eye contact with my mum, letting her know that I'm being deadly serious.

"Yes, please, I'd love one." And then I sit down and start looking at my phone.

"Okay, love."

A book called *Feminists Don't Wear Pink* pops up on my newsfeed. Sounds like the perfect way for me to get my groove back. I'm going to get it on Kindle and start it right away.

If I throw myself back into feminism, I will feel empowered and remind myself that there's so much more going on in the world than being ditched by some asshole.

7:40 a.m.

Oh god, can you even be ditched by someone you weren't with in the first place? Loser alert.

8:30 a.m.

Entering school via smokers' alley (or, per official school records, the back passage—LOLs)

The girls and I opted for our berets again this morning. It felt like an incognito day. If I'm going to face Trudy and Shit Josh, I need something to detract from my mournful facial expressions.

After starting *Feminists Don't Wear Pink* on my Kindle over my disgusting smoothie (I'm still hungry, by the way), I've been telling Millie and Sam all about it on the way in. I am brimming with confidence. Everything is tippity toppity okay fabby dooby, yessir, thank you very much.

"Oh god, Kat . . ."

Trudy is sitting on Josh's knee on a bench in the middle of the playground.

Millie turns to see how I'm coping with the absolute scene in front of me.

"She looks like a ventriloquist's puppet, babe."

Sam's correct, but I feel ashamed to note that I still wish I was his ventriloquist's puppet. Two minutes ago I was a feminist, now I'm a Stepford wife.

"Has she no self-respect? She's all over him like a syphilitic rash. What an absolute mess." Millie sounds genuinely appalled. I'm so lucky to have these two.

I take a deep centering yogic breath like I learned to do this morning, put my head up high, and steel myself. I remind myself: there are bigger things happening in the world. I don't need to compete with Trudy. I will not let this drag me down. I need to learn to take the high road or I'll never be a good person and good things will never happen to me.

152

8:35 a.m.

She's such a fucking prick.

8.36 a.m.

"You know what? It's okay. I'm okay," I say bravely.

Millie and Sam have their arms around me. We don't walk past them. We go the longer way around to homeroom. I am not going to cry.

9 a.m.

Homeroom

#Tim's left another note on my desk. This time with a rose. It says:

Katerina,
Thank you for making me a legend.
With love,
#Tim

Fuck's sake.
WHY ME?!

1 p.m.

Outside in the playground. Trying to be brave

I swear the teachers are afraid of Trudy too. They'd be breaking up anyone else who looked like they were dry-humping each other in the playground. They're just letting Trudy get on with it. A baby could be conceived right there, and everyone would be too afraid to so much as offer a condom.

Hot Shit Josh hasn't even looked in my direction. If I think about it too much I feel like I'm losing my marbles a bit, actually. I already feel like everyone knows, and everyone is laughing at me. Stupid Kat.

2 p.m.

English class

Every time I see them all over each other I just keep remembering all the times I imagined him all over me—kissing me, me sitting on his knee, laughing and joking with me . . . I think today is the only time I've ever seen Terrible Trudy properly smile. It's creepy.

Do I have the right to feel these things, though? He barely touched me on Saturday, and it was just one date that he didn't show up for, and I should have known that he wouldn't show up because he hadn't been in touch, and being realistic I'm not really what he would be going for anyway, am I?

I should have known. It's my fault and I'm an idiot.

3:30 p.m.

Trying to leave via the playground without having to witness another display

The vulgarity of watching Shit Josh and Trudy all over each other is really starting to wear a little thin now. #Tim seems to be really pleased with their PDAing too, which makes it even grosser. It's like they've become his personal porn channel. Bleurgh.

It's all a bit showy. I like to think I'd have been a bit subtler, more discreet.

I've definitely got more class.

At least it's the weekend now. I don't need to be thinking about either of them.

10 p.m.

In bed

I can't stop thinking about them. But I'm trying to distract myself by thinking about other things—more important things.

Any day now I'm going to get up the courage to ask Miss Mills about writing the blog. Any day. Maybe even next week.

Or the week after.

Unfeminist thoughts: 0

Actually had a few, what with wishing bad things on Trudy etc.,
but I'm choosing to ignore them.

Today I'm a strong feminist. I've got my girls, I don't need a
man, I am mighty.

I think I am mighty.

I want to be mighty.

I am trying my best to be mighty.

Monday, October 1

I_weigh:

Strength and positivity!

Who am I kidding? I've spent the weekend trying to better myself. Trying to distract myself with things but, in reality, no matter what I try, I start thinking about Josh and Trudy and how by now everyone in the school will know what happened and what an idiot I am.

Actual weight:

Humiliation

9 a.m.

Assembly

Monday morning assembly . . . again. Our weekly pep talk. How do these come around so bloody quickly? It's unnatural, the whole of Year Eleven smushed into one room for ten minutes to start the day while someone blathers on about how next year some of us will be getting jobs and out in the wide world and we can't behave like dickheads there.

Newsflash: we know. Tell us something useful, like how to do our taxes or something.

Oh, but wait, did I just hear the phrase "dick pic" come out of Mr. Clarke's mouth? Maybe I shouldn't have switched off. I turn to look at Millie and Sam who are snorting into their hands.

"And these, errr, 'dick pics' . . ."

Snicker, he said it again, and he's using those air quote things.

". . . as you young folk call them . . ."

Jesus, make yourself LESS relatable, sir.

"These 'DICK PICS' . . ."

Good, good, he's gaining confidence with the phrase, the air quotes are still in force, and the whole room is now in hysterics.

"They are not only FOOLISH because you don't know where on earth they might end up, but at your age they are also ILLEGAL. And it's the same with you lady folk . . . and your . . . er . . . BITS."

This is tremendous. It's actually cheered me up a bit. He's obviously been told he has to cover this stuff, but he's the least capable person to be doing it. I can see Comedy Krish videoing it stealthily on his phone. Marvelous.

12:30 p.m.

The toilets

"Great news! Dave's band has finally got a gig. It's the week-end after next, though, so he's stressing that it's so soon. Do you two want to come? It's at a pub but the music's out in back so you can generally get in without being IDed. Also we can just make sure we look older. Fancy it?" Sam is talking a million miles an hour, with excitement.

"Oh, yes! Maybe I should casually mention it to Nick? Maybe suggest it as a bonding exercise . . ." Millie's still insisting that they're not mixing personal and professional. Sure, Millie . . .

"Kat?" Sam and Millie stare at me expectantly, and I don't want to let them down.

I can't think of anything I want to do less right now than to go out to a place where both Trudy and Josh will definitely be, but maybe I'll have a nice time. Maybe I'll meet the man of my dreams, and he'll be in a band and he'll be better and hotter than Shit Josh.

Hahahahaha. As if anyone hotter than Josh exists—SHUT UP, BRAIN. HE IS SHIT.

"Yeah, sounds good to me. Do you think Trudy and Josh will be there?" I say, against my own will.

"Probably, everyone's going." Sam looks at me anxiously. "I'm sorry. We don't HAVE to go, if you don't want to? But maybe we can use it as an opportunity to show Josh what he's missing?" Sam looks devious.

"I like the sound of this! What did you have in mind?" Millie says.

"How about we all get ready at mine before? With Jas away, she won't notice if we borrow her stuff."

I don't want them not to go because of me and I don't want

Josh and Trudy thinking that I'm not there because of them either.

"Sure, why not. What's the worst that can happen? But I'm making myself look good for me. Not a boy. I've said it before. It's unfeminist, and I'm especially not doing it for a boy who ditched me for actual Satan," I say.

I should be making him regret his choices with my words and brain. But I also really want to look good and make him regret his choices. ARGHHHH.

12:35 p.m.

Google search:

Is it ok to want to look good if you're a feminist? 🔍

Why wearing makeup doesn't make you a bad feminist	V
Why being a man is hard	V

Why does it ALWAYS have to come back to men? I might as well go the whole hog then, if the internet's making it about men already.

Is it wrong to want to look nice for a boy if you're a feminist? 🔍

How to raise a feminist boy	V
Why being a man is scary	V

Oh, FFS. The patriarchy is ALL OVER the internet. ALL OVER IT.

Unfeminist thoughts: I'm losing track . . .
I HATE Trudy, and I'm not sure if this makes me a bad feminist? Is it okay because I also HATE Josh? So that's okay because I hate both man and woman equally? How does it work? Should I just not be hating anyone? But surely that's not feminism, that's just being a saint?

Friday, October 12

I_weigh:

All my failed attempts at feminism.

10 p.m.

My bedroom

I haven't written for a while. My head isn't in such a good place, and I don't really want to document how much of a spectacular fail this term is turning out to be.

I'm trying to be a feminist, but also wanting to look good for a boy and being miserable because everyone else has a boyfriend and I don't. So I'm actually FAILING at being a feminist.

Millie and Nick have been kissing—at rehearsals. I really want to be excited for her, and I am, I think. But all I can seem to think about is how now I'm definitely the odd one out.

So all in all, failing at both being a feminist and a friend.

In other developments, Matt seems to have loads of new friends in Sixth Form. He's started doing things like "going to the pub" and "hanging" at people's houses that aren't mine.

Dad says not to worry and that it's normal for him to move on a bit. I guess so. I think he's coming to Dave's big gig tomorrow so that's good, but I guess he'll probably bring all his new friends along.

Unfeminist thoughts: 2

1. Still worrying about looking good for a boy.

2. Still not being happy enough for friends.

   Basically, I'm failing miserably at everything.

Saturday, October 13

I_weigh:

All the happy and fulfilled lives everyone else is living, compared to me, sitting in bed alone, just watching on Snapchat.

9 a.m.

My bed

The gig is tonight. I should be excited. Instead, I seem to be surgically glued to Instagram and Snapchat, thinking about the things I'm probably supposed to be doing that everyone else IS doing. Le sigh.

3:30 p.m.

> **Emmeline Pankhurst's BAD BITCHEZ**
> Sam, Millie, Me

> **Sam:** When are you both coming over? I've just finished painting some trees so I'll be back home in about 30 mins?

> **Millie:** Just finished rehearsal. Can meet you now and we'll walk back to yours together? Nick's coming tonight BTW.

4 p.m.

Sam's house

Jas's closet is about the size of my entire bedroom. We've tried on everything in it and NONE of it looks good on me. Everything is very stylish and very lovely and a bit London Fashion Week, and I'm a bit more Greggs Sausage Roll on the Bench in a Small Town.

Sam and Millie keep telling me that I look good, but I know I don't, and I don't want them telling me I look nice just to spare my feelings if it means I end up going out looking like some artistic-yet-batshit bag lady.

"How was rehearsal with the lover man, anyway?" Sam asks Millie.

"It was good. Intense. We were doing the bit where they first meet. There's a lot of staring and swooning. I feel quite fatigued. And I've got jaw ache."

Urgh, I wish I had jaw ache.

4:15 p.m.

"Urgh, this is not going to work. I'm supposed to be looking hot, and right now I just look like a hot mess." I slump to the floor surrounded by sequins, feathers, and neon.

"You look well hot! Josh will feel like such a mug when he sees you!" Sam says.

"Exactly! And I know we're trying to be feminist but you're so much prettier than her!" Millie chimes in.

If that were true, I would have gotten the guy in the first place. Anyway, it doesn't matter if I'm going to be a great feminist journalist. I don't need the validation of a man liking me to be confident. And I will NOT compete with other women. MUST NOT.

Except I haven't worked out how to be confident at all yet.

"This is really terrible, but you know that scene in *Mean Girls* where she gets hit by the bus and everyone's happy?" Sam and Millie nod. "I really want that to happen to both of them."

"I think that's normal," Sam says wisely.

"I should be better than that, though. I shouldn't wish pain on another member of the sisterhood."

"Oh, I'm one hundred percent sure that her membership was revoked years ago, babe," Sam says. "If she ever had it."

6:30 p.m.

There's about an hour to go until we need to leave and we're almost ready, so a bit of restlessness has set in.

"We could dye our hair!" Sam says.

"In an hour?" Millie's right. Doing that at speed could end very badly.

"True. Also we'd have to bleach it first to get a color to take. Well, except you, Kat."

"This is the first time my mousey hair has EVER been a bonus," I say dryly.

"Oooh! Know what I've always wanted to try?" Millie gasps.

"DICK?" Sam says, collapsing onto the floor.

"No, vile woman! Contouring!" Millie says.

"Dick sounds more fun," I say. I'm quite funny today, even in my grumpy state.

"And that's coming from the feminist," Sam says.

6:40 p.m.

YouTube vloggersville

We're sitting in a line watching a video that we've found which describes itself as "the ULTIMATE CONTOURING GUIDE."

"Guys, whatever happens next, I think we should make a pact to share absolutely no photos of this with anyone. There are some experiences that should just be between us. This is one of them," I say gravely. I can't hack another bit of embarrassment this term.

"Agreed," Millie and Sam say.

"Right, I've got this palette I've borrowed from Mum which I will possibly never give back," Sam says.

"Your mum's so good at makeup. My mum wouldn't even know what a contouring palette was," I say.

"Black women didn't have many makeup choices when Mum was my age. She's got to make up for it now. God bless Fenty," Sam says. "And all praise Rihanna." She bows down to the beautiful palette in her hand.

"The Fenty lipsticks are fierce," Millie says.

"I could NEVER pull them off, though," I say before realizing what we're doing. "Wait, are we succumbing to some kind of crap stereotype? Should we, as feminists, even care what we look like now?" I think this is the first time I've ever vocalized this burning question with the two of them.

"Errrr, yes, we can talk about what we like and if we want to look good, we can look good!" Sam says forcefully.

"And be damn proud of it too!" Millie chimes in.

"YEAH! None of this! We look how we want to look. Being feminist is about not being oppressed. We're still being oppressed if we can't talk about what we want to. If we want to wear makeup and talk about makeup, we do it! And do you know what? We look beautiful!" Sam says.

God, she's good. I definitely should have asked sooner. So maybe sometimes the thoughts I torture myself with are just fine, actually.

"And right now I want to look contoured!" Millie says.

"Let's go!" I say.

6:50 p.m.

Postcontour

We sit staring straight ahead into the mirror—alarmed.

"We look like tigers," Sam observes.

"Sexy tigers, though?" Millie asks hopefully.

"I really like tigers," I say, and both girls look at me, surprised.

It turns out contouring isn't for us.

7:30 p.m.

"Ready to go, ladies?" We've taken all the makeup off and started again with a more natural look. I'm now one hundred percent sure that contouring's a myth.

"READY!" Millie and I sing.

I'm having fun with the girls and I don't really want to go out where there'll be other people, or specifically where Josh and Trudy will be. To be honest, I've got a level of dread now probably akin to one of Henry VIII's wives at the block, but I must soldier bravely on.

I'm a very supportive friend.

7:45 p.m.

On the train. Trudy and Josh are in the same carriage, snogging like their lives depend on it

I so wish I was a less supportive friend right now.

8:30 p.m.

The sweaty, stinky back room of the pub

We've arrived just in time to see Dave's band get on stage. This is completely in line with our strategy to look cool and not too keen. The pub smells a lot like a giant sneaker, if I'm being honest, and I'm very pleased that it's dark (except for two random spotlights on stage that don't seem to be directed at anyone). There's a sort of smell of sweat mixed with toilet and I think beer (?) but at least we're here, IN the pub, like adults. I just didn't know that being an adult smelled so bad.

Sam is hanging with me while Dave plays. (Their music doesn't seem to use many notes, just the same three played in different sequences. But I'm sure they know what they're doing, but the brass player is definitely distracting.) Millie is hanging with Nick, twirling her hair and pushing her chest out as far as it'll go. She's only just shy of rubbing her right tit against him right now.

Trudy and Josh don't seem to be all that interested in the band either. They're taking pictures of themselves at the side. I'm trying to tell myself that I'm not jealous of them because it looks really boring, and if you're updating your social media so often, when are you actually having fun? You're just leading a boring Instagram-admin-heavy lifestyle. At least I'm dancing.

Millie and Nick are getting quite cozy . . . in fact, they appear to be leaving. Millie gives me a little wave. INTERESTING! It dawns on me that when Dave gets off stage, Sam will inevitably leave me for him and I will be on my own.

Kat No-Mates, the spinster. This is why I'm worried about that cast party on my birthday. It'll be another party where I'm surrounded by people and still completely alone, but this time on my birthday.

I wonder when Matt's going to get here?

9:30 p.m.

The pub beer garden

The other bands that are on are a bit rubbish, really, so we're all hanging out outside. Nick and Millie have been sitting on a wall, making out for the last hour or something. I'd be surprised if she can breathe right now. I'm happy for her, honestly.

Sam's making out with Dave on an adjacent bench. Trudy and Josh are making out, well, all over the place, to be honest. They don't seem to be able to contain their making out to one area.

I'm literally the only person not making out with anyone right now.

9:40 p.m.

Matt's finally here! HURRAH! We're sitting at one of the tables talking to Comedy Krish who seems to prioritize being funny instead of engaging in any making out. I imagine if he started kissing someone, he'd take the piss out of it after a second.

It's nice talking to Matt, though. I've hardly seen him lately and I miss him.

10:30 p.m.

Fatigued from laughing after an hour with Comedy Krish

"Hey, this is pretty dead, and I'm wrecked. Wanna go home?" Matt says after Krish heads off to go and cause mischief somewhere else.

"I'm supposed to leave with the girls but I'm not sure if they'd even notice I was gone," I say, gesturing to them.

"I mean, I don't even know how you'd get their attention right now," Matt says, screwing his face up.

He's got a point. Is it okay to tap someone on the shoulder when they're mid–amorous embrace? Or is that like attempting a threesome? I don't want to add that to my list of sexual deviancies after the start of this term.

Think it's probably best if I just text them.

11 p.m.

Back in dullsville

We got the train back and now we're walking through the quiet, dead town toward home. There are only two pubs and neither of those seem particularly banging for a Saturday evening. Our conversation is the loudest thing happening.

"How are you feeling after everything the other week?" Matt asks.

"Yeah, fine," I lie.

"Oh, well that's good!" Matt says positively. "I'm sorry that I haven't been around much this last week or so. I guess everything's been quite full on. I've missed you," he says, as if he's speaking my thoughts.

He's right, though, it's actually only been a week or so since he's been around. It's not that long, and I've gotten myself so upset about it. Why is it that I can't seem to help myself feeling so low about things like this?

"Anyway, I've been thinking, and I don't think you should lose too much sleep over Josh. He's hot but he's not ALL that, is he? I mean he's school-hot, but he's not like Stormzy-hot, is he?"

I guess he's right, but I doubt I would ever get Stormzy either, somehow.

"That's true," I say, trying to pretend I agree. "I mean, I guess we've got a bit of a low bar?"

"Exactly! He's only an ASOS model! It's not Prada or Gucci!"

"Yeah, I guess this town is quite starved of hot men, so I just got overexcited."

"Imagine being in my situation! You try looking for a nice gay man to hang out with in this hole."

"I'm sorry. It can't be easy for you around here. I almost wonder if #Tim's gay and covering it with his creepy, overenthusiastic approach to women," I suggest.

"Oh god, I hope not," Matt says, cringing. "Also his 'the more you feel them, the bigger they get' line doesn't work for men!"

"Ha, or does it?"

"EWW, KAT. I've got the most disgusting thoughts in my head now!" Matt says, giving me a shove.

God, I've missed him so much. We're nearly at our houses and I'm not sure I feel ready to say goodbye yet.

"Wanna come back to mine and watch some *RuPaul* for a bit?"

"Sounds good. Can we make popcorn and tea?" he says.

"Deal!"

Unfeminist thoughts: 1
Constantly pitting myself against Trudy probably counts here, I think. Thou shalt not compare yourself to another woman, especially if they're a monster.

Sunday, October 14

I_weigh:
10,000 messages on my phone and a very needy dog.

10 a.m.

My bed

Alone . . . or so I thought.

I've woken up to Bea furiously licking my face. Sometimes when I sleep too late, she thinks I've died and feels like it's her duty to resuscitate me. Job done, girl, I'm awake now and definitely breathing, even though now every breath is tinged with the aroma of dog food.

I grab my phone. There are a lot of messages on there from the girls—asking if I got home safely and apologizing for not noticing when I left. Which is good because I was really nervous that they were going to be cross with me for not waiting for them.

> **We're sorry, Kat, please forgive us**
> Sam, Millie, Me

> **Sam:** Sorry, Kat, you'll understand when you get a boyfriend, though, for sure. You just don't notice that time's slipping away and before you know it you've been snogging for hours.

Sam: Hope you got home ok? <3 xxxxx

Millie: Yeah, sorry, Kat, I hope you got home ok. I've got SO MUCH TO TELL YOU! Nick asked me to be his GIRLFRIEND! AHHHHHH! <3 xxxx

Oh god, so that's official, then.

I'm the only one without a boyfriend.

Sad spare-wheel Kat. I'm trying to ignore the "you'll understand when you get a boyfriend" bit. I know I need to reply and be happy for them but . . . I can't face it just yet.

10:01 a.m.

I'm scrolling Instagram to see if there're any great pictures from last night that I can regram, to make it look like I've had a banging night out, even though Matt and I left early to come home and watch TV like an old couple.

The first picture that comes up is something Tiffany has reposted from Terrible Trudy. It's a group shot of her, Josh, and TB posing with Millie, Nick, Sam, and Dave. They're all grinning and/or pouting (grouting?) with their arms around each other like they're having the Best Time Ever.

I feel sick.

Against my better judgment I continue scrolling to the right. There are LOADS of them. Enough to make me worry that I'll get repetitive scrolling injury. In some of them Millie and Sam are blowing kisses to the camera, in others they're just smiling, but at NO point do they look like they don't want to be there, posing with the two people who absolutely humiliated me. In one Josh is even making bunny ears behind Millie's head.

So they did eventually come up for air, then? But when they did, they hung out with Trudy and Josh?! And they didn't even try to hide it. Do they just not care about my feelings AT ALL?

I'm so angry. I think I might cry.

10:20 a.m.

So they've basically gotten boyfriends and forgotten about me. Their earlier apologies are completely meaningless. They were feeling guilty. AND SO THEY SHOULD.

10:30 a.m.

I pull the covers over my head only for Bea to try to nuzzle her way in. She deposits a pair of my chewed-up knickers next to my face. FML.

11 a.m.

I've got English coursework on *Macbeth* due at the end of term, and I haven't been able to even think about it yet because I've been too caught up with things. Maybe I should distract myself with that. At least English is one thing I'm good at. Unlike friends. Or boyfriends. Or menstrual cups. And I know that my last *Inspector Calls* essay wasn't my finest work. I'm dreading finding out my mark for that. I need to focus.

Not sure how much studying Lady Macbeth's murder/ bloody hands scenario will help my current angry state of mind, though.

11:30 *a.m.*

My desk

I've put my phone over on the other side of the room. I don't need to hear anymore about last night. I'm going to knuckle down and get on with this. If they're ditching me for Trudy and Josh, I don't need them anyway. I am going to be a top feminist journalist.

11:35 *a.m.*

The question looks tricky so I'm just going to take it bit by bit. This is the first part:

Explore the themes of guilt and manipulation within the play Macbeth. *Particularly focus on Macbeth, Lady Macbeth, and the three witches.*

Right. Simple. I can do this.

12 *p.m.*

I've written nothing. I hate this play and its stupid guilt and jealousy. Do you think Shakespeare ever imagined that years into the future his literary meanderings would form the basis of qualifications which have the ability to make or break a person's life?

I feel like he'd be SHOCKED.

12:05 p.m.

Why. Can't. I. Focus?

Every time I try to sit still, I get itchy. I might look at my phone just in case they've messaged to say sorry or to explain that Trudy forced them to be in those pictures against their will. Maybe when they've apologized I'll feel better and be able to concentrate? They MUST have seen the pictures by now and KNOWN that they will have upset me? But then why pose for them in the first place?

12:10 p.m.

So there are no messages from the girls, and it looks like I have to unfollow the whole world on social media to stop seeing Shit Josh. Literally everyone is posting pictures of him and Trudy. Or reposting the pictures of them all together. I can't get away from them. I flip over to Snapchat and they're there with even more filter, looking even hotter.

Urgh. Again.

12:15 p.m.

Maybe there's something I can get to make my pores smaller. In this picture of the two of them, Trudy's barely got pores at all. Maybe I don't have a boyfriend because I have pores?

Do Millie and Sam have pores as big as mine? I've never really looked. You can't tell in the picture that Trudy posted last night. Maybe they're all now part of some kind of poreless club.

EMERGENCY UNFEMINIST THOUGHTS ALERT!
I should not obsess over my skin but should obsess over my essay instead. I should not be:
1. Competing with other women.
2. Trying to make my pores disappear for a boy (or anyone—I think they might have an actual scientific function).

12:30 p.m.

Right, this is good. I've got a few words down now. They're all rubbish but they're there.

I usually get these essays done as soon as we're assigned them. I'm the geeky one who submits things early and manages to understand everything easily for English. Why can't I do it now?

What if I've become stupid?

180

Or what if I've been stupid all along and I'm only just notic-ing? What if my teachers are just being kind and actually I'm stupid?

My mum must be so ashamed. She's won awards for how great she is at science, and the work that she's done in labs. And I can't even string together a couple of words for a play written by a guy who's been dead over four hundred years.

What if my mum's been secretly ashamed of me all this time? What if she's just biding her time with me? What if Dad's just humoring me whenever he says something I do is good or funny, and actually I'm more than just the sitcom character, I'm actually the butt of the longest running joke about an idiot ever?

What if that's me?

12:40 p.m.

> **We're sorry, Kat, please forgive us**
> Sam, Millie, Me

Sam: Kat? Are you ok? Xxxxxxxxxxx

Millie: Yeah, Kat, we're worried. Let us know you're ok? Xxxxxxxxxxxxxxxxxxxxxxxxxx

I should probably get in touch just to let them know I'm okay. I guess they either haven't seen Trudy's Instagram or they just don't think it's that big of a deal, which is even worse, really, because it's awful. It still feels like a punch in the face.

That should be enough. I'm so furious with them. If they can't work that out themselves then I don't know what I can do to help them, really.

Millie: OH, THANK GOD! WE'LL NEVER LEAVE YOU AGAIN, WE PROMISE! XXXX

Sam: Are you, though? You seem a bit . . . off? xx

Maybe I should just tell them. I go into Instagram and copy the link to the post, and just paste it into our WhatsApp group. I can immediately see Sam typing. Then stopping. Then Millie typing. Then stopping. Then neither of them are typing. I swear to god, if they're having a private message about this now, I will lose my shit.

I put my phone down and stroke Bea, my best friend, my trusty companion, my loyal chum.

I have become a middle-aged man.

12:43 p.m.

Typing . . .

12:45 p.m.

Typing . . .

182

12:48 p.m.

FFS

12:50 p.m.

It's taken them ten minutes of TYPING but they've finally gotten back to me.

> **We're REALLY sorry, Kat, PLEASE FORGIVE US**
> Sam, Millie, Me

> **Sam:** We're sorry. We tried to get out of them but Trudy was being awful and wouldn't let us leave and we didn't know what to do.

> **Millie:** You KNOW we'd never hang out with her willingly. We can't stand her. Please, Kat? We're really sorry? How can we make it up to you?

I'm finding it hard to forgive them, and I'm trying to tell myself to be a koala again and calm down but I just don't get it. Why not just tell Trudy to fuck off? Why not just walk away? The boys would have supported them, surely? Especially as they're such great boyfriends.

> **Millie:** Please, Kat? Don't let Trudy come between us Xxx

Sam: You know we hate her as much as you do. Please forgive us. We're really sorry. We'll never do it again Xxx

I'm starting to worry that I'm coming across a little bit petty or childish or something, and I don't want to be the only one without a boyfriend AND for people to think I'm really childish as well. I'm going to have to summon my inner koala whether I like it or not.

Me: No worries, guys. You're right, I know you'd never hang out with her really. Don't worry xx

Millie: <3 THANK GOD <3 We'll never do anything like this again xxx

Sam: <3 LOVE YOU, KITTY KAT xxxx

I know I've said I'm fine with it, but I'm not. I guess I have to try to get over it, though. Maybe I'll start by asking about Nick, see if that distracts me a bit.

Me: <3 love you too. CONGRATS on the new boyfriend, Mills. Tell me EVERYTHING xxx

10 p.m.

I've spent the majority of today trying to pretend I don't care about Trudy's pictures, or Millie and Sam both having boyfriends and the play together without me. I'm trying really hard to pretend that I'm not the odd one out now. But it really feels like I am.

184

I touch the light switch three times. Maybe that'll stop me from being alone forever. Or an old spinster living with her parents.

Unfeminist thoughts: 2
1. Why does everyone else have fewer pores than me? And why did I waste time thinking about it?
2. Wasting time thinking about boys instead of my coursework.

Monday, October 15

The burden on my parents of their only child without a partner. WTF?! How did this happen?!

10:30 a.m.

The playground

So far this morning has been normal (apart from Millie droning on about how great Nick is every five seconds, except this is actually quite normal, so I stand by my original comment), like any other until RIGHT now, when we went to the playground for break.

They say that sometimes when you become too obsessed with what's happening in your own life, you don't notice what's going on around you. Well, this has really proved that theory, because somehow we hadn't noticed that Millie's INNOCENT LITTLE SISTER ISSY. AND. MY. DISGUSTING. BROTHER. FREDDIE. ARE. GOING. OUT.

AS IN A COUPLE.

AS IN TOGETHER.

AS IN I CAN'T EVEN.

When we walked into the playground just now, there they were, BOLD AS BRASS—holding hands in public. Like they aren't even ashamed of it. Issy doesn't even look embarrassed to be seen with him.

I should have noticed. I'd clocked that he smelled a bit better recently but that had to happen at some point, right? Boys can't just smell like some kind of damp, trench-footed sock for ever? I just presumed that nature had intervened and he had finally learned how to wash properly.

Sam, Millie, and I are standing in a line, frozen to the spot, mouths open, eyes wide.

"Has something hit me on the head? Am I in a terrible coma? What is happening here, people?" I have to whisper due to the shock.

"SHIT," says Millie.

"I'm going right over there and I'm breaking this FILTH up immediately!" says Sam.

I'm glad that Sam and I are almost on the same page, but I'm not sure I'd be calling it filth because they're just holding hands. It's not exactly *Fifty Shades*. Sam's not even related to either of them and she's really taken umbrage with it. (What a great expression, by the way. I've taken UMBRAGE with it. *Are you okay with this, Kat?*; *No, sorry, I take UMBRAGE with it.*)

I'm looking at Millie and slightly concerned that her face has changed, and after the initial shock has subsided she now appears to be smiling at the scene in front of her.

"Actually, I think it's lovely. How well has this worked out! I've got a boyfriend, Issy's got a boyfriend, Sam's got a boyfriend! Kat . . . YOU CAN BE MY SISTER-IN-LAW."

I feel like I might vomit. Yes, Millie, that's correct. I am already a spinster dependent upon her family and friends to keep her company. I wonder which one of them will have me to live in their granny annex when I'm old and alone, puttering around with all my cats.

My disgusting brother is in a relationship before me.

And now (lucky me), I must sit in a room with Trudy and Josh for a period of double math in which they will flirt, throw things at each other, and make everyone feel like they're simulating sex across the room while the rest of us are merely some kind of CONTRACEPTIVE BARRIER CROWD.

Although I should make it clear that no one has ever orgasmed in a double math lesson, to my knowledge.

10.51 a.m.

Issy's Instagram:
picture of the two of their hands clasped together

Caption: *"When you know, you know."*

WHEN YOU KNOW WHAT?
YOU KNOW NOTHING!
YOU ARE CHILDREN!

10.52 a.m.

Does this mean my little brother is sexually active before me? I mean, he's underage!

Bleuurrghhh I can't even think about it.

I'm sure he's not.

10.53 a.m.

No.

10.58 a.m.

Please, god, no. Never.

I may pass out.

12:30 p.m.

The dining hall

Terrible Trudy is actually sitting on Josh's lap, feeding him his lunch.

"Do you think she cut it up for him first? Into bite-sized pieces so that he doesn't choke?" Sam asks.

"I always thought the act of feeding someone was supposed to be romantic, but she actually just looks like she's feeding a baby. She's one step away from giving him a little bib and scraping the mush off his chin as he dribbles," Millie notes.

I grab a forkful of rice from my plate and move it toward the girls.

"Here comes the airplane, nnnneeeeoooooooooowwwww."

Both girls burst into hysterics while I manage to spill rice everywhere. See, I'm funnier today. This is nice.

"The thing I don't get, though, is that when she's finished feeding him his lunch, will she then have to eat her own? Or will he feed it to her? Will we have to watch this whole thing again in reverse? Because I don't think my stomach can take it." Sam gestures with her knife quite aggressively.

"I have no idea, but it's ruined my appetite. Kat, another reason why I don't think Josh was the right man for you. If he needs assistance eating his lunch, he'll never find a, you know . . ." Millie says, gesturing downward.

"Clit," Sam says matter-of-factly.

"True story," I say. So wise.

"As much fun as this is, shall we go outside?" Sam asks. "Dave's playing football somewhere on the field, why don't you both humor me while I stand around fluttering my eyelashes and tossing my hair in his direction?"

Millie and I jump up. We don't need to be asked twice, given the view. I still have a niggling thought in the back of my head about those pictures too, despite them making fun of her with me now, so the less time I spend near Trudy, the better.

"How are things going with Dave, anyway?" I ask Sam as we stash our trays. I feel more positive about things since watching that absolute horror show. Better to be a strong independent woman who can feed herself and all that.

"Well." Sam's eyes flit from me to Millie. "We got to third base the other day, before his mum came home."

I'm actually a bit shocked because I thought that she would have told us if anything major happened. Third base is knicker-rummaging, and I feel like that's definitely major territory. Millie doesn't seem all that shocked. She's just nodding knowingly. Maybe she's gotten to the knicker-rummaging stage with Nick too, even though it's only been about two days?

It's like there's a whole world happening inside our friendship group that I know nothing about. I get the sinking feeling back in my stomach. Are they WhatsApping without me?

"Millie, did you know already?" I ask. I'm trying to measure my voice so that I don't sound quite as cross as I feel, but I'm very cross.

"Sam just asked if me and Nick had done anything like that yet, that's all," Millie says shyly.

"AND HAVE YOU?" I am aware that I'm bug-eyed right now.

"Well, a bit, but you know it's only been three days, and we're mostly limited to what we can get up to in the props cupboard. Things got a bit heated last night and then a cardboard sword dug into my back, and I just sort of fell into his hands, boobs first."

"Boobs first?! You just sort of fell, with your boobs first? I mean, I thought you would have both told me if stuff like that happened." I am aware that my voice is wobbling like I'm close to tears and that it is utterly ridiculous.

"Oh, Kat, we didn't think you'd want to know," Sam says, putting her arm around me.

191

"What with everything that happened with Shit Josh, we didn't want to seem like we were rubbing it in your face, that's all."

"We'll always tell you now if you want us to?" Mills adds her arm around Sam's, making me a sort of Kat sandwich.

"Um, yes please." I feel utterly stupid and childish now. But I really do want them to tell me. I don't like feeling like there's this whole world of sexual experience going on and I'm not even being told about it. It's definitely worse to be left out of it completely. Isn't it?

"Well, all I told Millie, just so that you're up to speed, is that he didn't seem to know what to do when he got down there. He sort of rushed his hand into my knickers and then right out again. A bit like he was afraid my vagina was going to munch him. He barely touched vulva."

Millie and I start giggling as Sam wiggles her fingers at us revoltingly.

"Poor Dave," I sigh. "Sounds like he's got a bit of fanny fear."

3 p.m.

Drama class

We're doing monologues. I'm doing Ariel from *The Little Mermaid*. #Tim keeps trying to tell me he's Sebastian so he can get closer to me.

He keeps snapping his pincer fingers at me and they smell vile.

Why do most boys smell like gone-off cheese?

4 p.m.

I've had a really nice day, so WHY am I STILL worrying about those pictures?

I can't stop thinking that they might just one day ditch me for Trudy now. They all looked pretty bloody happy in those pictures, after all. All the grown-ups with boyfriends together.

URGH.

4:15 p.m.

> What's the longest that a lonely dead person has gone before they find the body? Q

Just googling for myself and my future. This is the absolute pits.

4:30 p.m.

They're not even WhatsApping me because they're too busy being sexually active. I may as well join a nunnery.

4.32 p.m.

I'll text Matt. He'll be around.

Me: Did you hear the news?
Freddie's got a girlfriend. ISSY!

I stare at my phone expecting his instant reply, for him to be as shocked as I am. But there's not even any indication that he's seen my text.

5 p.m.

I've done three words of my *Macbeth* coursework.

I heard Freddie come home just now. He must have been out with his new girlfriend.

Everyone's at it.

Everyone except me.

5:30 p.m.

I wonder if I took my last tampon out the other week.

I probably need to check that quite urgently.

5:40 p.m.

No tampon up there. Thank god. Not that I could find, anyway. There's nothing to say that one hasn't, like, burrowed way up into my vagina all the way into my womb and is now swimming about in the wide-open space of my uterus.

5:45 p.m.

That's probably not possible, is it?

5:46 p.m.

Think I'll just google it.

5:50 p.m.

Nope, can't happen.

Didn't realize the bit that links the fallopian tubes is called the fundus, though. That's a funny word.

I wonder if that's because the fallopian tubes are so high up that they think, "No one will ever fundus."

Hahahaha.

5:55 p.m.

I'm so ashamed of that last joke. I'm sorry, and I actually think fundus sounds a bit gross, like fungus.

6 p.m.

Although it's actually not gross because I'm a feminist.

A fundus feminist.

I'll stop now.

6:05 p.m.

DINNER TIME!
Thank god. I've worked really hard here. I have written five words.

6:15 p.m.

Freddie's sitting opposite, staring at me. He knows I know, and he knows it's only a matter of time before I tell Mum and Dad. I'm a ticking time bomb. I could drop the "Freddie's got a girlfriend" news at any point, and there's not a thing he can do about it.

I feel like I've got so much power.

"Please could you pass the salt, Freddie?"

"Of course, Kat. Can I get you anything else?" Freddie's sucking up big time now.

I salt my dinner, all the while maintaining eye contact with him, replace the salt, keeping the eye contact, and start chewing, eyes still locked. I could blow at any minute, and I'm building the tension with my intense eyes. I really need to blink.

"Right, what is it? What's going on between you two?" Mum says, putting down her fork. She's onto us. God, why does Mum always have to be so perceptive? I wanted to drag the tension on a bit longer.

"Nothing!" Freddie exclaims cheerfully, scooping food into his mouth.

"There's only so long you can keep it secret, Freddie. You

shouldn't be ashamed," I say gently, pointing my fork at him, as if it's something serious.

I'm remembering all the things he's told my parents that I didn't want them to know about. ALL the things. In particular, #Tim.

I may never forgive or forget #Tim.

"What's your secret, Freddie?" Mum looks exasperated. Dad looks at Freddie with interest. I don't think he's ever had a secret from Dad before.

Freddie looks like he's about to cave, like he might be about to spill, and I can't let that happen before I've had my moment of glory. I just can't.

"FREDDIE'S GOT A GIRLFRIEND!" I shout, standing up and throwing my arms out into a big reveal pose.

Take THAT, Freddie.

"Ohhhh, that's wonderful news, love! What's she called?" Mum starts.

Freddie is HATING this. He's gone red from ear to ear. I think this is the only bit of him being more together than me that I've actually enjoyed at all, and I intend to milk every single second of it.

"A chip off the old block, son!" Dad slaps his back in a jokey way while Mum rolls her eyes at him.

"John, I'm the only real girlfriend you've ever had. None of the others would admit to going out with you."

"Not true, Claire. That's just what I wanted you to think. I used to be quite the ladies' man!"

"Name one lady."

Dad's gone quiet. He's shuffling in his seat. Mum's staring him down.

"What's she called, love?" she says again, turning back to Freddie. "Is she from your year at school?"

"She's um . . . well . . ."

"It's Millie's little sister!" I blurt out because I want to try to prolong my win and Freddie's embarrassment for as long as I possibly can.

"Well, Issy's a lovely girl. Why don't you invite her over for tea?"

Oh my god. Mum's just nailed it.

I cannot wait for this to happen. I'll have to remind Mum to get the baby pictures out. I'm pretty sure there's one where he's not only naked in the bath as a baby, but he's done a little poo in it too.

"I hate you." Freddie nudges my foot under the table.

It's strange because it's very much the opposite of how I feel about myself now. For a change, I think I'm pretty great.

9 p.m.

My bedroom, at my desk, poised for work that will never happen

My joy at rinsing Freddie was short lived. I still have not finished my *Macbeth* essay and Matt still has not texted me back. Not to mention that I've got a history project to think about. Bea appears to have gotten onto the bed next to me and is lying on her side. Like she wants me to spoon her. I worry that Bea is the only living creature on earth that will ever want to spoon in bed with me.

10:30 p.m.

Bea's just gotten really annoyed that I woke her up reaching around her to touch the light switch. Now my little quirks are annoying others as well as me.

Unfeminist thoughts: 0
Unless wanting to bump off your more successful brother is unfeminist? Where have I gotten this MURDEROUS streak from?

Tuesday, October 16

I_weigh:

Loneliness. When you realize everyone else in the world has someone but you.

1 a.m.

At my mirror

I'm sitting here trying to work out what's wrong with me and why everyone else has a boyfriend and I don't.

Here are the things that I have thought of so far:

1. My nose. Why do noses always have to be so protruding? And how do people end up with those ones that are literally just a little cute bump on their face? Always accompanied by freckles? They can't all be nose jobs.

2. My eyes. They're too normal. They're not wide and sparkly, and they're not an interesting shape or color. They're just eyes. No one wants someone with JUST eyes.

3. My hair. Again, it's not really a color. It's not really a style. Whenever I've tried to style it, it just falls out within seconds. I have the kind of hair that you can't do anything with, it just *is*.

4. My mouth. I don't have full lips. I just have lips. They're not plump. They're just there. Functional. For talking.

5. The light switch. Who is going to want to go out with a girl who can't go to sleep without touching a light switch three

times and who constantly imagines bad things happening to her loved ones?

Four of those points are based on my looks.
I'm a terrible feminist and possibly a lunatic.

7:30 a.m.

Maybe today is the day to ask about starting Feminist Friday in the school blog? To make up for my own self-obsessed, shallow behavior. There are people dying (quite literally) to go to school and I'm over here in my privileged position making lists about how my lips aren't big enough.

8 a.m.

On the way to school

"So, we're booking our waxes for Friday evening. Do you want to come with, Kat?" Sam's asking while she looks at Millie. I can see they're really trying to make sure I don't feel left out.

"Sure! I'll come along for the ride," I say, more enthusiastically than I feel.

"Okay!" They both seem disproportionately happy with this answer. Like it's somehow absolved them of any guilt, and we can all go back to normal again. So that's good.

"Oh god, is that Freddie and Issy holding hands up ahead?" Sam asks.

Urgh, it definitely is. It's too weird.

"Mum gave Issy THE TALK last night after I told her about them. I felt bad subjecting her to that," Millie says.

"Oh my god, can we not talk about this out loud!" I was already disgusted at the world before this news came out, but nothing has repulsed me more than this thought.

"Kat, they're in a relationship now. They may want to, you know, explore."

When did Millie become some kind of sex therapist? What on earth is happening here? And why is she okay with this? It's disgusting.

"All I'm saying is that as his older sister I just really don't need to know about it. EVER."

"I think that's reasonable, actually," Sam says. Thank god that someone understands plain and simple rules of decency.

"Oooohhh kayyyyy. But just because you don't talk about it, doesn't mean it's not happening," Millie says.

For god's sake. I don't need to be reminded that it's happening. I know it's happening all around me. I need to change the subject.

4:30 p.m.

My bedroom

I can't remember the last time I managed to focus on just one thing at a time.

Right now, for instance, I'm looking at my phone while also trying to do my coursework. I can't stand the silence in my room so I have the TV on for some background noise. Every time I try to focus, I end up just scrolling and scrolling through Insta. A lot of the time I don't even remember picking my phone up. I see pretty pictures of models and then go deep into their profiles, trying to work out how I can be just like them, how Shit Josh will regret the day he ditched me for Terrible Trudy.

Then two seconds later I'm trying to focus on my work again, before repeating the cycle. I'm like a hamster in a very nonproductive wheel.

6 p.m.

The dinner table

I don't really feel hungry, but I can't be bothered to tell anyone that I don't feel hungry because that would result in someone asking what's wrong, and what's wrong is that I'm me.

Thankfully, Mum's still got plenty of information that she needs to get out of Freddie about Issy, so the heat has really been taken off me, and I reckon it'll stay that way for a good few days if I keep my head down.

"So, Freds, when is Issy going to come round for dinner?" This is a repeat of yesterday's question, which Freddie has already answered. Mum knows this but she's hoping to break him down with repetition.

His face has screwed up, he's gone bright red, and he's dropped his fork.

"Um. Hm. Well, I mean, NEVER!" His ears look like they're on fire.

"Well, Freddie," Dad starts, "if you're going to be 'busy' with this girl . . ." he puts "busy" into little bunny ears with his fingers and I CAN'T COPE ". . . we should really meet her."

"Your dad's right, Freddie. If you're going to be 'busy' with her, we'd really like to meet her first."

Okay, this is no longer amusing, just HORRENDOUS. Freddie is dying, I am dying. Why is she repeating what Dad just said? Why are they doing this? He's fourteen. He's not getting "busy" with anyone.

They've definitely scripted this little chat. Are they trying to be funny? Oh god, I think they're trying to be funny. A small part of me is angry that they get to do it to Freddie before they do it to me.

Freddie looks like he's about to run out of the room.

"The thing is, Freds," says Dad, chomping on a sausage, "we can't rely on her parents to have spoken to her about contraception, so we thought we should probably sit the two of you down and have a good chat together. Not to mention that you're underage, so obviously we'll need to make sure she understands the importance of waiting as well as you do."

"And when the time comes, I can talk to her about the pill,

or the coil, perhaps. I don't mind." Mum looks really serious, but I can see the corners of her mouth twitching.

Freddie's pushing his chair back, shaking his head like his brain might be boiling over. Might he be having some kind of fit? Should we be worried? I reckon this much sex talk could overload a teenage boy's brain to the breaking point.

"ABSTINENCE!" he shouts, and runs away.

Mum and Dad collapse into a fit of giggles at the table. I stare at them in disbelief.

"For most parents, their child having sex is a real trauma, and something that they are afraid of. You two just turned it into ten minutes of comedy for your own pleasure. You are a pair of sick, sick individuals," I pronounce. "Someone needs to analyze the two of you."

They laugh even more with Dad doing impressions of Freddie's scared face and shouting "ABSTINENCE!" at the ceiling. Are all parents this deranged?

"Really, though, they're not going to do anything, are they?" Dad asks suddenly. "They're much too young, aren't they?" He's looking at Mum, slightly panicked now.

"Yeah, don't worry, John, he can't even get his underwear on the right way around most mornings," Mum says.

For some reason this makes Dad look even more alarmed.

11 p.m.

In bed

I don't think I can be a journalist. In order to be a journalist, you have to be pretty smart, energetic, and fierce. I am none of these things. What sorts of jobs can a person whose brain feels like it's going a million miles an hour at nothing specific do? If you were to compare my brain to an animal, it would be a kitten chasing its tail and then pooping on it.

I touch the light switch three times. Sometimes I really miss being a kid; at least then it felt like there was loads to look forward to. Now I'm not even a proper adult and I've already failed at everything.

Unfeminist thoughts: 5
I think the list of five things I hate about myself probably counts here.

Wednesday, October 17

I_weigh:
Trudy.

3:30 p.m.

The girls have headed off to work on the play again. So, I'm just going home. I still haven't heard from Matt and I still can't get my head around my coursework. Maybe I'll just get under the duvet.

I can see Trudy up ahead as I come out of the alleyway, and I know that she likes to prey on people the most when they're on their own, so I'm just going to keep my head down. I'll be fine as long as I don't make eye contact or show any sign of weakness.

I can hear her trying to get my attention, but I will not give in.

"Katerina! KATERINAAAA! LOSER!" And then I feel something hit me on the head and I realize she's started throwing ACTUAL STONES at me. I'm going to have to stop and engage with her before the stones turn into rocks. I wouldn't put it past her to actually brain me.

She's started walking alongside me anyway with The Bitches. Up front, Amelie and Tiffany have joined in with shouting my name.

"Where are your friends? Hanging out with their boyfriends? Is it sad that everyone else has someone? Everyone except you?"

I'm trying to ignore her but what she's saying is essentially completely true, and she's now blocking my path with her horrible little robot crew.

"Josh sent me your silly little chat with him, when you thought he ACTUALLY wanted to go out with you."

He what? Of course, he did, because it turns out that Shit Josh is actually Extra Shit Josh. I'm trying to remember if I said anything embarrassing. I'm just going to try to keep my cool, even though with Amelie, Tiffany, Nia, and Tia circling me like evil crows, my head is starting to spin.

"He sent them to me when he realized he might actually have to go as far as going on a date with you to make me jealous."

She's waving her phone in my face, which is massively unhelpful when things already seem quite blurry. My head feels like it's about to spin off and I feel really hot. Why can't she just leave me alone? She won. She got the guy.

I finally focus on the screenshot she's shoving in front of my eyes, texts from idiot, gullible me from the past.

I'm trying to propel myself to keep walking, but my legs feel really heavy and I'm afraid that I'm about to fall over. Every breath I take evaporates into nothing before it reaches my lungs, so I'm trying really hard to focus on not passing out because it feels like the whole world is closing in on me.

"You know, your friends were telling me how awful it is that they can't hang out with you anymore now that they have boyfriends and you don't. That they feel like you're a third wheel. Who no one fancies. That's why they stayed on Saturday and hung out with the grown-ups after you'd gone. You know they're over you. They're excited about the big cast party and you're still hung up on silly, babyish surprises for your silly, babyish birthday. They've moved on and you're still silly little Kitty Kat."

I need her to stop talking. Her voice feels like it's scratching at my brain. I can't even work out what she's saying now, it just sounds like noise.

I need to get away, but all of them together are blocking me in and the effort of putting one leg in front of the other seems too hard. I see a gap and push through them and their circling and taunts. I start running.

4 p.m.

I keep running until I realize that I really can't catch my breath now and I'm getting so dizzy that I might fall over, so I sit down on the curbside with my head between my knees like you're supposed to if you feel faint in gym class.

I don't know how long I can sit like this, though. I need to get home to where I'm safe and I can lock myself in my room.

Why would the girls say that to Trudy? Why would they have said all those nice things to me before we went out and then be saying that behind my back? Millie and Sam have always hated Trudy. They've always been there when Trudy's been horrible. They've always agreed with me that she's a witch. I don't understand it. What's changed?

I wouldn't normally believe they'd tell her stuff, but if they didn't then how would she even know about the birthday surprises? And also how would they know I was upset? I didn't even say anything. I can't believe they'd talk to her about that stuff, but there's no other way that she'd know.

5 p.m.

Face down on my bed

What happened? A few weeks ago everything was fine. I had Millie, Sam, and Matt, and I knew that nothing would ever come between us, that we'd do anything for each other. Now everyone's moved on and I'm left alone while they're bad-mouthing me to Terrible Trudy? Or, in Matt's case, just disappeared into some Sixth Form black hole.

Trudy's right.

They're the grown-ups and I'm the kid who's been left behind.

5:10 p.m.

I'm sitting at my mirror staring between my reflection and a picture of Trudy on Instagram. What does she have that I don't? What is it about me that's so rubbish that everyone has left me?

There must be some kind of fault with me and it just took the girls a little longer to realize it than most, but now that they've figured out I'm a faulty human, they've moved on to better things.

And I KNOW it's not feminist to pit yourself against another woman and try to work out ways that you're better or they're better, but I'm not sure even feminism wants me right now.

I don't feel very womanly. I don't feel like I'm feminine or attractive. I don't feel like the women in ads with perfect nails, wearing pure-white cotton floaty shirts, with their long thick hair and beautiful skin and smiley teeth. I don't feel like I can really be a proper woman, not the way I am.

So I don't feel like "feminist" is a title that I can really have any ownership over. That's a title for women and, no matter how hard I try, I'm still a silly little girl playing at being an adult.

5:15 p.m.

I get it now. Josh knew I was rubbish just like Millie and Sam do, that's why he only used me to make Trudy jealous and why he was never really interested in me in the first place. All I'm good for is to be used as a prop to get an actual woman.

At least last time I had Matt to cheer me up after Trudy's vileness. He still hasn't responded to my text from yesterday and I really want to text him again, but I also want to pretend I've still got some pride.

5:30 p.m.

My phone's vibrating.

Millie: THIRD BASE ALERT, GUYS! THIRD BASE!

Sam: TELL ME EVERYTHING!

I can't even with this right now. It's too confusing. They're texting me but telling Trudy they're bored of me.

5:35 p.m.

So I just need to be better at being a woman—not throwing my menstrual cup all over the place because I can't make it work. It's no wonder Sam and Millie don't want to be friends with someone so embarrassing.

I must just try to be better.

I need to know how to do that, though.

    Search: How to be better   Q

Google's decided that it's going to finish that sentence for me because apparently you can't just want to be better in general, you have to want to be better AT something.

"How to be better at Fortnite"

Has Freddie been using my computer again? Little shit.

"How to be better at sex"

Sure. Rub right into my face that I'm not ever going to get the opportunity because I'm too much of a troll for a man to ever want to do that with me.

"How to be better at math"

Oh, just throw another worry into the mix there, Google—thanks, mate. As if worrying that I'm not a complete person isn't enough, you're trying to remind me that I'm crap at math, too.

"Kat?" Dad's knocking on my door. "You okay, love? Didn't even hear you come in."

"Fine, Dad," I say firmly, trying not to sound like I'm about to cry.

"Hmmm, okay." I can hear him hesitate outside the door, but I really don't want to talk to anyone right now. I think running to my parents would just cement me as the biggest loser-child in Year Eleven.

6:30 p.m.

Dinner

Dad keeps asking well-meaning questions like "How's Matt finding Sixth Form?" and "Where are Millie and Sam this week?" and each question hits a painful nerve.

I can't answer properly so I just keep nodding and giving short one-word answers. The last thing I want to do is start crying into the tofu on my plate. Even though it may give it some much-needed moisture.

I eat fast so I can get back to my bedroom and being by myself.

8 p.m.

Back in my room

The girls have messaged to say they have a play meeting before school so they're going to walk in early together.

There's probably no meeting. It's just part of trying to phase me out.

8:30 p.m.

I want to tell the girls how angry I am that they were talking to Trudy, saying horrible things about me. But that would just be another example of me being childish. Silly little Kat, not able to keep up with everyone else and then complaining about it.

10 p.m.

Bed

Maybe if I touch the light switch an extra three times tonight, tomorrow will be better. Josh will break up with Trudy and realize it's me that he should have been with all along. (I know I shouldn't want this and I'm trying not to.) The girls will apologize for ever excluding me because of their boyfriends, and things will go back to how they were. The three of us, just hanging out together. And I'll finally be able to do at least some of my English coursework without my brain melting.

Why do things have to change when I'm not ready for them to? I feel like I'm doing everything wrong.

It's like everything's just plunged into darkness all of a sudden.

Unfeminist thoughts:
I don't think I'm good enough to be a feminist anymore so maybe it doesn't matter?

Thursday, October 18

I_weigh:

Everything and it's all too heavy.

8:20 a.m.

I still haven't responded to Sam and Millie. There's no point if I'm walking to school by myself anyway.

10:30 a.m.

> **Emmeline Pankhurst's BAD BITCHEZ**
> Sam, Millie, Me

Sam: Emergency! The fucking cardboard trees keep collapsing. I did good with the visuals but the physics of it is FUCKED. Am going to have to stay in the art room all lunch and break time trying to work out how to make this fucking thing stable.

Millie: No worries, there's a huge bit of dialogue I don't understand so I need to be working on that anyway. I think it's about someone dying but I don't really understand who. Kat, I need you!

Sam: Fuck. The Fucking Tree thing just knocked dirty water all over my portfolio. SOS!!! SOS!!!

> **Millie:** I'm coming!

They haven't even noticed that I'm not even responding. They're so busy in their own worlds.

11 a.m.

Double science

Millie came in late, probably too busy kissing Nick goodbye. So there wasn't anywhere near me for her to sit, which I guess I might have sort of accidentally planned, and she looks pretty puzzled as to why I didn't save her a seat.

11:10 a.m.

I can feel her behind me staring at the back of my head.

12 p.m.

Emmeline Pankhurst's BAD BITCHEZ
Sam, Millie, Me

> **Millie:** Sorry I was late. Play drama! I have to run out to a rehearsal as soon as class finishes. I've worked out it's the bit in the film where her cousin dies, though, so at least I know what I'm talking about now.

They still haven't noticed I'm not talking to them.

12:30 p.m.

The library

I've decided to spend lunch in the library trying to do my course-work, again. I don't know what made me think I was capable of doing that, though, when I can't seem to focus on anything at the moment apart from staring at my phone, anxiously watching the rest of the world having a life while I do not.

2 p.m.

English class

I'm staring at the worst mark I've ever been given for anything in English and, unfortunately, it's probably the most important piece of work I've ever done. It's the result for my mock exams from last term. And if this is anything to go by, I may not even pass. Adding insult to injury, my *Inspector Calls* essay is back too, and as predicted I did NOT do as well as usual. I seem to be screwing up right when it counts. I can't be a journalist if I don't get an English GCSE. I don't understand how this happened. I've always been really good at English.

I want to talk to Miss Mills about it, but I also feel like if I open my mouth I'm going to cry. I have to sit here for another hour and a half without crying or running out.

I can't believe it.

2:30 p.m.

> **Emmeline Pankhurst's BAD BITCHEZ**
> Sam, Millie, Me

Sam: My portfolio's ruined. I don't have time to start again. What am I going to do?!

Millie: Don't worry, I'll come and help you after school, Nick'll come too.

Sam: Dave said he'd come along as well but he seems annoyed because he wanted us to hang out tonight, without the play or my portfolio or any of that going on. I think he's starting to get bored of us never just hanging out by ourselves.

Millie: Don't worry. He's besotted with you. He won't be annoyed. He'll just want to help. We'll all help.

2:45 p.m.

I feel my phone vibrate. A private message from Millie.

> **Millie:** Where are you today? Sam needs us! Why aren't you helping?

I don't know what to say. I'm furious. They tell Trudy they've moved on and I'm too much of a baby for them and then they need my help?

I don't have time to deal with their problems when I've got problems of my own. Especially this English grade.

3:30 p.m.

I grab my things as soon as the bell rings. I'm just going to run straight home. I want to turn my phone off but I'm too worried about what might be happening while I'm not looking, and I can't think about anything else.

> **Millie:** Are you coming to the art block, Kat? Sam needs us. I don't know what's up with you or why you're not replying, but it's really childish. Sam's got bigger things to worry about right now than you throwing some kind of toddler tantrum.

I feel something inside my head snapping and before I know what's happening, I'm heading over to the art block. I just hope the boys haven't gotten there yet because I don't want an audience for this.

3:35 p.m.

The art room

I march through the door, fists clenched and head pounding. I'm still so angry that I can't get my thoughts straight and I'm worried I'm going to cry and give them even more reason to call me a baby.

"Hey, Kat! You finally graced us with your presence!" Millie says sarcastically, and that's me, I'm off.

"You've got a nerve! After everything you've said to Trudy about me? About me being a baby and about how you're too grown up for me now? All day all you've done is want things from me, when the whole time you're bitching about me behind my back?" I rage.

Sam looks up from what she's doing, a deep furrow in her forehead. "What are you talking about, Kat?" she says innocently.

"You KNOW what I'm talking about. On Saturday, after I left, you told Trudy that you've both moved on and don't want me third-wheeling on your relationships, and that you can't hang out with me anymore!" I shout.

"What?" Millie says.

"Trudy told me herself that you think I'm a baby for still wanting a birthday surprise, and don't try to deny it because you literally just called me a baby over text!"

"Well, that's because you're behaving like a baby!" Millie says. "We've all got stuff going on, and you're the only one not helping and making it all about you."

"I've got way too much to do for this right now, Kat. I'm sorry. I'm so stressed, I just don't have time," Sam says.

"WHAT'S NEW?" I shout, about to leave just as Millie starts up again.

"AT LEAST TRUDY'S A GROWN-UP! NOT SOMEONE WHO GETS IN A MOOD AND STOMPS OFF FOR THE DAY BECAUSE WE'VE GOT BOYFRIENDS AND SHE DOESN'T! OR BECAUSE WE'VE GOT WORK TO DO THAT'S MORE IMPORTANT THAN LIS-TENING TO YOU MOAN ABOUT A BOY YOU DIDN'T EVEN GO ON A DATE WITH!" Her words sting as hard as if I've just been slapped. "AND MAYBE YOU COULD GET A BOYFRIEND IF YOU DIDN'T ACT LIKE SUCH A CHILD ALL THE TIME!"

Millie never shouts. The shock freezes me for a moment.

"OH, FUCK YOU!" I shout at both of them and pick up the nearest paintbrush, hurling it across the room just as Dave arrives, paintbrush splotching him on the head and covering his forehead in tree-green paint.

I run out crying, just like a baby.

Again.

3:50 p.m.

I'm trying to get home without seeing anyone. My throat feels like it's got something hard and dry lodged in it, while everything around me echoes and blurs, spinning out of my control. Maybe there is something really wrong with me? Or else why does this keep happening?

I feel dizzy and a bit queasy. A watery, metallic taste fills my mouth and my stomach's churning. Oh god, I think I'm actually going to be sick. I stop and bend over, retching as I feel the bile burning its way up, scratching my throat until I'm crouched down, throwing up in the middle of the pavement. I'm not sure what I'm throwing up because I've barely managed to eat a thing today, and soon enough I feel completely empty.

I wipe my mouth on the sleeve of my jumper and sit down on the curb, waiting for the spinning to stop. I've lost everyone now, and I deserved to because I'm a horrible, childish person.

3:55 p.m.

I race upstairs. I need to get out of these clothes and wash my face before Dad sees me. I can't face the questions about if I'm sick or not.

4 p.m.

"You all right, love? You ran up those stairs pretty fast!" Dad's shouting from the hallway.

"Loads of work to do," I shout back, and pray that's enough for him to leave me alone now.

"Hmm, still? Well, I'm just downstairs if you need anything."

I take off my sicky clothes and wait for the sound of his feet retreating so I can sneak into the bathroom to wash my face.

4:15 p.m.

We've never had a fight that bad before. Usually we just have a bit of a bicker and then make up. Nothing's ever lasted this long and they've never both been cross at me at once. I can't get how angry they looked out of my head. And they didn't deny what they'd done. Deep down I hoped maybe it was just Trudy messing with my head. But now I know it's true.

4:20 p.m.

Terrible Trudy's been right all along. I am an ugly loser. And now I'm a friendless loser.

They're probably all off together right now, triple-dating and laughing at how alone I am and how much they hate me for being such a big loner baby. Trudy's probably there with Josh, slotting in seamlessly as my replacement.

They're probably all laughing at how funny it was when I thought I was still getting a babyish birthday surprise. As if my birthday was more important than the play, than their boyfriends.

What if they've all been friends all along, really? What if Josh asking me out and ditching me and all that was an elaborate plan that they all cooked up to get rid of stupid baby Kat?

To defriend me? Maybe I've been supposed to get the hint for ages now and I just wasn't understanding?

4:30 p.m.

I'm scrolling through Instagram again with no idea when I started looking at it or what I'm looking at.

I keep seeing this "You are enough" quote posted on people's grids. It's just not true for me. Everyone else might be enough, but I'm not. I'm not good enough, not pretty enough, not strong enough, certainly not feminine enough, not feminist enough, not clever enough. I am not enough.

I might post that in a twirly font on my grid. Big letters, surrounded by hearts and flowers:

I Am Not Enough

5 p.m.

I'm never going to be a glamorous journalist living in London in her own apartment who meets the girls in town for cocktails after work. I don't have any girls to meet anymore and I can't even do GCSE English, let alone actual real journalism.

I always think Trudy's the terrible one, but maybe it's actually me? After all, I seem to be the one without any friends right now.

I'm a mess.

6:30 p.m.

"Are you coming down for dinner, love?" Dad shouts up the stairs again.

"In a minute," I croak, like a miserable frog.

I'm still crying, and I wanted to stop before I went down to dinner, but I don't think I can manage it.

"Kat? You sound a bit funny. I'm coming up," Dad says.

He opens the door and peers in. As soon as he sees me crying on the bed, Bea's paw on my leg, he comes over.

"Aww, no, Kat. What's wrong?" he says.

I feel overwhelmingly tired and like if I talk it'll make no sense because of the crying. I just don't know where to start and I doubt that Dad would understand, anyway.

"Not feeling great. Is it okay if I just stay up here?" I manage.

Dad sits down on the bed, shuffling Bea along as he does, while Bea raises a brow and grunts if to say, *What on earth do you think you're doing? I'm handling this!*

He puts his arm around me rather than stroking Bea, which is obviously his second mistake, and Bea looks proper annoyed about it. She puts her head down on the bed with a bit of a "hurmph" noise.

"What's happened, love?"

"Nothing," I say, my voice muffled into his shoulder.

"I don't buy that, unfortunately. Something must have. You don't normally cry like this for no reason. Do you just not want to talk about it?"

"Not really."

"Okay. Well. I can bring dinner up to you, I guess?"

I nod.

"And maybe you might want to chat later? Might help? If you don't want to talk to me, maybe to Mum? Or you can text one of us, if it's easier?" he says kindly.

I stare blankly at him because I'd love to, but I've got absolutely no idea what IS wrong with me. Why have I suddenly started losing the ability to breathe, and started shouting at my friends, and not being pleased for them, and generally behaving like a bitter lunatic?

"Thanks, Dad."

"And don't just feed your dinner to Bea and think I won't notice." He's smart. That's exactly what I was going to do.

Bea sighs.

6:40 p.m.

I'd like to tell Dad what happened, but I don't know where to start. I'm not really sure where the beginning even was, and I'm embarrassed. I don't want him and Mum to know how badly I've screwed everything up, from my English mock to my friendships with the girls and Matt.

I don't know how long I've been feeling like this because I can't remember the first time I had to touch the light switch before I could sleep. Or the first time I felt like the whole world was moving at a different pace from me. The feeling like something bad is about to happen is so constant now, I feel paralyzed by it while I watch the rest of the world getting on with things behind a murky film.

But maybe I was right to expect something bad to happen, because now it has. Everyone's left me, and at least if I stay here by myself, I can't do any more harm.

7 p.m.

When I imagine myself in the future, I find it really hard to see anything good happening anymore. The dreams of my own apartment and being a journalist have been replaced with something much darker.

That stupid fear keeps coming back—where I'm sitting in prison, arrested for something I didn't do. With no friends, and no family to care about me or visit me, and it's the life I deserve because I'm a horrible person. Now that the part about having no friends has happened, the rest of it just feels like an inevitability. Millie and Sam certainly looked at me like I was a criminal.

I can't tell Dad this. He'll either laugh at me or think I've completely lost it.

9 p.m.

I keep looking at social media expecting a post from Trudy where she's hanging out with Millie and Sam that just says "haha, my friends now." Or maybe something from Josh that's just a picture of my face with "LOL" and the crying face emoji below it. I feel relieved when I check and there isn't one there, but then two seconds later the fear kicks in again and I feel like I have to keep an eye on it, like if I stop looking, it'll happen.

9:10 p.m.

My bed

I'm trying to work out why I keep feeling like I can't breathe.

What if I've got cancer or something? What if the thing in my throat is a tumor, or there's something growing in my lungs that's stopping them from working? What if my lungs are deformed? Google:

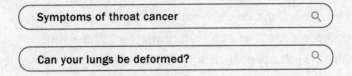

Google's very unhelpful. I should really go to the doctor before I'm in a situation where I can't breathe in the night and no one wakes up to help me, so I just die and then there's nothing anyone can do about it. What if that happens tonight? If I stay awake all night, would that make it less likely to happen?

Thing is, though, that right now it feels like my throat is

closing up or I've got something obstructing my airway again. What if this is how I die? The only things I'm going to be remembered for are #Tim and being the supporting role in my dad's Danny Dyer performances.

9:30 p.m.

"KNOCK KNOCK," Dad shouts through the door.

If I don't say anything, will he just think I'm asleep and go away? I don't want to talk to anyone—especially not about how shitty everything is and what a massive failure I am. He'd probably only turn it into material for his sitcom.

"Hey, love," he says, sticking his head around the door. What's the point in knocking if you're not going to wait for an answer? "You feeling any better?"

"Yep! Just trying to get some coursework done!" I say, overly cheerily.

"Ah, good. Don't stay up much later doing it, though. Your brain needs a rest!" he says, ruffling my hair as he leaves.

Great, a hair ruffle. Another thing people still do to me that they also do to children.

1 a.m.

When I was a kid, I used to lie awake worrying about monsters under my bed. This feels a lot like that. I'm completely alone, and I'm just waiting for the next monster to show up.

2 a.m.

I'm so pathetic. There are women who've spent years campaigning so that I could go to school, and I'm not even going to bother going because I'm weak and don't want to face embarrassment and feeling like I don't have any friends.

2:30 a.m.

Thing is, I don't remember a time before I was friends with Millie and Sam. We've never not been friends before. I don't know who I am at the moment, anyway, but I have even less of an idea without them.

3 a.m.

I just want to go back to normal.
    I want to be Kat again.
    But I don't know how.

3:30 a.m.

I've been trying to work out what to say to Dad tomorrow morning when I don't go to school. I mean, there's no way I can go to school. I thought I'd try the text thing he suggested. So far all I've got is:

> **Me:** I don't think I'm a very nice person and everyone hates me now. And I think there's something wrong because I keep not being able to breathe and I think I'm going to die. So I can't go to school.

I can't send him that. He'll think I've cracked. But maybe I have?

I've sent it. I hope he doesn't laugh at me.

I turn my phone off and put it in my drawer. I don't need a phone when there's no one to talk to.

Unfeminist thoughts:

There's not a feminist thing about me anymore.

Friday, October 19

7 a.m.

I hear Mum and Dad muttering together outside my room. I remember the weird text that I sent Dad last night and immediately want to throw the covers over my head and hide.

"Kat, love?" Dad says, knocking.

Their heads appear around the door, and I can tell from Dad's tone that he's actually worried and he might not be about to tell me to get up and get over it.

The two of them come and sit on the bed, shuffling poor Bea up again.

"I got your text, love. I'm sorry I wasn't awake to reply or come and sit with you. How are you feeling this morning?" Dad says.

I don't want them worrying—that's the last thing that I want, but I can't work out how to express myself properly. The more I try to refine my thoughts or make them comprehensible, the more scrambled things seem to become. It's unlikely that I could ever be a writer when I just don't seem to have any words anymore. At some point I've started crying again, and I don't know when it was, or if I'm just still crying from last night.

233

"I can't breathe," I blurt out between big gasps as Mum puts her arm around me. It feels just like yesterday except now I have an audience so I'm fighting harder to make it go back to normal more quickly.

"Okay, love, do this with me: breathe in as I count to three and out as I count to three," Dad says, and starts breathing along with me.

At first it feels harder because counting just seems to exacerbate the knowledge that nothing is going in or out, but as I focus on the numbers rather than the breaths, it does seem to get easier.

"Has this happened before?" Dad asks when I'm finally back under control a bit.

"Yes, a few times," I manage.

The words are coming out of me but it's a bit like an out-of-body experience. I still feel like I'm not in control. I don't feel coherent.

Mum stands next to me, stroking my hair, but I feel so detached from everything that I barely register it.

"Oh, love. Something similar to that used to happen to me a while back, and it was because I was really anxious at the time," Dad says. "Have you been feeling stressed about your exams? Or is there something going on at school?"

I'm a bit surprised that Dad seems so cool and calm about this and isn't laughing at me.

I stare at them. There's so much going on, I don't know where to start. So instead of using my words, I just start crying again.

Mum gathers me up into a big hug and Dad kisses the top of my head. She still smells like she used to when I was little. She still hugs the same too. It reminds me of when one of them used to scoop me up when I fell off my bike or grazed my knee. This is different, though, this time I've fallen off the world. The bike was so much easier to explain.

I pull away from the hug so that I can talk.

"I just keep worrying about things. I keep worrying about stuff that might happen to us. Like that you all might die and I'll be left alone, or that we'll all die, and I can't sleep because all I seem to do is lie here worrying about things and feeling sick and dizzy. I can't focus on schoolwork so I'm going to fail. What's wrong with me?" I look at them both and they hug me again.

"We're just going to go outside for a chat," Mum says. "We'll be back in a minute. Don't worry. We can sort this out."

7:15 a.m.

Dad comes back in first with Mum following behind and they sit on my bed with me.

"How would you feel if we went to talk to someone else about this? Someone who might be able to help?" Dad asks thoughtfully.

"Like who?" It comes out sounding a bit drunk because of all the crying.

"A doctor? I think you might be a bit anxious and there are people who you can talk to about it who will help to get you feeling a bit better, and I think the doctor can tell us who the best person would be."

"Okay." My voice is muffled because my face is in Mum's shoulder and I'm getting tears and a little bit of snot all over her work dress.

"I think it's a very good idea," Mum says, grabbing my hand. "And I really want to be able to come with you but I called work first thing and tried to get cover, and there isn't anyone to take my place. I'm really sorry, love. I'm going to call and text all day and see how you're doing. You're really brave telling us all this, now you just need to tell the doctor and we can get this sorted out. Try not to worry too much."

It feels better knowing that Mum and Dad are in charge somehow. This is what the girls were talking about, though. This is what Trudy was talking about. I'm too old to be running to my mummy and daddy. I shouldn't need them for this stuff. I should be a grown-up now and able to sort out my own problems.

"Why don't you get in the shower? I'll make us something for breakfast and we can go out into the garden and talk. How does that sound?" Dad says cheerily.

I nod, but I feel pathetic and scared.

8 a.m.

I head downstairs in a pair of jogging bottoms and a hoodie—a poor attempt to try to make myself feel comfortable.

Dad's made me a cup of tea and toast and he's sitting on the bench in our garden, which I love. It's small, walled, and a bit wild, but it's cozy and when Mum and Dad light candles around it, it looks dreamy.

"Here you go, kitten." He hands me the toast and ruffles my hair as I suppress the urge to shout that I'm KAT, not childish kitten.

"We've got a doctor's appointment at ten," he says. "How are you feeling now?"

"I don't know how to explain it," I say. "Bad."

"I know, but you've done the hardest bit now, you've told someone. We can help, and things will get better. You won't always feel like this. I promise."

I'm struggling to work out HOW it's going to get better. I don't have any friends anymore, I keep feeling like I can't breathe, and I'm going to fail my GCSEs. I try taking a bite of the toast but it feels huge in my mouth.

"Have you told Millie and Sam how you feel? I bet they'd want to help."

My throat tightens.

"We had a fight. They don't want to hang out with me because I'm a big childish loser." I'm annoyed that I've started crying again.

Dad's eyebrows raise. "I don't think you're a child. I'm sure they don't either. Why do you say that?"

"They've got boyfriends now and they've started hanging out with Trudy, who's going out with Josh, who I like. Or, at least, did like. I probably shouldn't like him anymore. She told me that's what they'd said about me."

"Oh, I remember Trudy," he says knowingly. "That doesn't sound quite right to me, though. How do you know they really said that?"

"There were pictures of them all hanging out together."

"Well, that doesn't mean they said anything, and I don't think we can trust Trudy."

I know what Dad's saying makes sense, and it does make me doubt what she said, but HOW would she know about the birthday thing if they hadn't told her?

"And what about this Josh?"

"He's new, started at the end of last year. Everyone fancies him. He asked me out. But then he didn't show up. Trudy turned up instead saying that he only asked me out to make her jealous and that they were together now. So now everyone has a boyfriend except for me because I'm too ugly for anyone to want to go out with and they all know what a loser I am." I take a breath. "I shouldn't even be worried about my looks because that's not what being a feminist is, and I know I'm a disappointment because I can't be a strong enough feminist not to worry about these things. I've got it all wrong. And Matt hasn't even spoken to me for ages because he's grown up and left me behind too."

My tears are falling on the toast, making it soggy. Dad puts his arm around me again.

"That simply isn't true, Kitty Kat, and you are NOT a disappointment. Firstly, it sounds like Josh and Trudy are made for each other. Both pieces of work. Two, you are beautiful. Three, I don't think any of what you've said makes you not a feminist. From what I know, being a feminist is more about supporting each other, lifting each other up, and getting equality. Four, you are SMART—you get that from your mum—AND strong. And lastly, you are LOVED. Not just liked. You are SO LOVED. By us, by your friends, even Freddie. And there will be even more people in the future who love you too. You can't see it right now, but you will feel better. You just have to stop being so hard on yourself."

"But I feel so foggy at the moment. I feel stupid."

"Well, you're not. Anxiety and stress play tricks on your brain. They can make thinking feel like you're wading through molasses and make you believe things that just aren't true. We're going to talk to the doctor and together we're all going to help you."

10 a.m.

The doctor's office

This waiting room's packed and I feel a bit like I'm taking up space that someone with a proper illness could have.

"Dad, are you sure I should be here? I mean, these people look properly sick," I say.

"Kat, just because you can't see your illness doesn't mean it's not real and you don't deserve help," Dad says, putting his hand on my shoulder.

I don't know if this is reassuring or not. I'm already starting to wish I could run out the door and go home and pretend it's all fine. I debate turning to Dad and saying, "Actually, don't worry! I'm fine now!" But I don't think he'd buy it.

There's a beep and the electronic board displays my name and a room number. That's that, then. Can't exactly leave now.

10:05 a.m.

"Hi, Kat," the doctor says. "Take a seat." She looks friendly, at least. She's got a short gray bob and really cool glasses, the kind with thick dark frames. She's smiling and doesn't look like the sort of person who's about to judge me or tell me to get out.

Dad shuffles me into my seat like a pushy parent at a swimming gala.

"How can I help?" the doctor asks, smiling at me and Dad.

"She's been having trouble breathing and I think she might be anxious!" Dad says in a hurry. My parents talking for me is just yet another sign that I'm not grown up.

"Right, okay. So, maybe if Kat could explain to me what's been going on?"

I don't know how to explain it. I feel hugely embarrassed. I think I'd rather have piles than this. Or some kind of STD. At least then it'd be easier to explain. And I'd be a normal having-sex type person. Not a loser.

"Erm, I keep feeling like my chest is really tight and I feel dizzy and quite sick and everything goes a bit blurry around me. Also, noises seem really loud and it's like they echo around my head." At least I've managed to say something.

"Okay. And is there a lot on your mind at the moment? Exams?"

I nod and she sits for a little bit.

She asks some more questions—how often do I feel like this? (ALL THE TIME.) Am I eating well? (NOT REALLY.)—while tapping away on her computer. I'm starting to feel pretty tired when she stops, makes a few more notes, and turns back to me.

"Everything you're describing to me sounds like anxiety. The experiences that you describe sound like panic attacks. They can be quite intense and scary, but they are manageable."

Panic attacks? I had no idea. But what do I do now? How do I stop them? How do I go back to how things were before?

"What we need to do is to address what's causing them. I'm just going to ask that you fill out this form for me so we have a better idea of what our next steps should be. Don't worry, it's all completely confidential. I just need you to read the statements and score how relevant they feel to you, as honestly as possible." She hands me a pen and sheet of paper and I try my best to fill it out without showing Dad anything.

The statements feel like someone's reading my actual mind. Things like: "I feel hopeless and like I've let myself and my family down." It's so accurate, I'm surprised it doesn't have the statement: "I feel completely left out because all of my friends have grown up and have boyfriends and I'm still wearing the cotton knickers from Marks & Spencer that my mother bought me."

I hand the survey back to the doctor, not looking her in the eye. I feel like she's got a page of my darkest secrets. She looks at it and writes little notes at the side of it.

"Okay, Kat. Your responses would indicate quite a high level of anxiety, and some mild depression."

I'm hearing the words she's saying but I'm not sure that I am able to apply them to myself. I smile and laugh. At school I'm one of the funniest people. I don't think I'm depressed, but Dad doesn't look shocked at all.

"So what we need to talk about is treatment. There is medication available, but I wouldn't recommend that course of action straight away. I think what we should try is some therapy."

Therapy sounds okay. It sounds less scary than medication, anyway.

"I'm going to suggest CBT. That's a type of talking therapy. It would be completely confidential and you would go and speak to someone once a week. What do you think?"

"Okay," I say, not sure how I feel, really, because all this is so new and overwhelming.

"There's a bit of a waiting list so it might be a few months. But I'll refer you now and we'll get the ball rolling. How does that sound?"

"Good," I say, nodding, although none of this feels good.

"Would there be any way of getting her seen sooner?" Dad asks.

"Only by paying for private treatment, I'm afraid," the doctor says. "Is that an option you'd like to explore?"

Dad nods and squeezes my hand.

"Okay, well, I'd really recommend the first doctor on this list of therapists that I'll give you. She sees a lot of younger patients, and she's very good. Just let me know if you decide to take that route and I'll cancel the referral."

She prints out a list and hands it over to Dad.

"We'd usually recommend twelve sessions initially. But I'd also like to see you back here in about three weeks to see how you're getting on if that's okay, Kat?"

I nod.

"I've also printed out this sheet for you—some breathing exercises that can be quite helpful. Why don't you try them when you get home?"

"Thank you," I say quietly, taking the sheet.

I haven't cried since leaving home but I feel like as soon as we walk out of the doctor's office, I'm going to burst into tears. At the moment I feel like I'm just watching a film, like I've detached myself from this and it's actually happening to someone else. I've read about anxiety, obviously, but I don't know that much about it. People talk about mental health so much on Instagram. I've seen it on @I_weigh posts a lot.

But it always seemed like something other people have.

Am I going to be like this forever now?

12 p.m.

My bedroom, with Bea

I don't know if I feel better now, or worse. I told Dad I needed a little bit of time alone, but I can hear him puttering around and listening outside my door every now and then.

I keep running the words that the doctor used around my head over and over again and googling them.

"Panic Attack." "Mental Health Disorder." "Depression." "Anxiety."

Okay. This is kind of interesting. One of the results is celebrities who suffer from anxiety.

I click through and Emma Stone comes up. I've always thought she was really cool, and I didn't realize she had mental health issues.

There's also:

Ariana Grande

David Beckham

Oprah Winfrey

Zayn from One Direction

Kendall Jenner

The list is HUGE and for once the more I google, the better I feel—somehow stronger knowing that these whole, adult and successful people suffer from the same thing as me.

Jennifer Lawrence is in there. She always seems so smiley and badass. I had no idea.

Maybe it's not so weird. I mean, I don't think any of these

celebrities are defective or shameful for having anxiety. When they talk about it, they actually seem brave—fearless, even. Can I be like that too?

12:30 p.m.

Dad knocks on the door, distracting me from the first thing I've focused on properly for days. I'm reading more about how the celebrities manage their anxiety.

"Hey!" he says, sticking his head around the door. "Do you fancy some lunch, kiddo?"

"Sure," I say. I'm going to let the kiddo bit go after everything he's done for me today.

"Beans on toast?" he asks.

I mean, again, it's the kind of thing you give to a FIVE-YEAR-OLD, Dad! But actually, it sounds kind of good right now.

"Thanks, Dad. I'll be down in a bit."

12:45 p.m.

"I spoke to your mum," Dad says as we pile beans onto our forks. "We're going to see if we can go private and get you to see someone a bit quicker, like the doctor said. You see, before we had you two, I was in a bit of a bad way." He takes a deep breath. "A lot of the things that you described this morning are exactly how I felt, and I remember how hard it was. Therapy really helped me get back on my feet and it gave me some coping strategies that I still use."

"But. I mean. I don't want you to have to go to any trouble if we can't afford it," I say.

"We can find a way for you, love. It's important. You mustn't add that to your list of worries!"

"Okay." As if I'm not going to worry about that. . . . As if I'd ever NOT worry about something.

3 p.m.

The sofa

Dad and I have been watching a lot of Netflix to try to distract me. But I can't get rid of this rising feeling of panic. It's like a tap I can't turn off.

What are the girls talking about at school without me? What's happening while I'm not there? Should I put my phone on and find out? It's nearly the end of the day, and then it's half term next week. I won't see anyone for ages. What did Mum and Dad tell Freddie about me being off today? What if Freddie's told everyone I'm loopy and that I spent all night crying in my room?

I decide to run upstairs and turn my phone back on. I'm going to have to face it at some point, and it's better to know what's going on than not.

I watch the screen go bright, a sight that instantly fills me with dread. I start counting my in- and out-breaths like the exercise sheet suggests. It's not exactly working yet.

I don't have any messages. I check social media as well to make sure that no one has written anything nasty about me there.

Nope, that all seems fine too. I do a long exhale just as my phone FINALLY GETS WITH THE PROGRAM and I see that I've got forty-six messages from Millie and Sam, and three from Matt. Shit.

I'm almost too scared to look at them.

Emmeline Pankhurst's BAD BITCHEZ
Sam, Millie, Me

Millie: Are you ok, Kat? I know we're fighting but Miss Mills said you're off sick?

Sam: Please just let us know you're ok?

Millie: I'm really sorry about yesterday and everything I said. I didn't mean it. I just didn't understand what you were talking about. Please explain it? We need to understand? xxx

Sam: We pinned down Tia (she sang like a budgie or whatever the phrase is). She said you and Trudy had some kind of standoff? What happened? What was the stuff about your birthday you mentioned? What did she say? Xxx

Millie: Whatever it is, we've got your back Xxx

247

Sam: We love you, Kat. Please talk to us?
We just want to understand what happened? Xxx

The last message was ten minutes ago. I feel a mixture of relief that they've gotten in touch and also confusion about what happened with Trudy. I think I'm just going to have to tell them. I start working out how to respond, but it's not easy.

Me: Hey, I'm ok. I'm sorry. Trudy told me that you'd told her at the gig you felt like I was a third wheel who no one wanted and that you were excited about the party and I was still hung up on a babyish birthday surprise xxx

Millie: We would NEVER say that! NEVER xxx

Sam: OF COURSE NOT! xxxxx

Sam: We honestly didn't speak to her. Those pictures make it look like we were all hanging out and we weren't. We wouldn't say that to her anyway. We were talking about your birthday but NOT to her and not in that way. We were saying that we still wanted to try and do the birthday surprise even though we have the play Xxx

Millie: We were explaining the surprises to the boys. They thought they sounded funny which surprised us because we thought they'd think we were losers. She must have heard us Xxx

Sam: Honestly we'd never talk to her about anything and we'd certainly never say any of that stuff. And we absolutely don't think you're a third wheel who no one wants! We love you! Xxxx

Millie: Triple MEGA LOVE YOU xxx

I feel relieved and also silly. Trudy's been scamming and torturing me for years, and I couldn't see this was another one of her nasty tricks to mess with me. I have some apologising to do.

Me: I'm so sorry. I don't know why I believed her, or how I couldn't see it was another of her schemes. I'm sorry for shouting at you both. I love you both too xxx

Sam: No, WE'RE sorry. We've been so caught up in the play and everything else we haven't been around much xxx

Millie: Agreed. We're going to be better friends and better at protecting you from Terrible Trudy xxxx

Me: You've got nothing to be sorry for. I should have been more supportive of you both and less in my own head Xxx

Sam: Let's never ever fight again Xxx

Millie: Seconded <3 xxx

Me: Thirded <3 xxx

I feel so relieved that I nearly forget to read Matt's messages.

Matt: Are you ok? Freddie says you're sick? X

Matt: And the girls said you had a fight? WHAT? X

Matt: Kat? I'm really starting to worry now, tell me if you're ok or I'm going to come around after school X

Me: Hey, no need for that. I'm ok, just not feeling that well. Have made up with the girls, don't worry x

Matt: Oh thank god! I was about to send a search party! I'm sorry I've not been around much lately. Can I come over later? Pleeeaseeeee? Xx

I don't know if I can face seeing people yet. I'm going to have a bit of a think before I reply.

3:30 p.m.

My room

Dad knocks and pokes his head around the door.

"Well, you look a bit brighter," he says, looking at the phone in my hand. "Have you spoken to the girls?"

"Yeah. We've made up."

"Ahh, that's good. I'm pleased. I don't think you girls could ever stay mad at each other for long. You need to remember that when the little gremlins in your head start playing tricks on you."

"Matt texted too. He wants to come over later. I don't know if I'm up for seeing people, though."

"I think it might do you good. He doesn't have to stay long if you don't want him to," Dad says.

"I guess. But what should I tell him?" I ask. "You know. About the doctor. And stuff."

"Tell him whatever you feel comfortable telling him. He's your friend—he'll only want to help you, so tell him whatever feels right. That's really something that only you can decide," Dad says, patting me on the back. "I'll leave you to it, but I'm just downstairs if you need me."

"Thanks, Dad. And Dad? What's a gremlin?"

"Google it!" Dad says.

> **Me:** Come over. I'd like that X

4 p.m.

The sofa

Matt squashes himself into the cushions with his cup of tea and looks at me thoughtfully. He's waiting to find out what the hell is going on with me.

I take a deep breath and close my eyes. If I'm going to tell anyone, I think Matt is the best place to start.

"Sooo . . . I've not been feeling so great," I say, words coming very fast and quiet. "I keep having these, kind of terrifying episodes, and Dad thought he knew what it was so he took me to the doctor and she said that they're panic

251

attacks, and that I'm anxious and depressed."

Once I've gotten it out I feel relieved, but when I was saying it I felt like I should stop, like I'd said too much and like I needed to crack a joke or start being silly instead.

"Oh, Kat," Matt says slowly, putting his tea down, like it would be wrong to enjoy it now. He looks a bit shocked. "Why didn't you say anything? I'm so sorry. I've not been around and I should have been. What did the doctor say they can do to help?"

"She suggested therapy but the waiting list is really long, and Mum and Dad want to pay for me to see someone privately, but I don't want them spending money if we don't have it and getting themselves into debt because I'm stupid," I say. I can feel tears threatening to come again so I swallow hard.

"You're not stupid, Kat! They must just want to get you the quickest help. They wouldn't offer to do anything that they weren't able to. Just worry about getting better. Is there anything I can do?" he asks.

"Nah, thank you, though. You're the first person I've told and I'm still getting my head around it. But thank you."

He grins and gives me a massive hug. "Hey, fancy an episode of *Drag Race*? This week's one'll be up now." he says.

And just like that, I am not a freak, and I am not alone. Unbelievable.

5:30 p.m.

Quite a lot of Drag Race *later*

Emmeline Pankhurst's BAD BITCHES
Sam, Millie, Me

Sam: So pleased you're ok and we can all be friends again! Love you, babe xxx

Millie: BAAAABBBBBBEEEEE, we missed you so much today. Let's never fall out again! Agreed! LOVE XXXXXXXX

Sam: We asked Freddie what was up and he said you were menstruating. Why do boys always think that's the only thing that's wrong with us? xxx

Me: For god's sake, FREDDIE! I'm not menstruating

Me: That's not even for another two weeks! He's going to face the full force of my PMS next week now. THE FULL FORCE xxx

Millie: LOLLLLLL should we warn Issy? Those two have been together almost constantly. I'm really not sure about our siblings getting married before we do?

Me: I know. When did my smelly little brother get his life all together, while I'm just paddling about over here trying to get a boy to notice me?

Sam: You've just not met anyone good enough for you yet. And I promise we'll be a bit better about not bringing Dave and Nick everywhere. We're sorry Xxxx

Millie: Yeah we are. We may have boyfriends but it's friends who are important. I watched an old TV show called *One Tree Hill* once where the woman said HOES BEFORE BROS. It's terribly sexist and I think would get me kicked out of the sisterhood, but HOES BEFORE BROS, YO. Xxxx

I send a big heart GIF over to them. They're the best. I don't know why I ever fell out with them. My stupid brain. But now I'm just worried about telling them what the doctor said. What if they see me differently?

6:30 p.m.

Matt's staying for dinner tonight, which is nice because it's been so long since he last did that. Mum just got home and gave me a big hug, Freddie's telling us tales of glory from the playground as if he's been away at war or something, and we're eating spaghetti and tomato sauce that Dad made and is bloody lovely. Everything feels just a little bit brighter. I might even be able to be funny.

"It sounds like you've had a busy day, Freds," I say, "and YET I hear that you STILL had time to tell everyone I wasn't at school because I was MENSTRUATING!"

Dad immediately drops his fork. Mum looks terribly disappointed in Freddie. Matt looks terribly disappointed in the universe for bringing vaginas into dinnertime.

"FREDDRICK!"

She only ever uses his full name when he's trailed mud

254

through the house or been caught playing computer games at three a.m. This is the first time he's been told off for a menstruation-related incident. Dad is now giggling into his pasta. I don't know what is so funny.

"JOHN? WHAT IS SO FUNNY?"

"I . . . I just . . . don't know if tomato sauce is . . . the right . . . dinner to be having . . . when we discuss . . . menstruation . . .?"

Oh FFS.

7 p.m.

My bedroom with Mum

"So Dad said you spoke to the girls?" Mum says, touching my hair. We're sitting on my bed for a chat while Dad and Freddie do all the cleaning up from dinner as their punishment for laughing at menstruation, and Matt is choosing a suitable movie for us all. (It will not be suitable.)

"Yeah, we made up, but I haven't told them everything yet. You know, about the doctor. And the therapy."

"Well, you will when you're ready, and you've told Matt, which is a huge thing. It takes strength to talk to people about your feelings like you have. Your dad and I are so proud of you."

I lean into her shoulder. "Mum?"

"Yes, love?"

"Do you ever feel like you don't know if you're doing a good or a bad thing? Like sometimes I spend ages worrying about what I look like, and I know that's not feminist, or I compare myself to other women and I know I'm not supposed to do that. Does it mean I'm a bad person?"

"Oh, Kat. Of course you're not a bad person! We all judge ourselves against other people sometimes. You can't just switch off thoughts because someone says that you shouldn't have them. That's not how it works. Feminism isn't about shaming each other for our feelings about ourselves," Mum says. God, she sounds so WISE sometimes.

"That makes sense, but sometimes I feel like there's constant stuff telling us what to do and how to act, and I never seem to get any of it right?" I say, as Dad comes in with a bowl of popcorn, like he's come to watch the Teenage Disaster Show.

"Well, you girls have it coming at you from all angles," Mum says. "All those bloody Insta-snap filters to be dealing with all the time." I don't have the heart to tell her that Insta-snap is Not A Thing. "We should all be less influenced by the media, especially when it comes to our bodies, but don't shame yourself for the way you feel. You can't just decide to be confident and that's it."

"Also," says Dad, popcorn spraying out of this mouth, "you have to remember that no one can get it a hundred percent right all the time. You'd have to be a robot to do that. Sometimes you have to just trust yourself and have faith that you'll do the right thing."

I sit taking this in and thinking how, actually, they might have a point. At least three times a day I see something on social media about how to do feminism right, how to be a modern woman, how not to do this or that. And maybe that in itself is overwhelming?

10:30 p.m.

My room with my best dog friend

As predicted, the film Matt picked was not suitable. A cheesy rom-com about friends who fall in love. I think he thought that I needed something light. It was terrible. One of the worst I've ever seen. Would not pass the Bechdel test. But I still love him.

There's a knock on my door. It's a nice thing. I feel a bit more respected. Although I'm definitely surprised that it's Freddie who pokes his head around.

"Ummm, hey." He looks kind of sheepish and weird.

"Hey."

"Um, are you, like, okay?"

Ohhhh, this is a new thing. He's worried about me!

"Yes, I'm okay."

"Dad says you've got anxiety and I did some googling and it doesn't sound very nice. Um, yeah, like, I just thought I'd come and just say, or whatever."

This might be the nicest thing Freddie has ever done. I'm not totally sure that the two of us have ever had a chat like this, and I can tell it's really hard for him.

"Thanks, Freds. That's really kind of you. I'm okay, though.

Just things got on top of me a bit. I'll work it out."

"I also, um, Josh is a twat. I mean, he's just an absolute twat. I'm glad things didn't work out between the two of you. The things he tells the other guys at school about Trudy aren't very nice and I'm glad it's not you that he's talking about."

"Wow. I mean, thanks, Freddie." My annoying little snotty brother suddenly seems so grown up. He edges closer to me on my bed and gives me a tiny awkward hug. Maybe more of a pat, if I'm honest. I can't remember the last time we hugged. It was probably for a picture Mum took when we were tiny where she used to force us to hug because it was cute. Cute, maybe, but absolutely not voluntary.

"Night, Freds," I say as he shuffles out, still slightly red in the face.

"Night, Kat."

Well, that was unexpected.

11 p.m.

In bed

Now that I know that a lot of what I've been thinking lately is because I was so anxious, I'm left staring at the light switch and wondering: Does part of getting better mean I have to stop touching it three times?

I was reading about the symptoms of anxiety earlier and I think it might be a compulsion. If I don't.do it, I feel sort of incomplete, like something's missing from me. Knowing what it is doesn't seem to stop me from needing to do it.

Right. I'm just going to turn it off, lie down, and go to sleep. It's been an exhausting day.

11:05 p.m.

I can't seem to turn my thoughts off. Questions churn endlessly like: *What if I tell the girls and they don't want to know me anymore?*

I think I'll try to find something to read. Maybe I'll be able to concentrate on something light.

11:10 p.m.

I've had a look through Mum's bookcases and found this old book called *Tales of the City*. It's set in San Francisco in the seventies and is about a single woman who moves there on her own. I think that's the sort of thing I need to be reading about now.

11:30 p.m.

I started to drift off so I turned the light off, but it's as if my hand's developed some kind of twitch. What if this isn't part of anxiety? What if tonight's the night when something bad happens? And it happens because I haven't touched the light switch, because I've messed with the system and, even worse than that, the things that I do have been keeping everything balanced, and so my selfish need to get better means that bad things happen to everyone now?

I turn the light on and sit up. This is silly. I'm silly. I need to stop this. These things need to stop.

I lie back down again and turn the light back off. This time I'm just going to fall asleep.

11:31 p.m.

I touch the light switch three times.

I've told people most of my secrets today—that's enough change, surely? I say "most of my secrets," because telling anyone about the light switch would be a step too far.

It would feel like betraying a small imaginary friend.

Saturday, October 20
7:30 a.m.

Lying in bed after a proper sleep

I can hear my phone vibrating. Millie and Sam are clearly talking to each other about something. I just don't know if I can bring myself to take a look yet.

My head starts to swim with the stuff I'm still worried about:

· _How am I going to tell the girls about the mental health thing?_
· _What if Mum and Dad have to pay loads for me to see a therapist and they can't afford it?_
· _What if, when I see the therapist, she's lovely but immediately has me locked up because I am clearly a complete weirdo?_
· _How am I going to face school now? I know it's over a week away, but what if someone heard my argument with Millie and Sam?_
· _How am I ever going to be a proper feminist and a proper writer if I can't even talk to my girlfriends or go to school?_

I can hear Dad coming up the stairs with Freddie yelling at him from the landing.

"How come she gets a tea brought to her and I have to get my own?"

"Because she is unwell, and YOU are perfectly fit and healthy. So GET UP!"

Dad's laughing and Freddie is tutting at the injustice of the whole thing and how awful it is that he's being treated so unfairly. Back to normal, then. That's a relief.

Dad knocks on the door and comes in with a big mug of hot tea. He hands it to me as he settles himself onto the bed.

"How did you sleep, love?"

"Okay. I kept waking up and thinking about things. I feel better than this time yesterday, though."

"That's good. I just thought I'd see if you have any plans for today? Probably be good to get up and about."

"Yeah. I think the girls might be trying to get ahold of me," I say, reaching for my phone.

"God, your phone's about to vibrate off the side there. What's going on?"

"I don't know, they've been texting like that all morning. There'll probably be about ten thousand messages."

When I look at it most of the excitement seems to be about me. They've missed me. They're looking forward to seeing me. What am I doing today? Can they pop over later?

I think it's time for me to face the music.

9 a.m.

I read on a mental health help website that when you're anxious or depressed, simple tasks can feel overwhelming, so you should break things down into lists.

Here is today's list:

- *Invite the girls over*
- *Write down what I'm going to say to them*
- *Say it to them*

    I wonder if they'll miss me as much when they find out I'm a big old crazy.

10:30 a.m.

The kitchen

"What time are they coming over?" Mum asks, looking up from her paper.

    "After twelve. I'm still not sure what I'm going to tell them," I say, fiddling with the stack of papers. Dad's making me my favorite pancakes. I mean, I feel about five years old again, but I'm going with it.

    "Why don't you send them a text before they get here?" Mum suggests, putting the paper down entirely. "Just thinking, it might be easier for you to say it the way you want to and then you'll know that they already know when they get here."

    I actually don't hate this idea.

11 a.m.

My bedroom

I've tidied my room up a bit and put all Bea's trophy knickers in the laundry basket, much to her dismay. God knows what she'll start parading around the house with in their place. It's interesting (and intelligent) that she'd never go near a pair of Freddie's boxers, though.

Now I'm just sitting writing and rewriting this message to the girls so many times that it's starting to get a bit ridiculous. I'm hoping I'm nearly there.

Emmeline Pankhurst's BAD BITCHEZ
Sam, Millie, Me

Me: I haven't been totally honest with you. I went to the doctor yesterday because I've been feeling super weird lately. I can't seem to sleep and sometimes I get really stressed out and worry about things so much that I can't breathe. The doctor says I'm suffering from anxiety and depression and I've got to see a therapist. I didn't know whether to tell you in case you didn't want to be friends with me because you think I'm weird. I completely understand if you don't want to come over anymore. I'm sorry for not telling you yesterday xx

I take a deep breath and press send. I can see the ticks turning blue as the message is read by both of them and that sets my heart racing out of my rib cage. But they start typing instantly. And then they stop. Then they start again. And then they stop. I can feel my chest tightening and my head starts to feel as if I'm underwater.

Just as I get to explosion point with my nerves, my phone vibrates underneath me.

Emmeline Pankhurst's BAD BITCHEZ
Sam, Millie, Me

Sam: Oh, Kat, of course we'd never stop being your friends and of course we still want to come over and see you. I'm just sorry we didn't know that something like that was going on. We were too wrapped up with our own stuff to see that you had things going on and you needed us
Xxxx

Millie: I'm so sorry. Of course we're still coming round, you doughnut. I don't really know much about anxiety except that someone from *TOWIE* once said she had it. I'm googling like mad.
LOVE FOREVER XXXXX

Sam: Don't worry. We've got this 🖐🩶 xxx

Millie: Can't wait to see you and we can have a proper chat about it xxx

Me: Can't wait to see you too <3 xxx

OH, THANK GOD. I remember the breathing exercises that the doctor gave me yesterday. Now seems like a good time for them.

12 p.m.

I hear the front doorbell go off and my palms are actually sweaty. It feels weird and I know that they said such nice things, but what if they were just saying them and then when we're face-to-face it's still awkward and horrible?

I open the door and am instantly overwhelmed by the two of them as they burst in and leap onto me with a hug.

"We're so sorry!" Millie cries first.

"We didn't mean it—we were just angry and stressed and let's never fight again!" Sam continues.

A lot of what they're saying I don't actually hear because they're talking over each other and the noise is muffled from where I am sandwiched between the two of them.

But I already feel like a more complete person.

12:10 p.m.

My bedroom

Sam and Millie are sprawled around my room, just like always. I'm so relieved that I've told them and that we're all back together.

Bea's got her head on my lap, mourning the loss of her knickers.

"I'm sorry for everything I said," I start. "Trudy said you told her that I was holding you back and you didn't want to hang out with me anymore now that you both have boyfriends, but I have no idea why I listened to her."

"We'd NEVER say that. NEVER. And we should ALL ignore ANYTHING that comes out of Toxic Trudy's mouth," Sam says, and Millie nods enthusiastically.

"I know. I think it's just that my head's been such a mess. I feel worried about things all the time and I think the reason I believed it is because I do feel like a loser. I feel like everyone else is maturing faster than me. I feel like I'm a letdown. I'm not massively clever like my mum and I'm not pretty like either of you, I can't get a boyfriend. I can't even be a good feminist." All of a sudden, it's too much. I am exhausted, and I start to cry.

"Oh, Kat," Millie says as they both put an arm around me. "I wish you'd told us all this sooner. You ARE pretty, and Josh is just a nasty prick, which is the only reason he ended up with Trudy. They're made for each other. Someone made for Trudy is definitely not good enough for you."

"And you ARE massively clever. I bet your mum's so proud." Sam looks down and takes a deep breath. "If it helps, I had a huge meltdown at my mum last night because she is constantly comparing me to Jas, so I am constantly having to prove I'm as good as her or as talented as her. I'm sick of it," she says quietly.

"What? I had no idea your mum was doing that!" I say, genuinely shocked. They always seem like the perfect family.

"Me either," Millie says, studying Sam's face.

"She didn't even realize she was doing it," Sam says, starting to cry too. "I mean, the good thing is that she was mortified and told me a story about how her mum used to do that to her. She's promised to try to stop. It's not just her, though, is it? It's the whole school, as well; everyone knows how amazing Jas is. So I need to find a way to let it bother me less."

"I'm sorry. I guess I'd never thought about how that might make you feel," I say. "I'm always so blown away by what you can do!"

"Yeah, if people are comparing you against your sister, that's really their problem. You're unique with your own talents," Millie says. It's properly thoughtful for our Mills.

"Well. Anyway! We're meant to be talking about you!" Sam says, wiping her eyes so a tiny bit of mascara runs onto her cheek.

"Nah. I've done enough talking about me these last couple of days," I say. "What about you, Millie? How's the play?"

"It's okay." She picks at the carpet. "I'm just worried that I've got this one opportunity with Sophie's mum and I don't want to blow it. I'm worried she'll just think I don't look attractive enough to be a proper actress too."

"WHAT?" Sam and I say at the same time.

"Millie! What are you talking about?" I say. "First of all, actresses need to ACT, not be some kind of weird eye candy, and second of all, you're bloody beautiful anyway!"

"I'm not Instagram beautiful," Millie says quietly. "All the girls on there that have loads of followers and have 'actress' in their bio are stunning. I don't come close."

"Those girls have MILLIONS of filters and photoshop their

actual faces," I say. "But I get it. I spend so long comparing my face to people who don't have pores or spots, and actually they probably do. It's just that we can't see them because they're under so much faff!"

"I guess we've all been feeling it a bit lately, huh?" Sam says.

"I guess." Millie and I both nod, and she hugs her knees.

"Well, you know what we need to do?" I say, having a brainwave. "We need to pick each other up. We need to tell each other we're clever and we're talented, and we need to have no shame in it. AND we need to stop comparing ourselves to other people and get to know who we are OURSELVES. That, my friends, will make us true feminists."

"YASSS!"

"Ooh, that reminds me!" says Sam, cramming a biscuit in her mouth. "We started making you a list on the way over here, Kat. It's advice that we found on the internet for ways to deal with anxiety. Maybe it's something we could all use together?" Sam says. She taps on her phone and shows me the screen.

Kat's Calm List:
· Cut down on caffeine *[it's all about the turmeric latte, apparently]*
· Daily meditation using a meditation app or similar
· Long, hot baths *[ha, Freddie! It's medicinal so you can't complain anymore!]*
· Exercise *[devil, no thank you]*
· Yoga *[also exercise . . . and I always just end up staring at*

the videos alarmed because NO ONE can do that stuff?
SURELY? And I've heard that actually if you're doing it properly
you ALWAYS fanny fart. Though that may be another urban
myth thingy]

· Walking Bea *[exercise dressed up as hanging out with a friend]*

"I can't believe you've done this. It's so sweet!" I say, genuinely shocked.

"Of course! We said we're going to help, and we are!" Millie says.

"And we figured it wouldn't hurt for us all to give some of this a go!" Sam says.

"So, as it's half term next week, we've booked us for a yoga class on Tuesday!" Millie says.

Wow. I can't believe I'm going to have to suppress a fanny fart in the name of my own well-being, but it's so amazing of them to help me like this that I can't exactly say that. Maybe we can all fanny fart together.

10 p.m.

Bed

The girls stayed for pizza. We watched *Lady Bird* for the thousandth time curled up on the sofa. Freddie was at Issy's house, Dad was out at a gig, and Mum made us hot chocolate and salted caramel popcorn. It was perfect.

We've made plans for next week, and I've agreed to hang

out with Dave and Nick on at least one of the days. I'm relieved that I've got a week to work on things before I have to head back to school. I don't think I'd be ready to sit in a classroom or be around the whole year just yet.

There's some party that they're all going to with the Sixth Form lot tomorrow evening that they've invited me to as well, but I'm just not sure I'm quite up for that. So they've told me that they'll text me and tell me everything that happens, and Sam said she'd Instagram Story it all too so I can feel like I'm there IRL.

I feel bad saying no to it, because what if I stop being invited places? But I know that I'm not ready to face Terrible Trudy and TB, and they will inevitably be there. They're always there.

10:15 p.m.

I'm going to read some more of the *Tales of the City* book. It's pretty good, even if it is one of Mum's really old books. I like that the main character has a best friend who's gay. Like me! Matt was texting a lot today. He's visiting his dad today and tomorrow and said that's probably for the best because I'd just be rebonding with the girls and doing some kind of howling at the moon situation.

11 p.m.

The thing is, no matter how much I've achieved today, I still haven't told anyone about the light switch. Still my crazy little secret. A thought twists in my head that I've failed, again.

Tuesday, October 23

I_weigh:
My amazing friends. Who needs anything else?

9 a.m.

My boudoir. Sun streaming through the window

Today is going to be a GOOD DAY. I have friends, I have support, and I'm going to do some mindful yogic exercise and definitely not fanny fart.

I woke up with Bea padding next to my bed, staring up at me. This is her "pretending she hasn't been fed" look. She thinks she can cheat me out of some food even though I know that Dad—and probably Mum as well—have fed her already. It's nice that whatever else has changed this week, Bea hasn't.

I shuffle downstairs and make myself a cup of tea and some toast and settle down at the kitchen table with my laptop. The last couple of days have been spent doing nice stuff. On Sunday we went around to Sam's and painted a tree or two for the set, and yesterday Matt and I had a rom-com marathon while it rained. Perfectly timed, and all the films we chose passed the Bechdel test.

Dad's working on a script, Mum's at the shops, and Freddie's still in bed, so I've got the place to myself until the girls show up. I'm trying to remind myself what I used to do, before

I spent all my time googling and comparing myself to people I've never met on Instagram.

Nothing to do but to try to keep my brain in check and remember how to be by myself.

10 a.m.

Have been reading this "Truth about Instagram influencers" piece online, and the thing is, it seems like most of them don't even have their shit together, anyway. I guess we all think we see their whole lives on Instagram, but all we actually see is a small square. A tiny, curated piece of the picture. Filtered and cropped. When all the stuff outside that square can be really messy, and flawed, and difficult. They're just people like everyone else and they have issues just like everyone else. I almost feel bad for thinking that they were perfect. Like I'm one of those responsible for heaping all the pressure on. Constantly lapping up more and more flawless content. But they continue to only post curated stuff. It's a horrible, vicious circle.

It feels like we should all be being more real in our profiles and our pictures. Taking the pressure off each other and ourselves a bit. That couldn't hurt, right?

I go to Instagram and take a picture of me and Bea. I'm not wearing any makeup, my hair's a mess, and I'm in my pajamas. I caption it: "Me and my dawg #reallife #imperfect #feminist #dogsofinstagram." It feels brave of me to post it, and not put a filter on it, but it's just my ACTUAL face.

I'm doing a better thing than putting myself out there as something that I'm not. At least this way, if someone sees my profile, they see the real me. Pores, spots, eye bogies, and all.

1 p.m.

The living room

The three of us are sitting at the dining table, staring over at Issy and Freddie as they hold hands on the sofa.

"It's so gross. They're actually touching each other." Millie recoils. She looks as if she's just stepped in dog poo.

"SO gross," Sam joins in. "Why can't they go somewhere where we don't have to see them? No one needs a PDA."

She's right, no one needs a PDA, but especially not a very single, unloved older sister.

"FREDDIE! Can't you go somewhere else?"

"Why don't YOU go somewhere else? WE were here FIRST!" Freddie shouts back.

Ah. Arguing with Freddie is starting to make me feel a little like my old self again. Although I do feel a bit bad after he was so nice to me the other night.

"FINE! We're going soon anyway. But don't do anything gross over there. The whole family has to sit on that sofa!"

"OH MY GOD, KAT! REALLY? THAT'S MY LITTLE SISTER!" Millie covers her eyes.

"OH MY GOD, GUYS, SHUT UP! WE'RE JUST HOLDING HANDS!" Issy shouts back.

"OH MY GOD, GUYS, STOP SHOUTINGGGGGGG!" I hear Dad shout from his study where he's supposed to be writing Nat's latest scenes.

God knows what she's up to this week. Last week she did, in fact, decide that she wanted to be a feminist . . . original, Dad. I should really get a cut of his writing fees, although after the last two days, I suppose I owe him.

"WE'RE GOING OUUUUUTTTTTT!" I mimic his style of shouting back.

"I'm GOING DEAF!" I hear him shout after us and then chuckle to himself. It's sweet how parents amuse themselves sometimes. Sweet, but sad.

1:15 p.m.

My bedroom

We get ready into our workout gear, which is basically just a trendier version of my PE kit for me, but Millie seems to have a whole lycra thing worked out. Sam's gone for some baggy tracky bs and a vest top, though, because like me, she's not some kind of Hollywood diva going off to lightly glisten in the gym before being snapped by paparazzi while drinking a kale smoothie.

I guess Millie IS an actress in training, after all.

I feel better than I have in days, but I still can't quite shake this feeling of impending doom sitting at the bottom of my stomach. I feel nervous about going out into the big, wide world (or small, tiny town), but I know I have to.

1:45 p.m.

The yoga studio

Another Insta lie is revealed: I thought yoga was all glamorous yummy mummies and shiny six-pack-endowed people. As I'm looking around this studio at the other participants, all I'm seeing is old folk. Lots and lots of old folk. In fact, if I didn't know any better, I'd think that the girls had accidentally booked us in for an OAP class or something.

"LADIES!" shouts a LADY who also looks old (older than my mum, anyway), while clapping her hands.

She's wearing a sweatband around her head and a leotard over her leggings, with leg warmers. I've only ever seen people dressed like this in the ancient film called *Fame* that I watched with my mum once while she mooned over one of the main male characters, saying things like, *Isn't he dreamy?* to me every five seconds. He was okay. But nothing to change my knickers over.

"Grab a mat, everyone, and let's get started!"

"All right, eager beaver!" Millie whispers to Sam and me as we observe that the lady does, indeed, have a bit of a front wedgie situation going on.

As feminists we shouldn't judge the camel toe sitch, and should probably tell her about it, but I'm scared of her.

1:55 p.m.

Here's the thing about yoga: it REALLY relaxes people. Sam, Millie, and I have all our mats in a row, and I have managed NOT TO FANNY FART thus far. But in front of and behind us are rows of OAPs, and every five seconds it would seem that at least one of them passes wind.

I say "passing wind" rather than "farting" because these are old women. Elegant old women do not fart, they pass wind. Delicately. And, it would appear, loudly and smellily too.

At first it was funny and we were struggling to keep in snorts of laughter while maintaining our frankly horrific balance. But now it's become a bit of a health hazard, especially as the instructor keeps telling us to breathe in deeply.

I once read that the gas from farts can kill you if it's in huge quantities. I wonder if it might be advisable to crack a window.

2 p.m.

I guess they've all relieved themselves now because I haven't heard anyone let loose for at least a few minutes.

Although I think Millie's shuffling around in a bit of a weird way . . .

I hear a noise emanating from Millie's butt that is frankly

louder than ANY of the noises that the old people made and forces all three of us to fall out of our downward dog positions and collapse onto the floor laughing.

"Pardon moi!" Millie giggles.

The teacher is giving us an absolute shocker of a look. But then I guess I would be extra miserable too if my leotard were wedged that far into my vagina.

2:30 p.m.

Still high on the fumes of old people's farts

"Annnnd when you're ready, slowly open your eyes and come back to the room."

It doesn't really make any sense to me as we definitely never left the room, but I guess the instructor means spiritually. It's hard to do anything spiritually in a room that smells this bad.

3 p.m.

Walking through the park to get a post-yoga ice cream

I definitely feel more relaxed and calm after the yoga, even though we giggled our way through all the positions. And it feels good to be out of the house in the sunshine.

"You know what we haven't done for a while?" Millie says.

"Feminism! We should do some activisting! Weren't you going to ask if you could write a weekly post on the school blog, Kat?"

My heart beats a little faster. "Yeah, but . . . I don't know now. My brain feels a bit too scrambled to come up with ideas," I say. I'm suddenly filled with dread at the idea of doing something that may not be very good, or will draw attention to me and encourage people to make fun of me.

"I bet you could. Why don't you just write about a feminist you really admire? Or do a brief timeline of feminism or something? Something really factual that you could take in stages?" Sam says. "I was reading a website about anxiety and depression last night and it was saying that when you feel like you can't think clearly, you just need to break things down into bite-sized, manageable chunks. Maybe you can do that with Feminist Friday?"

Great minds, Sam.

I feel really touched that she's been doing more research and looking at ways to help. I'd feel ungrateful if I told her I couldn't do it because I'm too afraid.

"That sounds good. Maybe I'll talk to Miss Mills about it when we're back at school next week."

"We can come with you for moral support," Millie says, as if she's actually just listening to my thoughts.

"Yeah!" says Sam. "The three muffskateers do everything together, especially feminism!"

"MUFFSKATEERS!" All three of us burst into hysterics.

"I think that might actually be a porn film," I say.

"BLEURGH!"

And with that, there shall be no more muffskateers.

3:10 p.m.

I hear her before I see her.

It's my own fault, I got too relaxed, and now Trudy is heading right for us with her gang of TB.

I wonder if there's a time when they're not together? Imagine not even getting school holidays off from being in the most horrible group.

Millie and Sam have grabbed my hands.

"Don't worry, we'll just walk past quickly," Millie says.

But Trudy has other ideas, obviously.

"Well, LOOK WHO IT IS!" Trudy says, the glee radiating off her.

"We're a bit busy, ACTUALLY, Trudy," Sam says.

"I didn't see you around the last couple of days of school, Kat. I hope you weren't sick?" Trudy says with ZERO sincerity. "Or perhaps you were just avoiding someone?"

"Shut up, Trudy," Millie says. "We haven't got time for you today."

"I'm just concerned. Aren't I allowed to be concerned?" Trudy says. "So, what was up?"

"I just feel like that's really none of your business," I say.

"Why don't you go and harass someone else, Trudy? You're not wanted here," Sam says.

"Unless, of course, it's that no one ever actually WANTS to talk to you, apart from your lame followers?" Millie's really getting going now. "And even then I heard you have to PAY them to hang out with you."

"That's not true!" Amelie says.

"Yeah, we hang out with her because of all the cool stuff she gets us," Tia says. Facepalm.

Suddenly I can't be bothered with this shit. I'm having a nice day, and recently I've had so many crap days because of Trudy, because of the things she's said. I'm not taking this any more. I have the girls beside me. What can she actually do?

"Anyway, we'd love to stay and chat so that you can be a prize twat, but like we said we've got places to be, people to see, and fun to have," I say, stepping around her to walk away. "And Trudy? If your boyfriend's so great, why don't you spend more time with him instead of harassing me?"

"Bye, Trudy!" Millie and Sam wave at her sarcastically and the three of us walk off into the sunshine, away from Trudy's dark cloud of tyranny.

3:30 p.m.

Scoops ice cream parlor

I love ice cream. I love my friends. We've both exercised ourselves and exorcised the demon of Terrible Trudy. Today is a GOOD day.

"She looked like she'd swallowed a hairy turd when you said that!" Millie says.

They are both SO PROUD of me for standing up for myself. I am proud too.

"She's going to have to get used to it, I'm not standing for her shit anymore. She can't just have a go at people she thinks are lower than her on the food chain to make herself feel better. She needs to get a normal hobby," I say.

Unfeminist thoughts: 1?
It probably wasn't massively feminist of me to make fun of the yoga instructor with the camel toe. Oops.

Thursday, October 25

I_weigh:

Being brave and going out with the couples even though I feel like crap about it.

1 p.m.

We're on our way to meet the boys at Cindy's. I've been sort of dreading it, if I'm being honest, because I feel like I'll be the odd one out. The big gooseberry. A. LOSER.

I'm starting to wish I'd convinced Matt to come with me.

1:30 p.m.

Cindy's cafe

The boys are watching something on Nick's phone when we get there. They clock us and Nick immediately jumps up to greet Millie, dropping the phone and looking INCREDIBLY SHIFTY.

Unfortunately for him, the vid is still playing on the screen on the table. It's a women's beach volleyball tournament. Nick snatches it away. I mean, really? We need to spread our feminist influence wider, it would seem.

"Hey!" They kiss their girlfriends and sort of awkwardly pat me on the shoulder.

I already feel exactly how I was afraid of feeling, like a spare part, a big old fuzzy gooseberry. I don't know how this is going to make me feel any better.

"Guys, what coffees do you want?" Nick says, heading to the counter.

Millie and Sam give him their order and then he looks at me. "Kat? What can I get you?"

I really wasn't expecting that.

"Oh, um, that's really kind of you. You don't have to do that," I find myself mumbling.

"Don't be silly—we're all together. What can I get you?" Nick asks. He seems really kind, actually. Maybe he's all right, after all.

"Oh, um, in that case, um, just a green tea please, would be good. Thanks," I mutter. Millie gives me a little squeeze.

I think this is probably why we've never done this before, hung out all five of us. Because I just don't fit in. I knew I didn't already. I'm not sure why the girls thought this would help. I feel out of place and foolish.

"We thought we might hang out at the park. Sun's out and there's bound to be stuff going on? It's also got that nice autumn vibe going on. WE CAN HAVE A LEAF FIGHT!" Dave says.

"Sounds good!" Millie says.

"Although, could we maybe check those leaves for dog shit first?" Sam says. Yet again, she's so wise.

4 p.m.

The park

I feel surprisingly relaxed and grown up. We walked all the way to the top of the park and I didn't even worry about bumping into Trudy because I'm bigger than her now.

I might even be having a nice time. I think I am, anyway. Dave and Nick are actually quite funny and have been doing impressions of people at school, and Matt's going to come and join us in a bit too.

They were telling me how #Tim nearly got lucky with a new girl at a party last weekend before she googled to check whether breast size has anything to do with how much people feel them. I feel like the fact that she had to look it up probably means they are made for each other. Which is nice.

4:30 p.m.

Lying on the grass, which Sam has checked for dog poo

"Urgh, Mum's new boyfriend's coming over this evening and she's asked if I'm going to be in," Dave says, looking at his phone.

"What's he like?" Sam asks.

"She met him at the bank where she works, so I imagine he's a complete douchebag. The ones she's met there before have mostly turned out to be secretly married."

"My mum has a habit of dating ones like that too." Matt nods sagely.

"Terry and his todger," I add, and we all cover our eyes at the memory.

"My oldest sister does, as well," Nick says.

They all look at each other, back at us, and then collectively sigh: "Women." Like they think they're hilarious. The three of us are obviously appalled and stare them down. Millie starts throwing items from her handbag at them.

"Er, did you ever stop to think it's the secretly married men who should take a long, hard look at themselves?"

"Hey!" Dave says, fending off quite a hard hairbrush. "We're only joking. My mum actually thinks what you guys did at school was pretty cool, and I do too. She's always having to deal with sexism at the bank: men talking over her, asking to see the 'man in charge.' She got passed up for promotion so many times because men got it first."

"My sisters always seem to be dealing with some kind of painful women's affliction too," Nick says. "There's always period cramps or cystitis. It's a never-ending cycle of shit for you guys, on top of the patriarchy stuff. We get it."

But DO they, though?

"Um, what is cystitis, please?" Sam asks.

"It's, err, this thing mostly women get where you feel like you really need a wee and you can't go and it burns like fire in your, erm, you know," Nick says shyly, but clearly trying to be matter-of-fact about it.

"Um, WHAT?" all three of us say at once.

"Erm, no, that is not a thing. They would warn us about that. There would be a memo, or something. WOULDN'T THERE?" Millie is FRANTIC.

I take out my phone.

> **What is cystitis?** 🔍

Why does my wee burn?	v
Has anyone ever died from cystitis?	v
When will the burning end?	v
Will I ever wee again?	v
Why am I pissing razorblades?	v

Matt's reading over my shoulder and I hear a sharp intake of breath.

"How do you know about this and we don't? Is this the sodding patriarchy again?" Sam asks.

"Um no, it's just I hear my sisters screaming and shouting about it all the time," Nick says.

"AND SO THEY SHOULD!" I gasp, my eyes still wide from everything I've learned.

"How do we stop this from ever happening to us?" Millie asks.

"I'm starting to understand why my mum painted my whole house red," Matt says solemnly.

11 p.m.

In bed, wrestling Bea for at least a tiny scrap of duvet

It's weird to admit it, but I've had a really nice day. I feel like I need to note some things that I've realized, so I don't forget them when the terror strikes, like I know it will:

1. Just because I don't have a boyfriend and they both do does not mean that the girls want to stop hanging out with me.

2. Hanging out with their boyfriends can actually be quite fun.

3. Sometimes it's okay to let new people in, as long as they're good ones.

4. ANYONE can be a feminist. It's not just for women.

5. Cystitis? What the fucking fuck?

Point four was massive. Dave, Nick, and Matt all know quite a lot about feminism from their mums and sisters, and they all think boys and girls should be equal, so they are totally on the feminist bus. Amazing. And they all agreed that Feminist Friday on the school blog is a really great idea. So now I have to do it. Fuck.

Dave said that because it was just him and his mum, and she talked about her period so much, for a whole year aged about ten he was basically waiting to start his period, until he finally worked out that periods were something only women have. And then he felt like men really shirk the workload if they don't even have to deal with bleeding once a month on top of the patriarchy.

He seems like a good guy.

I can't believe that Nick had to be the one to tell us about cystitis, though. I need to let Mum know that she's really dropped the ball there. It should be the first thing that trainee feminists are taught. I mean, what the hell? As if thrush and periods weren't bad enough! It says you need to wear cotton knickers to help prevent these things, which is fine because I've recently started to suspect that the people who make the other ones—you know, the nonbreathable ones made from suffocating, shiny and scratchy material—either work for thrush companies OR are the bad kind of men trying to prevent women from thriving. I mean, for fuck's sake, YEAST? IN MY VAGINA? RAZORBLADES IN MY URETHRA? No. Do fuck off.

They should put someone in charge of feminist communication to all women. Maybe Caitlin Moran? Or maybe one of the suffragettes watching over us could help us out with all this shit from the sky? Oh my god, what on earth did women do before medicine?

11:15 p.m.

Dear Emmeline Pankhurst,
If you're up there, I've just purchased a new menstrual cup to give it another go. If you could do your magic to help things go a little smoother for me, that'd be great.
With feminist thanks,
Kat

11:30 p.m.

If there is a God, then he's definitely a man. There's no way that a woman would allow cystitis to happen.

I'm so nervous about therapy tomorrow, though, so at least the thought of cystitis is a welcome distraction for now. I think I'm in denial about having to tell yet ANOTHER stranger about the inside of my head, but this time my parents are paying a LOT for it so I need to make sure I do it right.

11:45 p.m.

I turn off the light and find myself once again reaching out to touch it. What if I didn't, though? What if, for one night, I just didn't?

I'm not going to.

My hands are doing some kind of weird muscle-memory thing where they feel like they're going to jump out and touch it without my say-so. I lie on top of them to try to stop them from leaping out against my will and touching it.

Bea makes a loud sighing noise to let me know that she's not happy with all this movement, and that she's trying to sleep, actually.

Sometimes she can be quite the fusspot.

I'll probably end up getting cystitis if I don't touch it.

Think I'll just touch it so that Bea doesn't have to put up with my fidgeting anymore.

Unfeminist thoughts: 1
Is it unfeminist that I'm less pleased to own a vagina after finding out about cystitis? I mean, FFS.

Friday, October 26

I_weigh:

Nerves about meeting my therapist.

3:50 p.m.

Dad's car

I'm so nervous. I've spent all day trying to pretend that this isn't happening, hoping that if I got myself really into my book, this event would just happen in the background without me really having to know anything about it. Maybe I'm fine now and I don't need therapy and I especially don't need to put Mum and Dad into debt to see someone quicker?

Then I get really anxious about that, my chest starts to go tight and everything goes a bit swimmy, and I realize that's probably a good example of why I need the therapy.

4 p.m.

The therapist's office is quite nice. There are plants everywhere, and they're actually alive, rather than the ones in the office at school that are all dead.

The waiting room is all pink and chrome and has velvet cushions, and there's a scented candle giving off a nice expensive smell to mingle with the inspirational quotes on the walls:

"You can do this"

"Be still"

"It's going to be all right"

I guess this is what you get when you go private and bankrupt your parents.

I'm still really not sure what I'm supposed to tell this therapist. Do I just launch straight in and tell her my whole life story? What if she thinks I'm weird? What if she tells my parents I should be locked up for the safety of the universe? What if she is mean and tells me to stop being silly?

A woman's just come out of the door opposite and I wonder if it's her. She looks nice, not mean at all. I really hope it's her.

"Kat?" she asks.

It MUST be her! Thank holy One Direction.

Dad gives me a little shove and I realize I haven't moved.

"Go on, love. Good luck."

I'm not sure whether "good luck" is the appropriate statement for your daughter going to her first therapist appointment, but whatever.

"Hi," I say, slightly in slow motion, still willing this not to be happening.

"Hi, Kat, I'm Sarah. Nice to meet you." She sticks out a hand for me to shake, which feels very businesslike. "Come through."

She's around Mum's age, I reckon, long dark hair, big brown

eyes, wearing a lovely floaty dress. She's a lady who looks like she has her shit together. But then I guess you have to have your own shit together if you're going to dissect someone else's shit.

I follow her through into a room that's cozy and also smells amazing. Will I ever be able to smell another scented candle without thinking of my therapist's office? Will this ruin candles for me forever?

I take a seat on another lovely rose-pink armchair. It's like the whole room is an Instagram post. For some reason I imagine it as a post on my own account:

Just telling someone how cray cray I am. How's your Friday going, folks?

Probably not allowed to Instagram the therapist's office, though, especially as there are signs everywhere telling you to turn your phone off and "be in the moment."

We're sitting opposite each other and she's looking at me, which I find really uncomfortable. Has it started? How do I know when we've started? Should I be talking? Maybe it has started? Am I doing it wrong? Have I already screwed up therapy?

"So, Kat."

I do an audible sigh as I breathe again, no longer afraid of the silence and whether I'm expected to fill it with everything in my brain—like unpacking a very personal suitcase and then waving my arm over the contents with a *behold!* gesture.

"For the first session, I like to do a bit of background context and cover the basics. Am I right in thinking you've never been to therapy before?" she asks and I nod. "I'm going to give you some questionnaires to fill out and ask you some simple questions about yourself. Does that sound okay?"

I nod again.

"Great, just one rule first!"

There are rules? What kind of rules can there be? Is she about to tell me that she doesn't actually deal with certain things or that she doesn't want to hear certain problems? What if she cannot listen to light-switch-based issues?

I'm not sure that rules are going to make me more comfortable in this situation. The surroundings are comfortable. I am somehow a jagged and uncomfortable dot in the middle of all this crushed pink velvet and chrome.

"Everything you say to me is completely confidential. Nothing goes outside of these walls. Unless you tell me something that makes me worry that you are about to hurt yourself or others, then I have to tell someone. Does that make sense?"

"My mum and dad won't know any of it?"

"Not unless you tell them or you want me to tell them for you, no."

I'm massively relieved. Even though I've told Mum and Dad most of it already, there are obviously some bits that I left out on purpose because I just can't tell them. I'm glad that they won't receive a postsession report, like at school. *Congratulations, your daughter is an excellent level of crazy!*

"Why don't we start by you telling me why you're here?"

Oh god, I'm instantly uncomfortable again. Great.

"Erm. I thought that my dad had explained when he booked the session."

"Oh, he did, but I need to hear from clients in their own words what's going on. This room is about you having a voice, Kat. About you explaining your feelings and experiences to someone who you can trust and who may be able to help you. But I can only help you if I know exactly what's going on. That might be overwhelming for you or feel too big, so if it helps, we can start with small steps. What's been going on for you these last couple of weeks? I gather they've been tough?"

I take in a big gulp of air. And then I start.

5 p.m.

Back in the waiting room

The time seemed to pass quite quickly once I started talking. I gave the therapist the lowdown on my family; I talked about the way that I sometimes feel like everyone hates me, about how I don't think I'm very feminine and I worry that I'll never feel like a proper woman. I talked about how everyone else is getting waxes and boyfriends and all I seem to be doing is becoming more of a loser and spending more time on my own. And that I think probably I'm just not a very nice person and that's why no one wants to be with me. I surprised myself with the things I was brave enough to tell her. I even told her about the light switch. I guess if my parents are paying all this money, I need to make sure I'm not wasting it.

The thing was that she didn't seem at all surprised to hear about any of it. I didn't feel like a weirdo talking to her. She's given me some more breathing exercises to help when I feel panicked or stressed and has suggested I try practicing them morning and night as well. It makes me feel a little silly that I need to practice breathing—which most people seem to manage automatically—this much, but I'm willing to give it a go.

At the end, she told me that she thinks we'll be working to tackle my intrusive thoughts (like me thinking I have to touch the light switch). And it feels AMAZING having someone else in the world know my secret.

Dad stood up as we walked back into the waiting room and a copy of *Good Housekeeping* fell to the floor. Also reassuring because I kept having images of him leaning up against the door with a glass when I was talking. I nearly went and opened the door to see if he'd fall in like they do in films.

"Okay, Kat, so if it's okay with you and your dad, I'd like to continue to see you once a week for six sessions in the first instance?" Sarah asks.

I look at Dad and he nods.

"Yes. Thank you," I say, feeling bad AGAIN that Dad has to pay for this.

My mouth is exceptionally dry and I feel exhausted, but somehow . . . a bit free.

5:10 p.m.

I can tell Dad wants to ask what we talked about and knows he can't. So instead, he's asking other questions, like: "Did you like her? Do you think you'll feel comfortable talking to her? If you don't, don't feel like you have to stick with her. We can look around and find someone else."

"She was great. I really like her."

"Okay, that's good. How do you feel now?"

"Really tired, actually. Like, REALLY tired."

But I also feel lighter, much lighter. I'm no longer carrying this all on my own.

Sarah told me that an estimated six million people in the UK suffer from mental health conditions. So I immediately feel less alone. If there are that many people, I must know other people like me. There must be people passing me in the street all the time who are dealing with the same thoughts as I am (well, probably not EXACTLY the same), and we just don't know it because you can't see anxiety or depression. It's inside us.

"I think that's probably normal," Dad says. I hear Sarah in my head saying that normal isn't a thing; we're ALL different. "Why don't we head home? I'll get some dinner on and you can get into bed."

I lean into him and feel safe, just for now.

5:30 p.m.

I've got homework for the week from Sarah. I have to make a list of all my negative thoughts and then next week she'll help me to try to "reframe" them, which she says means look at it all from a more positive angle. So when I think things like "I won't ever get a boyfriend," I have to write them into this grid. It seems straightforward so far.

I definitely feel less hopeless this week. I never thought I'd be able to tell someone all that, and yet I did. And I can sort things out piece by piece. I don't have to do everything right away. There's no perfect, quick-fix way to recover. I still find it hard to imagine that I'll ever feel any different, but now I have hope.

Unfeminist thoughts:
Might do fewer of these, actually. Save it for when it's a really bad thought. I think judging myself too much might be what gets me in trouble.

Sunday, October 28

I_weigh:

Going back to school tomorrow and facing everyone now that I know I'm depressed and anxious.

9:15 p.m.

I've had a really relaxed day, possibly too relaxed considering what's happening tomorrow. Mum and Dad decided we should all go for a walk, so we ended up a bit lost in some fields somewhere, which was annoying, and then Dad fell over into a cow pie, which was really the highlight.

Tonight we all watched *Antiques Roadshow* with Matt, and Dad said he could still smell it. Then he sneezed out a bit of cow pie. A shit sneeze, if you will.

But now I'm just lying in bed worrying to death about school tomorrow. What if people find out how loopy I am? I KNOW it's silly because how would they know? But still. What if?

Monday, October 29

I_weigh:

Fear. I'm not sure I'm ready to go back to school after all. I feel very much like something heavy has sat on my chest and is preventing me from breathing again. My throat feels clogged. Oh god.

7:30 a.m.

In my room getting ready for school

Every time I think about today, I get freaked out and climb back under the duvet. Bea gets excited whenever I do this and settles herself in, only to find me attempting to get up again five minutes later. It's a good thing that she loves me unconditionally, really.

I'm sitting reading @I_weigh posts. Images of women standing, with words like "self-harm," "abuse," "bullying," "grief," and then the big one, "anxiety," around them. And here's me. I just need to go to school. I imagine my own @I_weigh post:

- Anxiety
- Depression
- Lonely
- Loopy
- Loser
- Ugly
- Unwanted

I need to stop it. Immediately. I'm spiralling, and those things aren't true. I've got my friends, I've got my parents, I've even got Freddie. I've just got to get through today.

8 a.m.

Dad emailed the school last week to tell them why I was off and explain things, and now the two of us have to have a meeting with the well-being officer before school starts. Which is not ideal because I wanted to walk in with the girls so that I felt protected with them on either side of me. But now I have to go in with Dad and hope that no one sees that I've:

1. Brought my dad to school
2. Got in super early like a keeno

8:30 a.m.

Outside the well-being officer's office

"I feel like I'm about to get told off by the principal whenever I come in here," Dad says as we both sit nervously waiting.

I just feel sick. I'm nervous that there might be people listening outside the door. I'm nervous that someone will see me with my dad and start asking questions, or worse still, tell Trudy or TB. Although I do feel a bit braver about handling her now.

"Mr. Evans? Kat? Come through," says Ms. Furmore, in a soothing voice. It reminds me of the yoga voices that annoy me so much. Also, I know she's putting it on, because I've heard her bellowing across the playground.

"Take a seat." She gestures to the chairs opposite her.

I don't know about Dad, but I still feel like a naughty schoolkid.

Her office is filled with posters of smiley faces, and there's some kind of incense machine pumping out the most oppressive smell I've ever encountered. The whole room is a migraine waiting to happen.

I let Dad do most of the talking while Ms. Furmore makes very sympathetic noises toward me and tells me that if I ever need to talk to her, I can. Which is kind but I'm not sure that I'd want to, if I'm being honest. She seems a bit too eager.

8:50 a.m.

When we come out I feel a sense of relief, and I'm not sure whether that's from having it done or from getting away from the overwhelming hippie scent in that room. Now I just need to get through the day as best I possibly can, and hopefully without having any panic attacks.

The girls come to meet me right outside the room so at least I'm not having to run the gauntlet of the playground by myself, and Dad slips seamlessly away, trying to draw as little attention to himself as possible. God, I love them all.

Two steps into the playground, I can see Trudy sitting on Josh's lap with TB surrounding them.

302

"Oh, look, it's the lapdog," Sam says.

I still feel that pang when I see them together—a bit of a should-have-been-me feeling.

"Hey, has anyone else noticed that they look the color of flamin' hot Monster Munch?" Sam asks.

"Oh my god, you're so right. Or, kind of, tomato soup?" Millie says.

"Have they gone for a couple's spray tan?" Sam chuckles.

"Two for one!" I finish, and the three of us collapse into giggles.

Once more we're being unfeminist/quite bitchy, but do you know what? After everything Trudy said to me and all the upset she's caused, I really don't care. I think she's been far more unfeminist anyway (not that it's a competition, that would be unfeminist too).

I already feel like today is going to be a better day.

9 a.m.

Homeroom

There's no assembly this week, which I'm so grateful for. I couldn't handle a whole room of people like that. I approach my desk with caution. I can't SEE any gifts from #Tim, but I know well that double English would be his time to do it, so he can sit being annoying for an hour and a half afterward. As I approach, though, I can see that the coast is completely clear—not a scrap of paper or a gift in sight. That is, of course, until I pull my chair out, and a massive "Get Well Soon" helium balloon comes floating out with a note attached to it.

Oh my god, this is SO EMBARRASSING. I yank it down and cover it with my jacket under the desk before anyone else gets here. I tear the note off it.

My dear Kat,
I have noticed your absence.
My heart has been empty and pines for you.
Please get well soon.
Yours forever,
#Tim (Your Legend)

I stuff it as far into my bag as it will possibly go so that it may never, ever resurface. Burning would be better.

This needs to stop. It's actually harassment now. Low level, but harassment none the less.

9:10 a.m.

I can feel the balloon bobbing against my leg, but as long as it doesn't go anywhere, and no one else sees it, and we all get out of here without it being found, it's completely fine. I'm trying to subtly tear a hole in it so that it will deflate in a cloud of helium, but it's not sodding working.

#Tim is staring at me. I think he's looking for his balloon.

Just then I realize I've lost control of it. Or rather, it's gone floaty bye-bye. It's bobbing up toward the ceiling, taking my jacket with it. The effect is quite ghostly, I realize, just as Stacey in the row behind me starts to scream.

"Oh god," I mutter as I hear #Tim get up behind me.

"Your balloon, Kat!" he shouts, grabbing it and bringing it back down to me.

The whole class is staring at me. They're not even laughing. I think it's probably because the whole thing is so weird. Miss Mills has stopped talking about Shakespeare, Millie and Sam have their heads in their hands.

Oh my god.

"Right. Well, let's carry on, shall we!" Miss Mills forges ahead with her chat about soliloquies, giving me a small wink, and as the class turns back around to face her, I lay my head in my hands on my desk, just like Millie and Sam.

9 p.m.

It was really hard to fill in this grid from Sarah while at school, so I'm trying to remember the things to put in it. It's starting to resemble something a little like thought bingo, if I'm being honest.

Sad	Anxious	Dizzy
Crying	Panic Attack	FULL HOUSE

Tuesday, October 30

I_weigh:

The weight of all my filth once again as I wait for my bloody brother to come out of the bathroom. He had better not be doing anything disgusting in that shower. I would rather burn the house down than use the shower after that.

7:30 a.m.

"FREDDIE! FREDDIIIIIIEEEEEE!" I scream, hammering at the door.

"At least things are back to normal," I can hear Dad saying to Mum. They're both just standing together with cups of tea, watching me rather than doing something to, oh I don't know, help, or intervene, or something?

I've got to leave for school in half an hour at the latest and I haven't even washed my hair yet, let alone attempted the task of drying and straightening, and then covering all my spots.

"FREEDDIIE, I WILL KILL YOU!" I bellow through the door. "I will fill your bed with used tampons and rub menstruating cats all over your pillows!"

"Menstruating cats . . ." I can hear Dad saying to Mum behind me. "She's inventive. I'll give her that."

"She gets that from you, John."

8:45 a.m.

The playground

As we walk into school, we see Trudy and Josh in their usual
spot, surrounded by TB. For the first time it strikes me they
never seem to be actually doing anything. They take selfies a
lot and hang out on that bloody bench, feed each other lunch (I
can feed myself lunch, thanks), and that's basically it. How
boring.

Josh is also looking really try-hard right now. He's got Ray-
Bans on when it's not even sunny; in fact, it's raining slightly.
He's got a leather jacket over his blazer with a Harley-Davidson
badge on it (you've not even got a scooter, mate. Don't pretend you ride a Harley), and he looks like a complete idiot. I
feel like I've FINALLY seen the light.

We join Dave and Comedy Krish in the playground. Comedy
Krish seems to be up to something. He usually is, but he looks
particularly suspicious today. I can't wait to see what it is.

10:30 a.m.

English

"Miss Mills?" I ask after English finishes and everyone has
left. I didn't really want to have this conversation in front of
anyone else in case she laughs at me, which I'm completely

convinced she's about to do. But I need to do it. I've waited too long, and Sarah said at therapy it sounded like a good idea. So what am I afraid of?

"Hi, Kat! How's your day going?" she asks brightly.

"Oh good, yeah, great, thanks," I say.

"Well, if you ever need to talk about anything, I'm always about," she says kindly.

How does she know? Is it written on my forehead?

"Oh, thank you. Erm. That's very kind." I feel like chickening out because I've been slightly derailed now. Before I can talk myself out of it, I plough on. "Actually, I was just wondering if I could talk to you about the school blog?"

"Of course, Kat!"

"So, I was thinking, erm, I'd like to do a post, maybe every Friday? Called Feminist Friday? And talk about a different woman or fact from history that might have been slightly over-looked or that people in the school just don't know about. I wondered if you thought that would be okay?" I'm suddenly really shy and I feel stupid.

"That sounds like a wonderful idea, Kat! I love it!" She seems really genuinely enthusiastic and it's surprised me a bit, to be honest.

"Oh. Okay, cool!" I say excitedly.

"How does a week from Friday sound for the first one? Give you time to do it at your own pace?"

"Perfect!" I say, like I'm not going to go home and start on it immediately.

"Great!" she says. "And Kat? I've been wanting to talk to you about your English mock grade. I'm worried that you might be feeling a bit disappointed by it. So I just wanted to reassure you, you did get the highest mark in the year. It's just that there's still a lot to cover and you haven't done it all yet, that's all."

"Okay," I say breezily, as if I'm trying to pretend that it's not what's been on my mind for the last week and a half, but this is EXCELLENT NEWS. I am SO RELIEVED! But also, WHY NOT TELL ME THAT AT THE TIME!

4 p.m.

Walking home

"What are you going to do the first one on, though?" Sam asks me, stuffing her hand into a packet of crisps.

"I think maybe Mary Beatrice Davidson Kenner?"

Both of them are staring at me blankly, which is exactly what I expected to happen, and it's good because it means I'm not about to write a blog about something people already know.

"She was a woman in the US who invented the sanitary belt in the 1920s. But even though she was able to raise enough money to patent the idea in 1957, no one wanted to work with her after they found out she was Black. Then when the patent expired, people stole her idea, and so she never got credit for it."

Sam nods sagely. "Standard," she says. "There are so many of those stories and I know I should be surprised or whatever, but hearing some of the stories that my mum tells me from her childhood, the way that they were bullied as kids, the way that things still are, this just doesn't shock me. I think she's the absolute best person to start the column with." Sam beams at me.

"Agreed!" Millie chimes in.

5 p.m.

My desk

I thought I'd get a head start on writing about Mary. I've tried to stick just to facts, which makes it easier for me to focus and write. I broke them all down into bullet points and rebuilt them to make my blog piece.

It feels like the first thing that I've managed to give any clear thought to for weeks. I can't remember the last time that I was able to complete a task like this. Which gives some hope to my GCSEs, thank god. Maybe after this I can give the coursework another try.

I finished the post with a bit about the Free Periods organization and period poverty, to see if as a school we can raise money and awareness for those who can't afford sanitary products. There are so many girls, even in the UK, who miss school because they can't afford to buy sanitary products. It got me thinking they could even be in our school. Maybe this'll help people somehow?

6 p.m.

I feel really proud that I've managed to finish that blog post, so I've printed it out and I'm going to take it in tomorrow and give it to Miss Mills at the start of the day—so that she has plenty of time to look over it and let me know if it's okay before we post next Friday.

While I've been doing this, I've realized I haven't once had any of the negative thoughts that have constantly gone around my head lately. I've not felt helpless or useless, because in a small way I am actually doing something. I am doing something to help other women.

The more I read about women and about feminism, the more I realize how amazing women are—how much we've been through, how much we can stand. But just because we can stand it doesn't mean that we should ever really have to.

Just because you CAN cope with something, doesn't mean that you SHOULD.

6:30 p.m.

The dinner table

"How was your day, love?" Dad asks.

311

"Yeah, it was good, thanks. I got Miss Mills to agree to my Feminist Friday blog so the first one's going to be next Friday. I've already written it," I say excitedly.

Freddie groans and rolls his eyes.

"More feminism! URGH!" he says dramatically. He knows exactly how to wind me up.

"That's great! When can I read it?" Mum asks, ignoring him, as we frequently have to do.

"After dinner?" I ask.

"Perfect! Your dad and Freddie can do the washing up as punishment for Freddie's rubbish response to feminism, AGAIN."

"Oh, thanks, son," Dad says, rolling his eyes at Freddie. "I'm a feminist too, I'll have you know." And I think that's very true. I think my dad is a pretty great feminist, actually.

7 p.m.

I sort of wish I hadn't decided to sit right next to Mum while she read it because now I'm watching her face to see if she's REALLY enjoying what she's reading. She lets out a little giggle, which is good because I tried to put in some funny bits, just to keep it relatable.

"Ahh, Kat!" she says, putting it down. "It's so great! SO great! I'm so proud of you!"

She gives me a hug and I feel like I can finally release the breath that I've been keeping in the whole time she was reading.

I'm so pleased that Mum likes it. I need to remember this

next time I worry that she thinks I'm an idiot or a disappointment.

"You know, I was thinking," Mum starts, "about what you were saying to me the other day, about not being feminist enough, and not being pretty enough. I think I just always take for granted that you know how proud of you I am, that you know how in awe I am of how smart you are. But maybe I don't tell you enough? And I should."

I don't know what to say.

"I always hoped that by the time you were a teenager, being a woman would be easier. But now, you've all got so many extra issues to deal with. You girls have to be so tough now and so savvy. And I think the way that you deal with it is amazing. You're so much tougher than I ever was at your age, and now with the way that you've faced everything, well, it blows my mind. I'm so proud of the woman you've become, Kat."

Oh Jesus, I'm going to cry again.

10:30 p.m.

Bed

I feel really grown up tonight. I faced my fears and went back to school. I faced Trudy and Josh in the playground, and I was brave and asked Miss Mills about the blog, and she didn't laugh me out of the school. And I've written my first bit of hard-hitting, feminist journalism.

But now, lying in the dark, I can't seem to stop myself from needing to touch the light switch or I know I won't sleep. I know that I can't do everything at once, I have to take my time and not everything will happen immediately. But I'd really like it if there was a magic fix.

What if when I get older, I still have to touch the light switch, and I get my first boyfriend and then before we go to sleep for the first time together, I'm like, *So sorry, I have to touch the light switch three times before bed to make sure that we don't get murdered by serial killers in our sleep or eaten by bears or something.*

I am a ridiculous human. I try to remember all the things that Mum said to me. I need to keep those in my head.

11 p.m.

Had a really funny idea. What if instead of Feminist Friday, I called it *The Vagina Monoblogs*? As it's a blog, and it's about women.

Hahahahaha. Imagine Mr. Clarke dealing with that.

AHAHAHAHHAHAHA!

Wednesday, October 31

I_weigh:

Anxiety. A day of the year when everyone is dressed in Hallow-een costumes and the weather is dark and moody is actually absolutely petrifying. Especially for someone who is very anxious anyway.

9:15 a.m.

I give the blog to Miss Mills at the end of the form period. I'm nervous because I really want her to like it and I'm not sure that I can cope with any bad feedback just yet.

12:30 p.m.

The cafeteria

"God, you had a lucky escape," Millie says as we watch Josh and Trudy obsessively selfie-ing every two seconds of them feeding each other their lunches, again.

Weirdly, I've had no desire to Instagram my soggy meat-balls and chips. It's so grim it's becoming a health hazard. Get a grip, people.

"Nick doesn't think Josh is even a model for ASOS either," Dave says casually.

"You what?" All three of us look at him in shock.

"What do you mean, babe?" Sam asks. "We're going to need more info if you're going to drop a bombshell like that."

"Well, have you ever seen proof that he actually is an ASOS model, or is that just what he's told you? Do we even know anyone from his last school?" Dave says.

"We do not," I say. "Because it is in London, but he does have a picture of himself modeling on the ASOS website on his Instagram, though, doesn't he?"

I ask this like a question to the girls because I'm not entirely sure if we have seen one or if I'm imagining it. Millie's already got her phone out and is googling.

"I'm on it, babe. I got this!" she says, holding up a hand. "Also, though, why has Nick never shared this insight with me?"

"It was just something we were talking about, saying all the girls in school have gone a bit loopy for him but no one's got proof, do they?" Dave says reasonably.

"All the girls?" I say, feeling a small bit of jealousy creep up along with a lump in my throat. Have I screwed up my one chance to date someone gorgeous and popular? NO! I go back to reminding myself how boring being his girlfriend would be and how I've had a lucky escape.

"Well, the girls in Sixth Form also seem to think he's a big deal. I think he's been flirting with one of them online from what Nick and Matt were saying the other day."

"SHUT THE FRONT DOOR! Why does my boyfriend never tell

me this kind of important information?" Millie is incandescent with rage.

"It's man talk," Dave says, like we should all agree that THAT's a suitable reason for the keeping stuff from us.

"WHO IS HE FLIRTING WITH?" Sam whispers urgently.

"Just some girl in Nick and Matt's year. I forget her name. He was flirting with her anyway, but she lost interest for some reason. I can't remember. Ask Nick or Matt about it," Dave says.

"Oh my GOD, WE WILL. You're all USELESS!" Sam pouts.

"Sorry, I guess I didn't know it was SO INTERESTING," Dave says, also sulking.

"You have so much to learn, Dave. So, so much," Millie says, patting his hand.

2 p.m.

Chemistry

If he's flirting with everyone, I guess that means he probably was flirting with me, but it doesn't make me special because he's been doing it with all the girls. I don't know if this is a good thing or a bad thing. I can't work out in my head if I'm a mega loser or if I should just feel good about myself because thank god I'm not with him when he's flirting with other girls. Poor Trudy, though.

I don't think I've ever felt sorry for Trudy before. I'm not sure I really should now.

317

Unfeminist thoughts: 1 (I know I said I wouldn't but this is a bad one)

Relishing in idle gossip about another woman's messy relationship, i.e., Josh being a bit of a cheating shit, apparently.

Thursday, November 1

Relief! That no one is dressed up like a horror film today.

4:30 p.m.

On the sofa

Today nothing really good happened, but nothing really bad happened, and after the last few weeks, I feel like being somewhere in the middle, without either extremes, is the greatest thing for me.

The girls are both studying with their boyfriends, Freddie's out with Issy doing whatever it is that young losers in love do, and Matt and I are watching *RuPaul's Drag Race* on the sofa with a massive bag of sweets.

"How are you feeling about your second therapy session tomorrow?

"Good. I think. I like her a lot. And I slept like a baby after last time, weirdly."

"I can pop over in the evening afterward, if you like? Catch up on more Netflix?"

"Sounds good to me!" I say.

Matt starts to shuffle like he's got something else to say. Sure enough . . .

"I have some news but it's secret . . ."

Oh thank god, a change of subject. What news, though?

"Tell me?" I say casually, but I can't help worrying that something might be about to change.

"I've met someone."

"Shut the front door! Who? Do I know him?"

"He, um, he goes to St. Augustine's." One of the other schools in our town, the more religious one.

I've sat upright, strawberry lace dangling half out of my mouth. I must look a bit like a baby bird with a worm. "Tell me everything about him immediately, please!"

"Well, he's called Si, and he's in the same year as me. He's good at art and I met him at life drawing class."

"Naked man or naked woman?" I interject.

"Man, very old, a lot of wrinkles. We bonded over the wrinkles."

I wonder if it was the same man that Sam drew naked. The Town Naked Man.

"It's super early days. We met at the start of term. We like the same films and music. I introduced him to Mum last night, although actually accidentally because I didn't realize she'd be home early from work. I think you'd like him and I'd really like it if you met him."

"AHHHHHH, I'm so pleased for you!" I say, giving Matt a big hug, and I realize that I really do mean it. For the first time in ages, someone's told me about their love life and I don't feel jealous, or petrified about my own—I just feel overwhelmingly happy for him. This is progress. Maybe I'm becoming a better person?

"I'd like to meet him too! I need to inspect him and check he's good enough!" I say, and Matt shoves his head in his hands.

"Speaking of relationships . . ." I start. "I have another question for you! Dave said that you and Nick don't think Josh is a real ASOS model and that he had been flirting with some girl in your year? What? Who? When? Where? Immediately, please!"

Everything is much more fun now that I've realized that Josh is just a mess that I don't want to be a part of.

"Well, I've been meaning to tell you for a while but didn't know if you were ready. So, it goes like this: One, I don't think he IS an ASOS MODEL because surely he'd just be A MODEL. He'd be doing other modeling jobs too, but he's never said anything about that. He doesn't seem to have an agency, and you can't see any modeling photos when you google him. That shot on his Instagram could have been put together by anyone with any kind of Photoshop skills."

This all makes total sense and I nod in agreement, already starting to feel foolish that I was in any way taken in by him.

"Two, he was flirting with Tracey Fowler in our year and she said that his stories just didn't add up. Like he'd always tell her he was off on a shoot and then she'd see him hanging out in town with Trudy. So, he's kind of a liar and not even very smart about it either."

"Oh my god. What a total loser. Why would he pretend to be something he's not when it would be so easy to get found out?"

Matt shrugs at me.

"Not a clue, Kitty Kat, but he's one fishy guy. He reminds me a bit of Terry, and I'd say you're well rid of him."

The more I hear this, the easier it is to believe it.

Friday, November 2

I_weigh:

A whole week back at school with no embarrassing incidents or panic attacks. HURRAH!

3:50 p.m.

Sarah's office

I thought it would feel weird coming here by myself, but it turns out that it was okay. I was nervous that I'd get lost and miss my appointment or something. But I got here with ten minutes to spare, so now I'm staring at the inspirational quotes on the walls and wondering what on earth we're going to talk about this week.

4 p.m.

"How's your week been?" Sarah asks.

"It's been . . . okay," I say, feeling a bit surprised that I can say that honestly.

"And have you had any anxiety attacks?"

"I've felt my chest tightening, yeah, but when I do my breathing exercises, it helps a bit," I say.

"That's good!" Sarah says. "Remember, though, it's a process. If you have a bad one, it doesn't mean you're going backward."

"Okay. Got it."

"I thought we'd go back and talk about some of the things we touched on last week, maybe start to look at them in more detail?"

"Okay," I say.

"We talked last week about feminism. Do you want to talk about that a bit more?"

"Er, yes, sure. I mean, Mum and Sandra, that's my friend Matt's mum, talked to me about it over the summer and I guess I thought I'd feel more like a woman by now, and maybe feminism would help with that? But it's just made me feel more confused."

"And what do you think it feels like to be a woman?"

5 p.m.

It's a bit weird when you've spent an hour in a little bubble, sharing your secrets with someone, looking at your thought bingo grid, and thinking about things you don't want to think about, and then there's the real world, waiting for you. I feel exhausted and a bit sad, even though most of it was positive. But talking about myself so much made me realize I don't feel so great about me.

8 p.m.

On the sofa with Matt

324

"So, I was wondering if you fancied coming for ice cream to meet Si tomorrow?" Matt asks.

"OH MY GOD! It's time to meet the parents?" I ask, clutching my chest.

"I'll revoke my invite if you can't behave," he says.

"Sorry, sir. Will absolutely behave! Please don't do that! COUNT ME IN!"

I'm so excited and honored. I don't think anyone has met Si yet. I'm going to be the first. I can't bloody wait.

Saturday, November 3

I_weigh:

URGH—*I didn't sleep well last night and now I'm struggling a bit. I feel more anxious than usual and a bit like I might cry for no reason.*

2 p.m.

Walking into town

I said I'd meet them both there, which means that I've walked into town by myself. The first bit by my house was really calm and relaxing, but as I got closer to town, I got more and more stressed out, because it meant that I was getting closer to potentially bumping into Trudy. I've been like a cat on high alert for the last ten minutes, but fortunately I'm nearly there now. Home stretch.

2:05 p.m.

Why does the outside world have to be so scary sometimes, though? Right, just got to get across the road, I can see Scoops now. I'm nearly there. I've just got to wait for the lights to change and get there. My vision's going a bit misty, though, and I think I might just need to do some counting of my breaths.

One . . . two . . . three . . .

Lights have changed. I'm going for it. Just one foot in front of the other and keep breathing . . .

I've realized that actually I'm quite nervous about what Si thinks of me. What if he doesn't like me? Will Matt have to choose between us? What if Si just highlights to Matt how much of a loser I am?

For god's sake, I haven't even met him yet and I'm already assuming the worst. Chill OUT, Kat.

I'm there. I just need to take some breaths before I go inside so that I don't meet Matt's new boyfriend in the middle of a panic attack.

2:08 p.m.

Scoops ice cream parlor

"HEY!" Matt says a little too loudly to me. I guess I'm not the only one a bit nervous about this meeting, then!

Si stands up. "You must be the famous Kat!"

He's taller than Matt, with dark hair and eyes. I mean, I don't want to make Matt too big headed so I'll probably keep this thought to myself—but he is a dreamboat.

"And you must be the famous Si!" I say back. Quite cheesy but I think it's okay.

"It's nice to meet you," Si says. "Matt says you're basically his sister."

I'm so touched by this that I think I might cry. But I keep it together. Come on, Kat.

3 p.m.

The last hour seems to have flown by. Si's really funny and friendly. It's made me happy to see Matt so happy and with someone who's clearly so into him.

We've told him all about Terrible Trudy and Shit Josh, who he says have the best names for a couple ever, and he's currently looking at Josh's Instagram.

"He's not a model!" he declares. "There's no way. That's just a mock-up of him on a page of the ASOS website."

I definitely feel dumb that he is now the third person to say this to me and I didn't clock it sooner.

"It's such a stupid lie, though!" I say.

"I guess he wanted to make a mark on his new school. I mean, coming into a new school at the end of the year is really tough."

For a moment, I feel sorry for Shit Josh, which I didn't think was possible. You'd have to feel pretty low about yourself to think telling lies like that is the only way people will like you.

But then I remember that he treated me like absolute crap, and I'm over it.

11 p.m.

Bed

I touch the light switch three times.

I wonder when that's going to feel less essential.

Unfeminist thoughts: 1

Pleased that Trudy was tricked by the fake ASOS model too.
Ooops.

Monday, November 5

I_weigh:

Being able to laugh even though things feel hard.

9 a.m.

Assembly

It's kind of horrible being in a room with everyone in your whole year. I've never felt this claustrophobic during assembly before. I'm glad that Millie and Sam are next to me, and I'm glad that I can just look down and think about my breathing if I feel panicked.

"Morning," Mr. Clarke starts.

I wonder what his topic will be this week. Nothing could be as good as dick-pic fest.

"RECYCLING!" he booms to the hall, and everyone immediately switches off.

I'm starting to feel much more comfortable, though. Just as everyone's staring at the floor, preparing themselves to sit for ten minutes in utter boredom, a noise comes from the back of the room.

"DICK, DICK, DICK, DICK, DICK PICS!" it repeats over and over again. It's Mr. Clarke's voice and it's been remixed.

The whole year group falls apart laughing while the remix goes on repeat before changing to "LADY BITS" loudly. I think I might actually be starting to enjoy myself.

Even Miss Mills has her hand over her mouth and seems to be suppressing quite the giggle.

"WHO'S DOING THAT? STOP IT THIS INSTANT!"

Clarke's gone bright beet red in color, shaking his fist, and all it's doing is making everyone laugh at him even more.

"DICK. DICK. D. D. D. D. D. DICK PICS."

It was definitely Comedy Krish and he's a genius, but I note that once again the patriarchy has taken over. Why does everything have to be about dicks?

I think this week might actually be okay. And I'm overthrowing the dicks and approaching it with a BIG VAGINA ENERGY, guys.

Unfeminist thoughts: 1

Dick jokes are funny. (Not as funny as vagina ones, though.)

Tuesday, November 6

I_weigh:

The gender pay gap—I'm pretty sure my little brother Freddie definitely gets more allowance than me and he doesn't even have to pay tampon tax. The patriarchy is real and in this very house.

5 p.m.

The bathroom

Why? Why, why, WHY? My period is early. I was hoping to be able to try out my new smaller menstrual cup for this one but it hasn't arrived yet. That's the thing about periods, they always make out on TV shows like they're predictable and everyone knows when they're coming. Do you know what? WE DON'T! Not all the time! It's one of life's great treats!

SURPRISE! You shouldn't have worn a white skirt today!

SURPRISE! You've woken up to a murder all over your bed!

SURPRISE! Should have sat on a plastic sheet!

THANKS, NATURE.

I repeat: God is definitely not a woman.

Unfeminist thoughts: 1

Hating my bloody period.

Wednesday, November 1

I_weigh:

The weight of mystery. How does this happen? HOW? It can't be that big up there, can it? Maybe I do have a horse's collar, after all.

7:45 a.m.

The bathroom

Where the fucking fuck is the fucking tampon string? As if it's not bad enough that my unpredictable period came a week early, I can't even find the fucking tampon I put in now?

This happened to Sam once and she nearly had to go to the doctor to get it removed. I remember her sister telling us that there really is nowhere for it to go so there's no point in panicking. There's no way it can swim up inside your body from your vagina and all the way out of your mouth or ear or something during polite conversation.

But WHAT IF I'm the one exception to that? No one's ever checked that my bits are all as they should be! For all I know, I could be the one person who has that body where the tampon goes for a swim and comes out of your nose a week later, accompanied by some toxic shock syndrome?

I just need to stay calm and remember that it's just a tampon. This may be worse than the whole menstrual cup thing.

Actually, no, nothing is worse than throwing a menstrual cup at the school hottie/dickhead. I'm lying to myself to try to make my past traumas seem less bad.

Okay, right, I'm going to have to have a bit more of a rummage. A deep dive, if you will. It's okay. I'm a modern woman and my vagina is part of me. I do not need to be afraid of it. I can do this.

I am not afraid of my own menstruating vagina

I am not afraid of my own menstruating vagina

I am not afraid of my own menstruating vagina

Oh my god, it's so icky in there. Right. I'll just find it quick and get out of there.

For god's sake, where could it be? COME ON!

GOT IT! SUCCESS!

Thank god for that.

I appear to be holding it aloft like some kind of trophy. Like a hunter with their prey. A small bloody mouse.

I literally cannot believe that after all that, I'm about to shove another one in there.

Unfeminist thoughts: 1

Why does my vagina have to be so contrary?

Thursday, November 8

8:00 a.m.

I grab the ten thousand tampons I'll need to get through today's heavy flow at school. Feeling so lucky that Dad always buys a healthy stock in his weekly shopping trips. I never noticed before, but I think he really is a feminist. I'm lucky I'm never caught without, and pleased that tomorrow I should be taking delivery of my new menstrual cup. A second attempt at stemming the flow in a more eco-friendly way. I've moved on from my previous embarrassment and I'm starting to feel better about things. I feel like I'm ready to try again.

And that's when it hits me. . . . A proper plan for some activism.

12:45 p.m.

The cafeteria

"So I was wondering if you guys wanted to help me with something after school tomorrow? Something for feminism?" I ask.

"OOHHHH!" Millie squeals. "It's been ages since we did some feminisming! What did you have in mind?"

"Have you heard of Free Periods?"

"Oh god, is that when you don't wear a tampon or menstrual

cup or anything and free-bleed everywhere? Because I don't think I'm down for that at school, babe . . . ," Sam says.

"Babe. No," Millie whispers at me while staring like a rabbit in headlights.

"Ha! No, it's not that! It's a charity for girls who can't afford tampons. Not just in other countries either, here as well. So this charity helps raise awareness and money to give out free sanitary products."

"What? But if girls can't afford tampons, what do they do? I don't understand. I don't know how I'd cope without them," Sam says.

"There are a huge number of girls probably not even that far away from us who can't go to school once a month and fall behind. It's awful," I say.

"That IS awful!" Millie's mind is obviously completely boggling at this.

"Also, sort of related, we're still charged tax on tampons in this country—they're classed as a luxury item, apparently."

"You what?" Millie turns around slowly. "HOW ARE THEY A LUXURY?"

"Right! So, what are we going to do?" Sam's always about the action. I love that about her.

"I have an idea . . . ," I start, with my devious plotting face on (which coincidentally looks a lot like my scared face).

Sam puts down her sandwich. "Babe, I've just realized. Why do we always have to talk about periods at lunch?"

4 p.m.

My bedroom

We have everything we need laid out on the floor. Millie, Sam, Matt, Dave, and Nick are all around, helping with a little bit of PR to go alongside my first ever Feminist Friday blog.

"Okay, so here's the plan: we draw sanitary pads and/or tampons covered in the red paint onto the posters—you can use Google image search if you need, but I'd use your imagination for the blood." I ignore the boys making immature faces. "Then we need to paint 'Feminist Friday supports FreePeriods.org' on them. Then place some tampons and pads into the small cloth bags and write 'Free for those who need them,' and staple the bags to the posters. I've calculated we need about twenty to go around the school effectively. So, GET BLEEDING, PEOPLE!" I clap my hands together.

Matt, Nick, and Dave are all looking at me like I'm the most disgusting thing on earth.

"This is why I don't hang out with them so much anymore," Matt's explaining to Nick and Dave.

Traitor. Also, with how his mum painted their house, you'd think he'd feel right at home.

Watching the boys trying to touch the sanitary products is one of the most amusing things I've ever seen. They all have a different way of dealing with it. Dave is holding everything between thumb and forefinger as if it might break. Nick is the most comfortable with it. I wonder if that's an age thing or just that having three sisters means that he's seen a lot of tampons in his life. His drawings are very realistic, anyway.

Matt is probably the worst one. You'd think the tampons were alive, the way he's behaving. At one point he lets out a yelp and throws a tampon and one of the little bags across the room. Poor Bea raises an eyebrow at all this. She's not impressed, not one bit.

Meanwhile, Sam, Millie, and I are very much enjoying tampon crafting hour. Very, very much.

4:30 p.m.

Still crafting

"We've run out of red paint!" Millie howls. "And we've still got ten posters to make!"

"It's okay. I'll sort it out." I know exactly what to do. I head downstairs to the fridge.

6 p.m.

Dinner with Mum, Dad, and Freddie

"Where on earth is the ketchup? Freddie! Did you finish the ketchup without saying anything again?"

Mum shall sadly never find her ketchup.

For the ketchup is on protest drawings of tampons, under my bed.

Sorry, Mum.

6:15 p.m.

Freddie can tell that the lack of ketchup had something to do with me. I don't know how he knows, because he wasn't here, but he definitely knows.

He's glaring at me as he eats his dry chips, swigging water between bites to get them down. The only reason he's not told anyone his suspicions is probably because the claggy mass of dry chip in his mouth is preventing him from talking. I know it is for the rest of us.

To be fair, Dad bought the healthier chips. So this is partly his fault. They've got no salt, no oil, no fat, just oven baked, dry potato. Not even ketchup could save us now.

11 p.m.

In bed

I'm a mixture of excited and nervous about tomorrow. I can't believe I've finally gotten Feminist Friday going, and it's actually happening tomorrow. A couple of weeks ago, this would have seemed completely impossible. Now I'm still anxious about it, but I've done it and I'm actually quite proud of myself for pushing through even though I'm nervous.

I touch the light switch three times, but I know that with how far I've already come, maybe one day I can stop doing that too.

Friday, November 9

Feminist Friday #1

I_weigh:

FEAR. How will the blog post go down? Will we get the posters hung up before school starts? And what kind of trouble will we get into this time? Although we're not actually defacing anything—we're not doing anything permanent. I don't think that we can get into trouble for this. Can we?

7:30 a.m.

"I'm off to school, byeeee!" I shout as I launch out of the door to meet the girls with all my posters concealed in a black bin liner.

I hear Mum and Dad making shocked and questioning noises behind me, but I leave so quickly that they don't have time to catch me.

"Ready?" I ask the girls.

"Let's paint this school red!" Sam sings with joy.

8:45 a.m.

By the time everyone showed up, two things were in place:

1. My blog post was live and ready to be read.
2. The posters were up around the school.

I can see people looking at them and then reaching for their phones. Mostly girls. I can see boys looking at them and making fun of them. Oh well.

I see Trudy making a face. She's so clearly disgusted by them, and yet that would have to mean that she was slightly disgusted by herself. Poor Trudy.

11 a.m.

The response to the blog has been huge. Quite a few boys have written in the comments, mostly the same sort of thing. "When's MAN Friday?" "Which day of the week is for masculinity?"

A bit sad, really, because it means they still haven't grasped quite how much power and advantage men have had up till this point. How women have been kept in the background, and how the patriarchy controls everything. They don't need a day; they have every day. Or they have grasped it and they think that's the way it should be, in which case they can get back to the 1800s where they belong.

Mostly the response has been really good, though. That is, until two minutes ago when I was sitting in biology and received a message that I needed to go and see Mr. Clarke at lunchtime. Oh god.

Last time I did something for feminism, he wasn't exactly over the moon about it. But I haven't damaged any property this time, I haven't defaced anything. All I've done is put up some sanitary products with ketchup on them. If he finds that so offensive, then I have to question how grown up he is, really.

12:15 p.m.

Outside the administrator offices. Again

Nervously waiting for Mr. Clarke to call me into his office. I'm trying to channel the suffragettes. I'm planning what I'm going to say, about how periods are natural and that this is an important issue. Screw you—that kind of thing.

"KATERINA EVANS!" I hear him shout from behind the big office door.

I stand up, take a deep breath, and walk in, more steadily and confidently than I feel.

"Sit down, Katerina."

I take a seat on the tiny chair opposite his desk—the tiny chair that I'm sure is supposed to make whoever is sitting opposite him feel even smaller than they actually are.

"Now, Kat, I read your blog and I have to say I'm very impressed."

That was not what I was expecting.

His face still looks weird, though.

"Oh, thanks." I am suspicious. There must be a catch.

"And I've seen the posters that you put up around the school. . . ." He's giving me a stern look (I think?) now so I probably am in a degree of trouble about that? Maybe? Oh god.

"Erm, yeah," I mumble to the floor. I so wish the girls were here with me too and that I'd not gone into this one on my own. Actually, how come they haven't been summoned too?

"Obviously, it would have been better for you to have gotten permission first, before you put up the, ermmm, essentials." He's gone bright red and I've realized that the weird look on his face is him being a bit EMBARRASSED.

"But it was incredibly, erm, effective and has had quite an impact on a lot of teachers this morning. I don't think I realized that it was such a widespread problem. As you know, we're committed to equality in this school, and this has really struck me. Miss Mills has suggested setting up donation boxes in the toilets where girls can leave, erm, items for other girls who may be less fortunate to use."

I can't believe it. That's such a great idea! It's a shame Mr. Clarke looks like he may die from embarrassment now.

"If you could announce it in your . . . erm . . . blog next Friday and explain how it would work, I would be most grateful. Thank you."

I'm literally BEAMING at him.

"I believe that is going to be a weekly feature as well. So congratulations on that. I will also be placing a box in reception to collect monetary donations from the staff and any visitors to the school for the Free Periods charity."

I'm quite shocked, mostly because I didn't think something that I did could have such a direct and quick response. I know it's just one school, but right now I feel like I've done something good, and if I can do this, what else am I capable of?

"Thank you, sir!" I say. I feel ecstatic.

"No, thank you. For bringing this important matter to my attention. Maybe we'll get those attendance numbers up a bit, eh?" He lets out a little uncomfortable chuckle.

The girls are NOT going to believe this when I tell them about it.

12:30 p.m.

The cafeteria

I'm chasing bits of pasta around my plate, far too excited to eat anything. I've just told the guys about the MOST AWKWARD BUT BEST PERIOD CHAT IN HISTORY.

"Oh my god, babe, you've made a change! You've done what people are always talking about—you've seen an injustice and you've fixed it!" Sam's over her Mooncup about it.

"I'm just glad that none of our art was in vain!" says Nick, who's joined us to celebrate, along with Matt and Dave. They are now fully fledged feminists and seem to be quite proud of it. I'm quite proud of them too. I need to find a way to thank Nick, Dave, and Matt properly, really. Especially as they were so hands on.

"Though may that be the first and last time I draw a tampon, please!" Matt says.

Maybe not Matt.

I also texted Mum and let her know that the blog post made

345

a difference. I didn't mention the posters, which makes me feel a little bad, but tiny white lies are okay, right? She's really proud of me anyway, and I don't think she'd mind sacrificing the ketchup to such a good cause. I can't wait to tell Dad later.

Even Freddie gave me a small nod in the cafeteria just now. He normally prefers to pretend I don't exist at school, so that really meant a lot, actually.

"Why don't we go and get some ice cream tomorrow before Salma's party to celebrate properly?" Millie suggests.

"As long as no one gets strawberry sauce, I'm in," Matt says, grinning.

Which surprises me because I thought he was hanging out with Si.

"Do you mind if I bring Si?"

Ahhhh. I get a fuzzy warm feeling for how happy he looks.

4 p.m.

Therapy session number three

I'm getting better at this now. It feels more normal to be coming here, and I wasn't distracted by the thought of it all day. Progress?

4:15 p.m.

Sarah's laughing because I've just finished telling her about the posters and the campaign, along with Feminist Friday.

"On a serious note, though, Kat, what you've done is amazing. You've not just written your first blog post, you've done something that's really made a change and is going to help people. So I have to ask, how do you feel about being a woman now?"

I did not see that coming. Jesus. She's good.

5:15 p.m.

Walking home

It's finally started to feel a bit more wintery, and weirdly I've realized I always feel colder than normal after therapy. Like my worries were somehow keeping me warm, or I've exposed myself so much that I need to layer up and protect myself once I head back into the real world.

Therapy got hard after Sarah's killer question. I'd had such a good day and it was great talking about it all. But then she hit me with that, and we started on how I feel about myself, and how I worry that actually I'm not a nice person, really, and that inside I'm horrible. And then I cried. Now I feel weird. Like I've had the nicest day, with the best things happening, and then I've cried and gotten upset about myself. I guess I can't always be progressing forward, sometimes there have to be some backward steps as well. Just gotta keep going, I guess.

Ack.

7 p.m.

The kitchen

Dad's really proud of me for my activisming and for going to therapy by myself, so he made my favorite dinner of all time (spaghetti) and now we're watching some *Schitt's Creek* because it's so funny it might take my mind off things. Freddie's over at Issy's, so it's just little old me sitting at home with my parents.

It's weirdly comforting, though, to be around Mum and Dad, who are acting like their usual lunatic selves. Even if it is Friday night and I'm supposed to be out being young and disruptive rather than in watching Netflix.

I might be the world's first fifteen-year-old spinster.

10:15 p.m.

I've paused before touching the light switch. Sarah and I talked today about if I didn't touch it tonight.

What would happen?

And then my mind starts playing out all the things that could happen if I don't. I've achieved a fair amount today. My first work as a journalist, tampon donation boxes at school, and my third ever therapy appointment.

Maybe it's not for today. But soon. I remind myself that it doesn't mean I've failed, it means that I'm working on it.

I'm doing my best, and that's what's important.

Saturday, November 10

I_weigh:

Anxiety about the party but I'm going to be with the others and who knows, I might even enjoy myself?

10 a.m.

I didn't really sleep last night because I was worrying about the party. There's a huge part of me that wants to make it simple and just not go, but I know that I NEED to go. It's part of getting better. I'll be with my friends and it'll all be okay.

2 p.m.

Scoops ice cream parlor

The boys seemed to be under the illusion that we were going to share ice cream with them. We've corrected them and they now thankfully know better than to ever assume such a terrible thing again.

Idiots.

"A toast!" yells Sam, raising her enormous sundae glass to the sky. "To Kat! QUEEN OF THE TAMPONS!"

I bury my head in my hands as everyone recites it after her even MORE LOUDLY, and raises their spoons.

Everyone turns to look at us, including a table of older

people who look a bit shocked. God knows what they'd think of menstrual cups and period pants.

Si's happily joining in while we loudly talk about menstruation—it feels like it's part of the initiation process if you want to hang out with us now.

We're all still messing around when Josh walks past the window with Tiffany, as in, Trudy's Third Bitch in Command. And no Trudy.

We look at each other, jaws dropped.

"What's Shit Josh doing with Tiffany on his own?" Matt asks.

We all know that Trudy Would Not Stand For This.

"Probably sex," I say flippantly.

"Oh my god!" Matt says. "What if he's sleeping his way around allll The Bitches. . . . Every. Single. Last. Bitch?"

We collectively gasp at him.

"Okay, so I missed him walking past," says Si, "but I've seen pictures, and he does NOT look that hot. I mean, he's all right, but he's not good enough for you, Kat. He looks too dull. He doesn't seem to ever actually do anything other than pose on his feed. Yawn."

Wow. Si's just done a full-blown assassination of the man who broke my heart in front of everyone, and I'm so unbelievably grateful. I could kiss him.

"I think I love you," I say to him, beaming.

"Hands off, he's mine!" Matt says. "You are quite right, though, and quite dreamy," he tells Si, laughing as the two of them kiss.

"Are him and Turdy Trudy going to be at this party tonight?" Si asks.

"Unfortunately, yes." I sigh, slightly annoyed with myself that I've never thought to call her Turdy Trudy (unfeminist thought alert).

"Wonderful. Nothing quite like meeting a pair of monsters in real life!" Si says gleefully.

6 p.m.

Millie's bedroom, hiding from the lovebirds

We're all at Millie's house, getting ready for the party, or in my case, trying to control my preparty anxiety. We're supposed to be keeping an eye on Freddie and Issy while Millie's parents are out, but they were feeding each other popcorn on the sofa so we made retching noises at them and they got angry. Which I guess is fair. But where did they learn that feeding each other was cool? I bet they got that from watching Trudy and Josh at school—proof that their disgusting displays of PDA are actually DAMAGING OUR YOUTH. I already feel a bit sick with nerves about the party, they might push me over the edge to actual vomsville.

We're nearly ready. I've gone for my staple of miniskirt, black top, and biker jacket, with my suede boots. Sam's wearing a playsuit and Millie's wearing a jumpsuit. I think we all look really cool. I felt dingy for recycling an old favorite but I really like it. Also, I'm just being eco-friendly, there's no shame in recycling outfits now that we know how harmful fast fashion can be for the environment. I'm still nervous, but feeling confident in my outfit helps.

7:30 p.m.

Salma's house

OMG, how does anyone get this rich? Salma's house is like some kind of surburban palace. And more to the point, why do parents with houses like these EVER go away and leave their offspring to their own devices? Have they never watched a teen movie?

When we arrive, we find Matt, Si, Dave, and Nick standing in the kitchen, watching as some absolute moron attempts to drink a yard of some kind of blue punch out of one of those wackily long glasses. Liquid is dripping down his mouth and chin like he's a toddler.

"He's going to be so sick," Matt says wisely, shuffling backward. "And when he is, I want him nowhere near me."

"Why do straight boys do these things?" Si says. "Do they think it impresses women? Because I can tell you, not one of these women here is going to drop their knickers for this specimen tonight."

We survey the room and they're right: all the girls here are looking on more in horror than anything else. One of them is asking whether we should be preemptively phoning an ambulance because it's actually very dangerous to drink that much punch, especially when several people have now spiked it.

"I can see we haven't missed anything then," says Sam.

"Not a thing. Just idiocy, laddishness, and embarrassment," says Dave.

"Shall we go to the garden before the hurling starts?" I ask.

7:40 p.m.

Salma's garden with many interesting (read: batshit) sculptures. I mean, I've heard about people having more money than sense, but now I'm SEEING it

We've been at this party for, like, ten minutes, and already I can tell it's going to be an eventful one. The therapist told me that alcohol is a depressant so I'm not drinking, and I find that I'm weirdly having more fun without it, but I can see everyone else getting nicely carried away. And I'm probably getting high off the weed cloud that seems to be hanging over the garden anyway. I mean, come on, this isn't the sixties, people.

Trudy and Shit Josh have just arrived with TB following in hot pursuit, including Tiffany, the sly dog. Trudy is wearing an almost identical outfit to me and as I've worn this one many times before, I can only assume that imitation really is the sincerest form of flattery.

One of the "pieces of art" is a giant fountain with a naked stone sculpture of a man in its center. A very well-endowed man, at that. I'm far more intrigued by his schlong than I am by watching Trudy attempting to make a grand entrance, to be honest.

I mean they're not all that big, are they? Si comes to stand next to me and sees where I'm looking. He puts his arm around me, and we stare ahead at the fountain together.

"I've never seen a schlong that long," he says, sighing.

8 p.m.

Back in the kitchen. We got intimidated by the long schlong

We're now watching the third moron from the year above attempting to drink a yard of a lethal blue booze concoction, and I cannot help but wonder if we'll need a whole fleet of ambulances. Turns out it is just a tiny bit dull watching other people drink when you're completely sober and in charge of all your faculties, but at least I've started to worry less what people think of me, mostly as most people are acting far more twatily than I ever could.

I think I'm going to just pop to the loo. Give myself something to do.

8:05 p.m.

Outside the toilet

The door's a bit stiff and I can't tell if there's someone in there or not. I've tried knocking and gotten no response, so I'm just going to give it a bit of a wiggle. I'm probably putting more force into it than is strictly necessary right now, but I suddenly really need the loo quite badly and I could do without adding WETTING MYSELF to my list of dramas for this term.

Just as I'm pushing all my weight forward, the door springs open—and so does my mouth.

On the floor in front of me, FROLICKING SHIRTLESS, is Shit Josh. But he's not accompanied by Trudy, as I would have expected, or even by Tiffany. His bathroom-banging companion seems to be none other than Second Bitch in Command, Amelie.

"Oh. My. God," I say.

Other people have noticed now. Everyone crowds around as we all watch Josh scramble his shirt back on like an awful horror show.

I'm sort of annoyed with myself that I was too shocked to focus on getting a better peek at his schlong.

URGH, what am I saying? I'm not some kind of female #Tim. That was super creepy of me. Although, you know, only human and curious. I've never seen a real one head-on like that.

"TRUDDDYYYYYYY!" I hear another TB scream at decibels that could probably be heard on the moon. "TRUDDDDYYYYYYYYYYYY!" She's really going to carry on with that until Trudy comes and sees this for herself, I guess. The rest of us have got our hands over our ears, protecting our hearing.

I see Trudy coming up the stairs.

She's not happy. "What on earth is your problem, bitch? Why are you making my name some kind of mating call from a deranged . . . oh . . . my . . . god . . . ," she says, slowing down and staring at Josh and Amelie, who are still scrabbling to make themselves look decent. They'd really gotten down to it. Josh has only just found his trousers in the bath.

Even as they're pulling on items of clothing, other bits are falling off. I've seen both of Amelie's boobs at least twice, like she can't contain them no matter how hard she tries, and Shit Josh's penis may be back in its clothes, but it's very much still ready for action.

I mean.

There seems to be some kind of standoff: Trudy staring into the bathroom wordlessly; Josh and Amelie staring at the floor, not looking at her. I finally understand the expression "You could cut the tension with a knife." Or some kind of machete, in this instance.

Out of nowhere, one of the booze-chugging losers from the kitchen appears, hurtling through the crowd. Clearly not realizing the importance of what's happening around him, he catapults himself into the bathroom, only to miss the toilet, leaving Josh and Amelie not just disgraced but now covered in vom as well.

I guess the hurling has started.

Tension Towers

The puke has broken the tension somewhat. Trudy no longer appears to be staring through the two of them with such a level of intensity that I was starting to wonder if she'd actually forgotten how to blink with the shock of it all.

"URGHHH!"

Trudy makes an indescribable noise, as if she's about to explode, and then stomps down the stairs. The rest of TB are following behind at a fast yet shuffly pace, all eager to be the most helpful, now aware that Amelie's place in the pecking order is up for grabs, I should imagine. Also, all looking suitably petrified. No one's ever crossed Trudy before—except me—and we all know what that got me, AND it was just over a bunny.

I turn around to see that Josh's erection still hasn't gone down and, frankly, if someone throwing up on you and being caught by your girlfriend having sex with her best friend doesn't have some kind of excitement-dampening effect, I really question him as a person. Again.

I start to dash down the stairs to find the others and tell them what's happened when I realize that literally everyone at the party is behind me, crammed on the stairs, watching Josh and Amelie in the bathroom.

I find Si and Matt shaking their heads at the back of the crowd.

"I repeat," says Matt, "you've had a lucky escape, Kat, and frankly I expected better, on all fronts."

Si nods at him. "Y-fronts," he says knowingly. "A disaster."

8:30 p.m.

The back garden, close to Schlong Fountain

After finding a vom-less bathroom, the girls and I are in the garden, watching Trudy screaming at Josh. They're pretty pleased for me about how this is all panning out. We're too far away to hear what he's muttering to her, but we can all hear exactly what she's SHOUTING at him.

She's called Amelie a skank more times than any of us can count. She's also called her an ugly hoebag, a beast, and suggested more than once that she has some kind of STI. She's doing a terrible job for feminism and womankind.

The other bitches are all flapping around Trudy in either protection or fear. I note that Tiffany seems to be vying for top position in the pecking order right now even though, if what we saw earlier is anything to go by, she certainly has her own secrets with Josh too.

Matt and Si have just appeared from inside the house, looking most excitable.

"You will not BELIEVE what we have just heard!" Matt exclaims wildly.

"What? WHAT? What did you hear?" I've not seen Matt like

this since the end of the last season of *Game of Thrones*.

"Well, there are at least twenty Sixth Formers in there with pictures of Josh's dick on their phones. That he sent to them," Si says.

"Oh my god!" I say. "How has he managed to spread it around so far?"

"Oh, I think they've all been talking about it but until now, it's never been such common knowledge, so out there," Matt says.

"Little slime bag," Si says. "If he's sent photos of his dick to twenty girls just in there, god knows how many more have been sent it. All while he's been going out with Trudy."

I feel a pang of something, not jealousy, but maybe something a bit like that, and that makes me a TERRIBLE feminist. AWFUL. My worst offense yet. Or does it just make me human? To wonder why I wasn't deemed hot enough to receive a pic and yet EVERY SINGLE other girl he so much as said hello to was? WHAT IS WRONG WITH ME?

"He never sent a dick pic to me," I say. "Thank god." That's more like it.

"Yeah, trust me, you don't want it," says Si. "I've seen better."

Matt's face during this exchange is priceless. I imagine their conversation later will be interesting.

Just then Trudy stomps past us and into the house.

"I can't watch this anymore," Sam says. "I don't like her but if he's sent his dick to all those Sixth Formers, and he's definitely fooling around with at least one or two of TB, I don't trust him not to be going even further. We need to tell her the extent of things. I repeat, I DO NOT like her, but I think maybe I dislike him even more now. And feminism . . ." She throws her hands up.

Millie and I nod and follow her in through the house to find Trudy.

8:45 p.m.

The study. Who has a STUDY, FFS? It's even got a huge globe in it, and a whiskey decanter. I feel like I'm in an episode of **Gilmore Girls**

We find Trudy sitting alone. What we weren't prepared for was that she's absolutely bawling her eyes out. I never even knew it was possible. Although our natural response to a crying person is to comfort them, with Trudy we're all standing in a line opposite her as she ugly-cries, staring at each other. None of us want to touch her because we think that might end in combustion or being turned to stone.

"Trudy?" I inch toward her. She's really in no position to lash out at me right now, and someone has to do something to help. Josh can't get away with his behavior.

My first advance seems to have been ignored so I just carry on, hoping that at some point she'll get on board and that she won't actually punch me in the face or something instead.

"The thing is, Trudy, we know that you're upset, but there's more that you should hear," I say.

Millie and Sam are nodding at me for encouragement so I carry on.

"We saw Josh earlier today with Tiffany. And then we heard that he'd been messaging a girl from the Sixth Form but that she turned him down, and then the last thing is that, well . . . after what happened just now in the bathroom, it . . . well . . . it got everyone talking. And it turns out . . . it turns out that he's sent quite a few people pictures of his ermmm . . . dick. He's sent at least twenty people dick pics." I tail off slightly at this point because I feel like I can't really end this on "dick pics," but I've got nothing else to say.

Trudy raises her tear-stained face slowly toward me, eyes narrowed. She looks like she's about to launch herself at me, because to be fair, she's always, always hated me. I have probably just earned myself a good bog-washing or, at the very least, a slap and another few months of being told daily what a twattish loser I am.

Her face is bright, bright red and she's been staring at me without blinking for longer than I thought was humanly possible now. I worry her eyes will be very dry by the end of this evening. If she's going to kill me, then my last words are going to be "dick pics." That is not how a feminist should die.

"You what?" she finally says.

"He's tossing it all over the place, babe," Millie says, waving her arms around. "Lording it about."

"And he's definitely cheating on you with at least one of

your own crew," Sam says. I think she actually just enjoyed sticking the knife in a bit there.

"ARGHHHHHH!" Trudy screams like an actual hyena. "He is going to regret that he was ever BORN! What should I do now? I need a plan. I need to make him pay for this. He needs to fucking PAY! No one makes Trudy look like an ass."

I'm trying not to laugh because in my head I'm imagining a giant ass with her face in the middle and it's giving me great joy. Also, though, what kind of person refers to themself in the third person? An ass.

I know that if I do start laughing, then I am completely dead. But I can see Millie's shoulders shaking slightly and Sam's got her hand over her mouth, suppressing some giggles. I bet they're imagining the ass thing too.

"I have an idea," I say.

9:15 p.m.

The back garden, gathered around Schlong Fountain

As soon as Trudy emerged from the study, people began to follow her. Now the three of us are walking in a line with her, everyone else following behind. It makes me a feel a bit like we're the pied pipers of drama.

No one's seen Amelie for a while, but I swear I can see her shoes over in the bushes and if I listen carefully I'm pretty sure that I can hear the occasional sob. I want to go

362

and see if she's okay, but I also don't want to draw unnecessary attention toward her at this point. She probably wouldn't thank me, and neither would Trudy, who I think is revelling in the fact that she's about to have a pretty big moment.

"Trudy!" Josh exclaims, leaping up from the edge of Schlong Fountain. Seems like a fitting spot for him to me. "I can explain. It wasn't what it looked like. I know you'll have questions, but I can answer them all, I promise!"

"I do have questions, actually!" she says.

"Ask them. I'll answer anything you want me to. Just let me explain! Amelie was throwing herself at me! I don't even like her. Let's go somewhere quiet, away from everyone, and have a proper chat. Without all these people watching."

"Actually, I'm okay right here, and from what I hear, you've already been quite public, anyway."

He's doing a really good impression of someone who doesn't have a clue what she's on about: eyebrows raised, shoulders lifted in an innocent shrug. But really, we know he's faking it, and so do all the girls here who have a picture of his knob to prove it.

"Who here has been sent a picture of my darling boyfriend's penis?" Trudy asks loudly, using a large plant pot for a stage.

"Me!" comes the first voice.

"Me!" the second.

"I have!" the third.

"Me too."

"Me too."

"Me too!"

Voices spring from all over the garden, some even coming from as far as the kitchen. At one point there's a loud bark from the next garden. I mean, none of us would be that surprised if the poor dog actually had received one, as well. It's our very own #TimesUp moment.

How on earth Shit Josh thought he would get away with this is beyond me. Did he think that no one would talk about it? That people would just receive a picture of his dick and never mention it to anyone? It's also really seriously at least ALMOST illegal, I think. It would be illegal to see one you didn't want to on the street, so why wouldn't it be illegal to be forced to see one on your phone? I'm starting to wish I'd paid more attention in that assembly and not just laughed about it.

There's a rustling in the bushes behind us, and Amelie appears.

"What the FUCK, Josh? You said I was special! You said you were breaking up with Trudy and that when you'd sorted everything out that we could be together. You said that Trudy had said I wasn't even a proper friend anyway, and that she's always bitching about me. What the FUCK?"

She's got tears streaming down her face. I'm not surprised. The bastard. Sam puts her arm around her.

"And me," pipes up Tiffany. "He said that you were cheating on him, Trudy, and that you were going to break up anyway. He also said that you were always saying how ugly I am and that no one could ever fancy someone as gross as me."

"That's such a lie! I'd never say that about either of you. I wasn't cheating on him!" Trudy is furious and it's possibly the most human I've ever seen her. I always thought her incapable of emotion before tonight, and now I've seen her have two emotions in one hour.

"Who here actually wanted that picture? Who asked for it? Longed to receive it?" Trudy continues.

Everyone in the garden is shaking their head. I look over at Josh and he's red in the face. He should be. Who taught him he can behave like that? I can't believe I ever fancied this absolute slimeball.

I look over at Matt and Si, who are both shaking their heads in a disapproving manner and giggling to themselves. I think they're a mixture of disgusted at Josh and also enjoying him getting his comeuppance. At the very least, whether it's illegal or not, it confirms what they've suspected about him for a long time: he is a SHITTY person. Not to mention that he pretended to be a feminist when he was talking to me. He told me he thought what I was doing was WOKE. Maybe that's why he didn't send me a pic? He knew as a feminist I wouldn't stand for it.

"You see, Josh, no one wants you, or your sad little penis. You'll never date at our school again, and I'm going to see to it that your life there is made a living hell." Fair play, she's made lives a living hell for much less. "Get out of here and never contact me or any of these people again. You sad, sad bastard."

We all watch as he starts to slink away—but then he seems to have some kind of second wind.

"I don't have to settle for you, anyway. I only wanted to go out with you because you were popular, but everyone thinks you're just some nasty bitch. You're only popular because everyone's afraid of you," Josh spits out.

Wow.

Everything that he's just said is technically true, but I still hate him. I see Si put a foot out as Josh turns to leave. It's as if things have switched to slow motion as we all watch Josh catapult straight into the Schlong Fountain. As he sits under the stream of what looks like wee coming from the massive stone penis, I can't help but think this is the exact, perfect kind of payback his crimes deserve.

"Oh, and Josh?" Trudy says as Josh watches her angrily from the fountain. "We all know you're not a model. Who photoshops a picture of themself modeling on the ASOS website?"

Everyone gasps. Shit Josh just goes bright red, his hair flattened and sopping, thanks to a constant stream of faux urine.

#Tim comes to his rescue and lends him a hand to get out of the fountain. He probably wants tips on how to become even more of a sleaze now that he realizes that the creep crown has been so spectacularly taken from him.

"Who knew?" said Matt. "Turns out that somewhat attractive boys can still be lying, sleazebag assholes."

"Amen to that," Si says next to him.

And I think I finally believe that I deserve much better than that.

10:30 p.m.

The rest of the party moves back to the kitchen now that the action has ended. Trudy and TB lock themselves in the study for some kind of crisis meeting.

I never thought I'd see the day I felt sorry for Trudy, but I can't imagine what it's like to be betrayed by your friends like that. All I do know is that mine would never do that. I feel very lucky.

12 a.m.

In bed

Who could have predicted any of that happening?

And, I DID IT! I went to the party and it was fun and good and nothing bad happened (to me, anyway)! I was so worried people would think I was such a loser for not drinking when everyone else was, and about being the gooseberry without the boyfriend, or that I'd have a panic attack or say or do something that made me a pariah—but somehow tonight:

1. I had a great time.

2. I didn't drink anything and it didn't matter.

3. Despite being the only one without a boyfriend, I didn't once feel left out.

And after all that, I found out what a sleazebag Shit Josh really is. I can't believe I ever wasted my time on him. I also can't believe we helped Trudy tonight, but I'm proud of us for that.

I want to go to sleep without touching the light switch. But then I think about what a great night I've had and I worry that all that will be taken away from me. That I'll wake up tomorrow and it'll all be gone. I need to make sure I'm doing everything I can to prevent that.

I touch the light switch three times, but I have hope that one day I won't have to anymore.

Unfeminist thoughts: 1
Wondering why I didn't get a dick pic too. My most ridiculous and worst thought yet.

Friday, December 14

The day of the play AND MY BIRTHDAY

I_weigh:
The weight of my full sixteen years. Oh, and three boxes of tampons (more on this later!).

7 a.m.

The birthday bedroom

I can hear so much rustling outside my bedroom door. What on EARTH is going on? The door handle jiggles and I hear Sam shouting, "ARE YOU DECENT? INCOMING!"

Oh my god! What are the girls doing here so early?

"YES, COME IN!" I shout back, my duvet gathered around me.

"Happy birthday!" Millie, Sam, Dad, Freddie, Mum, Issy, and Matt shout at me as they come in. Millie and Sam are inexplicably dressed as tigers. I don't even know why, but it's excellent. Poor darling Bea launches herself over to me wearing a little party hat and bow tie that I think she's hoping I'll rescue her from. I was expecting Mum, Dad, and Freddie but not the girls and Matt as well. They must have gotten up pretty early.

"PRESENTS!" Millie shouts, thrusting some small packages and cards my way as they all gather round.

A couple of months ago I thought I'd be spending my birthday alone after we'd fallen out, while they all hung out at a party with Trudy without me. It turns out that instead of feeling lonely on my sixteenth birthday, I feel incredibly loved. And I guess we're not too grown up for birthday surprises, after all.

"Why are you dressed as tigers again?" Matt asks.

"Kat loves them. She told us when we looked like them before," Millie says, clearing it up for no one except the three of us.

8:30 a.m.

The playground

It's FINALLY the school play tonight. Millie and Nick seem to be practicing their big kiss scenes, still. Everyone will be bored of watching them kiss by the time the play starts, if you ask me.

We're ending the year on a high. We've got something big, one last act of feminism planned for the end of term. It turns out that as Millie and Nick worked more and more on *Romeo and Juliet*, they learned that it wasn't the most feminist of plays. . . .

"MOVE!" Trudy slams into us from behind with TB parting the way.

It took a VERY short space of time for Trudy to get back to her normal self after we found out how much Josh had been whanging his willy about. For a short while after the Schlong

Fountain Fiasco, she did try to be nicer to us, but it was creepy and made us feel uncomfortable. She made Amelie and Tiffany pay by performing chores for her for a week before having some kind of pseudo-feminist realization that they were as tricked by Josh as she was, and now they seem to be back in the inner circle. I think it might have had more to do with her worrying that, with her group diminishing, her power was too. But she definitely has all that power back now, and then some. And it's as if we never helped her.

Today is the last Feminist Friday of the term and I wrote about women's mental health. It was scary but I wanted to open up the discussion. I can't be the only person in the school who struggles, and now that I know how isolating and lonely it can feel, how your brain tricks you into thinking that you're weird and no one else would ever feel like that, it felt important to me to be honest.

The girls and Matt have agreed to take on anyone who is rude about it, because it's not weird—it's common—and the more people talk about it, the more we can support each other. So far people have said that it's brave, but I think I've done it as much for me as I did for everyone else. It felt like an important way of taking control.

10 a.m.

Macbeth coursework handed in. Done. Finished. The end. So relieved. Will happily never see that again, ever.

7 p.m.

The Assembly Hall

Millie's been a wreck of nerves all day. Not that I blame her, it would be terrifying enough even without Sophie's mum in the audience. We've been summoned backstage by her three times since getting here at 6:30.

Firstly: so that she could run through the plan with us again and check that we still think it's a good idea—it's a GREAT idea.

Secondly: so that she could ask us for the millionth time whether or not we think she will be suspended for this. I said no. Sam said no. But neither of us are a hundred percent sure, and anyway, being suspended for feminism would be okay? Maybe? Probably not, actually. It's still a suspension. So, you know, fingers crossed! But if she goes down then we're all going down with her. That's the pact.

Thirdly: so that we could bring her a paper bag to breathe into. Fortunately, I have experience of not being able to catch my breath so I'm being quite helpful for her here.

I think Nick's also massively nervous, and now the two of them have been separated into men's and women's dressing rooms. Mr. Clarke said it was to avoid any "hanky panky." Him saying "hanky panky" was gross enough to be good contraception, anyway. Although, he doesn't seem to have realized that the two girls who are playing the nurse and Juliet's mum have just started dating. I imagine that would blow his dinosaur mind.

Dave's saved us some seats near the middle, so we're close enough to see, but far enough away that Millie isn't put off by just seeing our faces all the time from the stage. Sam's mum came over a little while ago to hug her and tell her how AMAZING it all looks. It really does too. She's done so well AND handed in her portfolio in time. She's a superwoman.

I saw Trudy and TB coming in earlier. She glided past me as if I was a nobody, which is actually comforting now.

She's sitting at the back with her minions, making sure it's clear she's absolutely not here because she wants to be, or because she's in any way actually interested in anything that anyone else is doing. She is just here because the rest of the school is. What a boring life, never doing anything you actually enjoy, just being led by FOMO.

7:10 p.m.

Twenty minutes till kickoff

Si and Matt have joined us and we're all getting a bit excited. I'm just thinking about how super nice it is to be here with everyone, supporting my best friend, when I see Shit Josh approaching me from the aisle. He's been doing this on and off for the last few weeks—sort of hovering around me, trying to get my attention with his new best friend #Tim. It's not totally clear what he wants but whatever it is, I'm not interested. I finally know for sure that it's actually him who's the loser and not me.

I'd definitely rather be on my own than with someone like him. You should never settle for someone less than you deserve.

No one's sure if Josh'll still be here next year, anyway. Some parents have complained after what happened and this week the school started investigating the allegations—basically, just collecting enough proof to expel him. It shouldn't be hard, considering almost everyone seems to have something from him on their phone. I don't know what's taking so long, to be honest.

He seems to have taken a seat next to me, and #Tim the one next to that. Three months ago, it would have sent a little wave of electricity shooting down my body, I'd have found it hard to breathe and made weird noises at him instead of speaking. Today, it just makes my skin crawl being near him. He's actually worse than #Tim. At least #Tim is sort of harmless. Now I almost feel like we need to rescue him from Josh too.

"So I've been thinking, we never did get a chance to go on that date. You know?" he says, without even saying hi first.

Wow. Is he doing what I think he's doing? Obviously I do NOT want to go on a date with him. I decide to let him carry on anyway and get to the end, though. I want the full satisfaction of turning him down in the most agonizing way possible.

"I just, I was wondering, if maybe? You know? If you'd? Well, you're not going to make me say it, are you?"

I am going to make him say it, oh yes.

I stare him dead in the eye. He's going to have to finish that sentence. The absolute nerve of him, after everything he's done. To me, to Trudy, to almost every girl in school who had to endure a picture of his gross penis.

374

My low self-esteem and anxiety weren't his doing. They were already in place before he came along—but I just didn't believe I deserved better, and now I know I deserve SO much better.

"So . . . would you, erm, like to go out sometime?" he finally finishes.

What a tosser.

"No, thank you," I say. Poised, dignified, eloquent. Three words. He doesn't deserve more.

"What? But I thought you liked me? And your friends all have boyfriends? I could be yours? We could even up the numbers a bit? And I wasn't ready before, I was still getting to know the school and thought Trudy would be the best person to be my girlfriend."

You what? As if that's a reason to go out with someone. I need a boyfriend to even up the numbers? I'm going to give him SUCH a talking-to.

"As I said, no, thank you. I very much doubt that me or my friends would find having you around preferable to having 'uneven numbers.' In fact, I'm pretty sure I'd rather be slowly eaten by a rabid bear, alone in the wilderness, while being pissed on by a squirrel, than ever go out with you."

Si, Matt, and Dave start clapping next to me, with Sam waving at Josh to signal to him that it's time to go now.

"Not to mention," I carry on, "that we've all seen how you behave in a relationship, and I'm really not looking for a weak weasel who can't be trusted as far as their weaselly self can be thrown," I finish.

Possibly a bit harsh. Or is it? Matt's just put his arm around my shoulders.

"Can we help you with anything else, Josh?" he says, smiling sweetly.

"Mad cow," Josh mutters, standing up and walking away.

"I BEG YOUR PARDON?" Sam shouts at him, getting to her feet.

"Everyone in the school knows she's mad," he says.

Dave stands up next to Sam, fists balled, followed by Matt and Si.

"You what?" Matt says. "I'd say the mad one here isn't the one who's just turned down someone who is SUCH a loser that they've had their penis rejected by almost every girl in the school. What's so mad about having enough self-respect to know that she can do a million times better than you?"

"Exactly," I say. "Please leave, Josh. You're ruining our evening with your bad juju."

"Losers," Josh mutters to himself as he walks away, #Tim in hot and pathetic pursuit.

Matt grabs me into a massive hug, which I'm very grateful to receive.

It makes me realize—if I did let anyone into my life romantically now, they'd have to be pretty great to match up to my life. I have my friends, my family; I have writing, Feminist Friday, and all the campaigning I have yet to do. I feel grateful just as I am. The bar is high, and it shouldn't be anything else.

7:30 p.m.

#Tim has taken Josh to sit in the back row. He's got binoculars and I'm one hundred percent sure that it's nothing to do with poor eyesight. All I'm saying is that I want to see two hands on that pair of binoculars at all times, please.

The lights dim and Sam, Dave, Matt, Si, and I all hold hands in a line. We're excited and proud and can't wait to see Mills (and Nick) doing their thing.

9 p.m.

Christ, Romeo and Juliet *is long. Get on with it*

Millie's lying on the stage, trying to be completely still and make it look like she's not breathing. But every now and then you see her chest heave up and down as she absolutely has to breathe because she's not actually dead.

Nick's beside her, clutching a bottle of poison.

"Thus with a kiss . . ." He kisses Millie (pretty sure I saw her slip him tongue from here), holds the poison aloft, drinks it, clutches at his throat dramatically, and then . . . "I DIE."

He falls to the floor in what I would say was a bit of an overdone death, if I'm being honest. Though not as bad as the guy playing Mercutio earlier, who, clearly livid not to be Romeo, made his death last SIX MINUTES, and used the full length of the stage.

Now is Millie's time—the thing that we've been planning for

these last few weeks running up to the performance.

She sits up, looks at Nick genuinely fondly (I really hope no one's told Sophie's mum that they're together. She'll think this is amazing if they haven't), and then, her face creasing into an angry frown, she begins:

"NOOOO! What did you do that for, you idiot? I put so many signals and messages in place, how could you not understand the plan? No more of this! I'll not kill myself to follow a man. Women have followed men for centuries, and we don't have to anymore!" With this, Millie reaches behind her, pulling down the secret cord that Sam hid in the set, unleashing a sign that says "#FEMINISTSOCIETY January 6th, 12:30 p.m., Room 404."

On the anniversary of #TimesUp at the Golden Globes, we'll be starting our very own movement right here.

"Join us on the sixth of January! It's time to take charge, AND SMASH THE PATRIARCHY!" Millie shouts.

"FREE PERIODS FOR ALL! BAN THE TAMPON TAX!" Nick shouts, springing back up to life and helping Millie grab an array of sanitary products from under their deathbed to throw out into the crowd.

This is also our cue.

We all stand up and make it rain tampons.

I look around, at my friends, watching teachers get hit in the face with tampons in slow motion, Mr. Clarke removing a rogue menstrual cup from his head, and Sophie's mum standing, clapping, with a tampon in hand. Actually, I think sixteen might be my best year yet.

How Not to Be a Confused Feminist

by Kat Evans

1. Feminism isn't about being right or being perfect. It's about helping other women, lifting each other up, not competing against each other. It's not about judgment, it's about support.

2. Men can be feminists too. But when they behave otherwise, it says more about them than it does about you. It's on them. It's not something that you (or I) have done wrong.

3. Menstrual cups come in different sizes. They can work for you—eventually, with a bit of serious jiggling—but everyone's different. Never let anyone else tell you how you should do your periods.

4. It's okay to be flawed. It's okay to feel unsure about things— your body, your future, the contestants of Love Island. . . . You're not always going to get everything right. Just remember that getting one thing wrong doesn't equal getting EVERYTHING wrong.

5. See also: it's okay to have unfeminist thoughts sometimes.

6. There's no angle from which a dick pic looks good. None.

7. Love from your friends can be far more important and enduring than romantic love.

8. Thoughts you think are weird aren't all that weird. You'd be surprised by how many other people have them too.

9. Telling someone how you feel, all the thoughts in your head, makes you strong. Possibly even stronger than the strongest of weight lifters. Never be ashamed of feeling depressed, anxious, sad, or like you don't fit in. You're human, and you are loved. Always remember this.

10. The vulva is the outside bit; the vagina is the inside bit.

You're welcome.